THE SPY SANCTUARY

Secrets of the Cherokee Hideaway
BOOK THREE

Wheeler Pounds

Bluewater Publications

Bluewater Publication
Killen, AL 35645
Bluewaterpublications.com

Published in the United States by Bluewater Publications.

This work is based from the author's personal perspective.

Editor – Sierra Tabor
Cover Design – Scott Campbell
Interior Design - Maria Yasaka
Managing Editor – Angela Broyles

Secrets of the Cherokee Hideaway

$\blacklozenge$

The Cherokee Hideaway
Book One

The Cellar Vault
Book Two

The Spy Sanctuary
Book Three

Acknowledgements

There are several people who helped this third book come to be and that I would like to thank. First, Terry Michaels, who painstakingly reviewed the book and offered valuable corrections and advice. Also Ricky Butch Walker, who has been with me throughout the time I have been writing this series.

I also want to extend thanks to Sierra Tabor for her meticulous editing and to Bluewater Publications for publishing all my books and insisting on getting them in the best possible condition for publication.

And as always, I am beyond grateful to my wife, Judi, who continues to overlook all my shortcomings.

Jenny's Family Tree showing her connection to the people in the Journals.

Jenny Riddle Walker

Abigail Riddle   Dutch Riddle

Mattie Jackson   Silas Jackson

unknown   unknown

Beatrice Abston   Simpson Abston   Rebekah Abston

Sarah

Woody   Buck   Sunny Abston

Evie   Gray Fox   Sunbeam   Joseph B. Stone

PREFACE

◆————————

The Civil War had long been fought in the United States and is part of our nation's historical past. It was certainly not a period of time that we could claim to be our proudest. Severe growing pains developed as the nation expanded westward, and the first victims were the Native Americans, who found their homelands coveted by the European newcomers hungry for land of their own.

In July 1829, gold was discovered in an area around Dahlonega, Georgia, which was in Cherokee territory. Less than ten years later, the Cherokee were forced to vacate their ancestral lands. Not only the treaties, but even the lives of the Native Americans were secondary to the search for wealth and prosperity. Included in this number were not only the Cherokee but all of the Indian tribes that inhabited this land. Thousands died on the Trail of Tears.

Slavery was another issue which brought shame upon the nation at that time. As the Native Americans were considered to be second class inhabitants, so were the imported black people who were brought from Africa as slaves. They were owned in a similar way to the work animals, and sometimes they were treated not much better. They were bought and sold, valued only for the amount of work which they might be able to do. Severe punishment when they were unable to fulfill expectations was commonplace. Some of the young females were delegated to be sex slaves when their masters so desired.

There seemed to be no improvement in the slavery issue until after the election of President Abraham Lincoln in 1860. The rich slave owners in the South were not willing to grant freedom to those who did the work for them, and this became the motivating factor of the civil conflict. President Lincoln declared them to be free, and the rich landowners revolted.

Southern history is weighted heavily toward the concept of the solidarity of the South toward the defeat of the Yankees and the retaining of slavery. While this may be true to a large extent, there were, however, a sizeable number of Southerners who were opposed to war. Many first requested to be allowed to remain neutral, but were not allowed to do so. Even those who opposed conflict with their fellow Americans were conscripted to join the Confederate Army and forced to fight against them. Many, on moral and religious grounds as well as being opposed to slavery, just wanted to be left alone.

Winston County was the poorest county in Alabama. There were only a few individuals who owned slaves as the hill country was not suitable to large scale farming. Many of the county's citizens considered that this was a rich man's war, and they had no desire to become involved. Consequently, the large majority of the residents refused to participate in the conflict, which resulted in their being branded as "Tories."

This writing contains the viewpoint of Union sympathizers who opposed the war and favored abolition. For a truly historical perspective, actual articles are copied from old editions of the *Florence Gazette*, the publisher of the papers which, for the sake of this story, were found after being stored in a box for over almost 150 years. A diligent attempt has been made to copy each article from the newspaper exactly as it was written—mistakes and all.

Therefore, the pronunciation, capitalization, excessive use of commas, spelling, spacing, and word usage will be recorded as written at that time, with any perceived mistakes to be those of the editor of the newspaper or writer thereof. This practice will continue throughout the entirety of the copied papers. In a few places the old newspapers were not legible, and therefore a "sic" is inserted.

In addition to these newspaper articles, it is stated in this book that several journals are found in the boxes. And while the articles are from actual newspapers printed by the *Florence Gazette*, the journals should be taken as historical fiction.

Thought was given as to whether or not to record certain articles which were highlighted in the old newspapers, as the journal is repetitive of many of them. The writer of the journal discusses her thoughts concerning them, but in order to present a more complete picture of the subject matter, many articles, as written in the *Florence Gazette* are recorded in the order in which they were removed from the container in which they had been stored. The reader may find the journal to be of greater interest but hopefully will realize the importance of knowing the actual contents of the newspaper articles to which reference was made.

It is the desire of the author to present this as a historically accurate novel depicting differing sentiments of those who lived in Northwestern Alabama during the Civil War. The editors of the *Florence Gazette* were strongly in favor of secession while the writer of the journal was fervently opposed. Hopefully, this writing will help to understand the state of mind of the opposing sides.

Part One

THE WAR

"War is the stinking excrement created by greed, oppression, hatred, and power, which has been consumed, digested, and defecated by degenerate humanity in an insatiable quest for domination! Prime young men are conscripted to offer their bodies to be served on platters of bloody battlefields while the influential cowards who create the conflicts gluttonously dine on the bounties gained by the slaughter of brave young men. While being shrouded in their personal security blanket, far removed from the bloodshed, the powerful feast while the oppressed are butchered."

Joseph Stone, AKA Reverend Stone, Master Stone, and Papa Joe, made the remark after having read of the carnage which had been inflicted upon the troops in the battle that had been fought near Franklin, Tennessee.

It was shortly before Christmas time, 1864, when Reverend Stone received the news of the battle, but many of the men and boys from the area would not be celebrating the holiday. They would not even be afforded the dignity of a proper burial.

"It is disgraceful that numerous soldiers who were enrolled from here are getting only a fresh new grave for a Christmas present. The news account which I heard is that both sides are claiming to have come out on top in the battle at the Carter's house.

"The Confederates say that the Union Army cut and ran back to Nashville during the night after the battle while both sides had stacks of bodies to be removed from the battle field. The number of deaths on both sides is appalling, and they claim to have been victorious?

"I hope that the news I got is not right, but the report is that the Confederate Army lost six generals and a lot of men, and some of them are from around here. If that is true then that is no victory for the South. I want to see the slaves go free, but I don't want to see nobody from anywhere get killed over them. The only victor in this whole conflict has been Satan himself."

While speaking to a group of his farm workers who had gathered at the combined school and church building which he had erected on his plantation, Reverend Stone was keeping his workers informed of the status of the conflict. He adamantly opposed the war from its beginning and had suffered because of his refusal to cooperate with the Confederates.

"It has been clear for some time now that the battles that are being fought by the Southern armies are hopeless. The Union troops have been in control of Nashville and all the way south to this part of the country for a while now. Even if General Hood is able to drive them back to Nashville, there is no way that they will be able to turn the tide of this war. It is a shame that so many of our fine young men have been forced to enter the fight against their wishes, and a large number of them will never return.

"Men from almost every family lie buried all the way from Bull Run, Pea Ridge, Shiloh, Corinth, Iuka, Fredericksburg, Perryville, Murfreesboro, and on and on, with fine young men being killed all over the Southland. There have been so many killing fields that I cannot keep up with them, and it is senseless to continue the slaughters. I am proud of my decision to shield many of those who had no interest in killing Yankees by providing a hiding place for them here on the farm. I am not ashamed that I have made available a spy sanctuary for men who want this war to be over and help to get this land back to sensible leadership."

These words spoken many years ago in an impromptu speech by Joseph Stone have long been forgotten, but the beliefs and feelings behind them still resonate today. They are held strongly by many, especially when looking back to this particular time.

The Indian removal from the Southeast, followed by the Civil War, was a low point in the history of the United States. Many of those who lived and survived during that period of time carried the scars of the removal and of the battles for the remainder of their lives, both physically and mentally.

To read their stories, preserved in ancient journals, is a sobering experience. Raleigh Walker, his wife Jenny, and her parents, Dutch and Abigail Riddle, along with their friends, Kurt Marshal and Cressy Alexander, have discovered the old journals which had been stored in a secret cellar vault on the plantation belonging to Dutch and Abigail Riddle. Join the adventures as they are read by descendants of the oppressed.

CHAPTER 1

◆

The war had ended, but deep scars were still visible all over the Southland. Rains had washed the blood from the soils of the battlefields, but the carnage left behind served as evidence of the conflicts that had occurred there. The Southern army had suffered defeat, and the losers were attempting to pick up the pieces while trying to come to terms with their failure.

At the farm which was then managed by Sunshine "Sunny" Abston, the illegitimate son of Joseph Stone and Sunbeam, a native Cherokee woman, there were no tears shed when the Confederate General Robert E Lee surrendered to the Union commanders.

Reverend Stone had refused to send his farm workers to die for a cause which he opposed and had hid them in a secret hideaway on the farm property. A spy sanctuary. He denounced slavery and advocated freedom for all people regardless of skin color or social status.

Because of sound management throughout the ensuing years, the farm built by Joseph Stone survived the turmoil following the bloody civil conflict. It continued to prosper and grew into the large plantation it is in the present time due to the work of Stone's descendants and their spouses.

Slaves had been freed at the conclusion of the war, but many blacks remained on the plantation, as they considered it their home. In those days their chances of finding better accommodations elsewhere were slim, and many, being born on the farm, were contented to stay where their families had lived for generations.

The plantation had its beginning shortly after the infamous "Trail of Tears," when Reverend Joseph B. Stone bought property that had once been Cherokee lands. After the Cherokee Nation lost title to all property east of the Mississippi River, there was a land grab where white settlers moved onto the forfeited property and made claims to the vacated land. This resulted in conflicts as there sometimes were multiple claims to the same plots. Land agents were brought in to divide the parcels, sell, and deed the land in order to quell the disputes as to who was the rightful owner of each piece of property.

Although others had laid claim to the fertile Tennessee Valley parcels of land where Cherokee farmers had prospered while growing cotton and corn and raising cattle, Reverend Stone, being an educated man, had maneuvered to secure a deed, probably by passing money under the table, and had developed a well-organized farming operation. Gradually he and his descendants had increased their land holdings, and as they prospered, they were able to buy out the deeds of others who were struggling to turn a profit. Slowly the plantation became the largest farming operation in the area.

The farm was labor intensive which forced Reverend Stone to acquire a number of slaves to meet the work demands. There were also several white families and a few Cherokees who called the plantation their home. He was diligent in his selection of workers, choosing only those whom he felt would serve him well. Unlike many others, when at a slave auction, he insisted that the family unit remain intact as he considered that this would solidify his laborers and make them more contented as they worked for him. He made a great effort to place them in adequate housing while maintaining a well-stocked pantry. His workers were supplied their basic needs and were treated with respect.

Reverend Stone took pleasure in having a good rapport with those that worked for him; he was careful that his workers be not compelled to do more than they were capable of doing, yet he expected them to do their best and carry their share of the work load. The slaves and other workers were consistently encouraged to feel included in the plantation family with everyone treated as equals. Places were provided for them to meet, worship, and relax. A building was erected on the farm to grant an opportunity for them to meet for church services and to have school classes for the children. Different events were scheduled regularly where food and recreation offered a break in the rigors of the farming operation.

There was one area of the farm in which access was very limited. From the onset of his farming endeavors, Master Stone, as his workers addressed him, saw a need to have a place which was off limits to all but a selected few. It was a secret hideaway in which he concealed those who were being sought for various reasons.

During the Indian removal, there were those Cherokee who refused to leave their ancestral homeland and went into hiding in order to avoid the long march to the West. The hideaway was initially utilized to provide a sanctuary for a Cherokee family who had first found refuge in a secluded cove in a canyon in the Sipsey Wilderness in order to escape the removal.

Shortly following their arrival on the Stone plantation, the hideaway also served as a "depot" on the Underground Railroad. Oppressed slaves fleeing ruthless masters were sheltered there for a short time as they made their way to northern "free states." There they had received food, shelter, and transportation to meet their next host while on their way to freedom.

During the Civil War, there became another useful purpose for the hideaway. The families who assisted Master Stone in the farming operation, all stood with him in adamantly opposing the war and refusing to send workers into the conflict. The hidden shelter was used as a place for them to hide to escape the Home Guard, Enrollment Officers, and Partisan Rangers who were sent to enforce the conscription order that required all able bodied men in the South to enlist in the Confederate Army.

Sunny Abston, son of Reverend Stone, assisted his father in the job of operating the farm, and they were in no way favorable of sending their workers out to kill Yankees and possibly lose their lives in the process. A second son, named Flash and born after Reverend Stone had married Sunbeam, was too young for military service or a substantial role in the operations of the farm.

Their opposition to slavery dictated that they do all in their power to ensure a Northern victory. Soon after the beginning of the war, the Union Navy seized control of the Tennessee River, which flowed through the plantation, and another useful purpose was found for Stone's hideaway. Union spies found a sanctuary in the hideaway and Yankee sympathizers, branded as "Tories" by the Rebels, were given a place of refuge as they made their way to the Federal lines where they were welcomed as workers for the cause of freedom for the oppressed slaves.

Later on, there was one more purpose found for the hideaway, which would remain a top secret. Following the conclusion of the war, with the Union Army victorious, there was no longer a need for a hideaway to conceal individuals, but there was still a need for the secret location.

The family was becoming quite prosperous, which resulted in an accumulation of valuables and important documents. With no trust in the government, which had failed to honor the treaties made with the Native Americans, Master Stone and his descendants were determined to secure their possessions so as not to allow the government to again take that which rightfully belonged to them.

They were careful to get legal documents for all their land and property dealings and stored them securely. They likewise put no trust in paper currency, dealing only in gold and silver as the country was then under the gold standard. Gold and silver were the backings used for the paper money and could be obtained upon request when payment was made for goods and services.

The role of the hideaway was transformed from that of being a place of concealment for people to that of a safety deposit location for those valuables, and thus it became known to a very select few as being the "cellar vault."

Those who knew of its existence, had bestowed upon them the title of "the keeper of the treasure." This title was entrusted to only males, and only to the operator of the farm and sometimes a designated family member.

Over generations, the wealth of the family had greatly increased, and the excessive bounties had consistently found their way into the cellar vault. Prosperity had allowed the cost of the farming operations to be paid out of the current income each year, often still leaving a surplus. Therefore, there were only deposits and no withdrawals from the underground bank.

Because the family dealt only in gold and silver, the years of the Great Depression had played favorably in behalf of the plantation. By owning gold and silver and having no money in the failing banks, they were able to add to their land holdings by buying farms whose owners had lost everything in the financial crash. With cash in hand, it was possible to buy ownership of a number of farms in the area.

Not only was money stored in the cellar vault, but there were also several boxes which contained deeds and other farm records. In the electronic age, the majority of the necessary titles and records had been transferred to computers, and there was no longer a need for the documents stored in what was once known as the spy sanctuary.

They continued to remain there, unmolested for generations. Until...

CHAPTER 2

◆───

Until a surprising turn of events which would set the wheels in motion to bring the keys out to unlock the doors that had been shut for a long time.

Raleigh Walker, a confirmed bachelor, or so he thought, had his life changed abruptly after attending a meeting of the Echota Cherokee Tribe. A beautiful young Cherokee woman, as though caught by a dream catcher and deposited in the amphitheater at the Oakville Indian Mounds, changed his mind about bachelorhood.

Jenny Riddle had turned his status as a single guy upside down. Until that day at the powwow, his passion had been centered on wilderness and outdoor adventures. In one day, he was tamed by a girl who had deserted the country for a life in the city. Raleigh had had no idea that a future in farming was in the cards, nor had he had a clue that he would return from an excursion to the old Cherokee capital of New Echota with a wife. His marriage had quickly led him from the forest to wide open fields – with only distant trees in sight.

After their marriage, Raleigh and Jenny had promptly traveled to Jenny's ancestral home where they delivered the news to her parents, Dutch and Abigail Riddle. The vast plantation on which she had been raised had come as a surprise to Raleigh on their first visit, but shortly thereafter he was made an offer to join Dutch to learn the operations of the farm with future ownership possible.

Due to time restraints and pressure on Jenny to complete an important project at the Marshal Space Flight Center where she was employed, it was a month before the newlyweds could find the time to break the news to Raleigh's parents. They had continued to live separately, except on weekends, as Raleigh's job was in Walker County. After a discussion, they both agreed that the announcement should be made in person, so that his parents could meet their new daughter-in-law while receiving the news of their marriage.

"I suppose that we should make time to let Mother and Daddy in on our little secret," Raleigh had informed Jenny while talking to her on the phone about a month following their marriage. "I think we should set aside some time this weekend to visit. I can't wait any longer for them to meet you and for you to get to know them."

"I was just thinking the same thing today," Jenny responded positively. "It's been long enough now, and you've never told me much about them."

"That's because I want you all to get to know each other in person," Raleigh replied. "I know they'll love you and that you'll really enjoy the time we spend with them."

"We'll see about that," Jenny said jokingly. "I hope they don't mind that we didn't tell them sooner. I may be getting off to a bad start with them as soon as we deliver the news."

"Don't worry about that!" Raleigh chuckled. "I'm sure they'll understand."

The trip was planned after Raleigh had verified that his parents had no plans for the weekend. The Walker's residence was located outside the city of Birmingham but was near enough that his father's commute to his work inside the city was not excessively time consuming. Located on a sizeable lot, the house was spacious but was nothing compared to the one in which Jenny was raised.

Richard Walker, Raleigh's father, was employed at UAB - University of Alabama Birmingham - Medical Center, where he was involved in research seeking remedies for physical and developmental disorders in the juvenile population. He had dedicated his life to working in the interest of helping children and found it very rewarding.

Richard's father, likewise, had been involved in early research in the same field and had encouraged Richard to follow his lead. Richard had also wanted Raleigh to continue the family tradition of compassion for the young, unfortunate children who faced a difficult start in life, but Raleigh was too much the outdoorsman to be confined in a lab.

A legend in the Walker's family had been passed down through generations that an unknown ancestor had taken an interest in a handicapped child, reportedly the male child of a family slave, and had resolved to make an effort to help him and other children who were born with disabilities. This evolved into a passion with ensuing family members wishing to help disabled children to achieve the highest level possible while coping with their infirmities.

Raleigh's mother, Jane, served as the librarian for one of the local elementary schools. Books were her interest, but her passion was the school children with whom she worked. She always arrived at school prepared to lead the pupils in extra activities which involved crafts and storytelling, and she was much beloved by her students.

During the previous year, the school's yearbook had been dedicated to her.

As their only child, Raleigh had enjoyed a happy family life in his formative years, but he had chosen the field of Criminal Justice as his profession, despite his parents' hopes of his joining a career similar to theirs.

After graduating from Harding University in Arkansas, he had secured a job with the Alabama Board of Pardons and Paroles and was contented in his role as a probation and parole supervisor.

During this visit, there was no way that he could have known that his occupation would soon make a drastic change.

"Well, I see that you still remember the way to get here," his mother quipped upon their arrival. "It's been a while since we've seen you."

Gesturing by throwing his arms up and dropping them to his sides, Raleigh countered, "Come on, Mom! I only made one wrong turn; give me a break!"

Smiling, he continued, "But I can't blame you for thinking that I had forgotten. I just don't seem to ever have enough time to do everything I would like to do. Don't forget, I did spend a weekend with you a few months ago, but I probably haven't been as diligent in communicating with you as I should be."

"Your mother is just trying to give you a hard time," Richard said, giving his son a slight wink. "I've learned to just acknowledge that she is absolutely right, whether or not she actually is. Which is seldom."

Then Richard suddenly raised his voice several octaves higher in an attempt to imitate his wife's speech. "Did you get lost coming home?" he said before returning to his normal voice and laughing. "I get that sweet little greeting if I work late at the lab and come in later than she expects. I just tell her that I misplaced my map and will try to do better the next time."

Richard's comments triggered smiles all around which compelled his wife to respond, "Like a map would do him any good. He doesn't even know how to unfold and refold one. The last time I saw him with a map of Alabama in his hands, he was trying to read it upside down with the Gulf of Mexico joining the Tennessee line."

Richard laughed again, put his arm around his wife's waist and pecked a kiss on her cheek. "Where would I be without you to turn my maps right side up for me?"

Jenny had yet to be introduced to her new in-laws, but the light-hearted exchange about the maps had made a favorable impression on her.

"So what's the latest with you? I see that you brought a friend with you today."   Richard looked between Raleigh and Jenny as he spoke.

"I would like for you to meet Jenny," Raleigh hesitated with the last name. She was now Jenny Walker, but he was not yet ready to make that revelation.

As they turned to enter the house, Richard looked at Jenny. "Welcome to our home. If you are the one who is responsible for getting Raleigh to visit his mother, you're already on her good side."

"If that's the case, I will take the credit." Jenny smiled while replying. "I certainly would like to stay on Mrs. Walker's good side."

As Raleigh entered the house, his thoughts replayed his initial meeting with Jenny's parents the week following their marriage. By agreement, she had done the talking as they broke the news to them that she was a married woman. Now it was his turn to startle his unsuspecting parents.

They engaged briefly in small talk before Raleigh summoned sufficient courage to reveal their secret.

"I would like for both of you to see this," he addressed his parents as he handed his mother their marriage certificate. "I didn't tell you Jenny's last name because you should know that it is now 'Walker.' I would like for you to meet and become acquainted with your new daughter-in-law. I realize that I have a lot of explaining to do, but we will have time for that before we leave."

Richard leaned over Jane's shoulder as the two examined the certificate which Raleigh had handed them. Both seemed to still be trying to digest the news, which had rendered them speechless.

After a long pause, Raleigh was the one who broke the silence. "You will notice that the date on the certificate shows that we have now been married a month. We have not purposely kept you in the dark about this; we can honestly blame time restraints on the delay." He hesitated a moment before continuing. "Mom, I realize that it's a poor excuse, but it's the main reason I haven't been here in so long. For what it's worth, you should know that we married without the knowledge or blessings of either her parents or you. We felt that the proper way to inform you of our marriage was to do it in person, so as to be able to have the opportunity to explain our actions and to answer any questions which you might have."

Pausing, Raleigh waited for questions. He got only puzzled stares from his parents. Continuing his explanation, he felt that additional clarification would be helpful to appease his parents. "Maybe it was not fair to you, but we informed Jenny's parents after I suggested that we should tell them first. One reason for that was due to her grandmother who is in her nineties, and I felt that she should be told of her new grandson-in-law while she could appreciate the information. There had to be a decision made as to who should be told first, and I think our choice was justified. Needless to say, they were completely surprised when we broke the news to them, but they were accepting of our actions. I have assured Jenny that you would be just as understanding as her parents were."

"I-I really don't know what to say," Jane finally spoke as she struggled reply.

This was more of a response than Richard could manage, who continued to stare at the marriage certificate without a word.

"I am sure that you would like to know something about our new family member, and why it is that you were not introduced or knew anything about her before today." Raleigh said, realizing that there was more explaining to do. "I could say that it's a long story, but that would be misleading. Everything happened so quickly that it still feels like I'm living in a dream world."

"As I told my parents," Jenny interjected, "Raleigh and I met and very soon realized that we wanted to be together for a lifetime, so we married. It's as simple as that. I must confess that I took an aggressive role in our decision to marry when we did, however, no one can contend that we married because we were young and foolish, or that we did not know what we were doing at the time. We are definitely mature enough to know whom we want to share our future with."

Raleigh added to Jenny's comment, "We are deeply in love and have total confidence that our love will continue to grow as we share our lives together."

"Neither Jane nor I would dispute that," Richard was finally able to respond. "It just came as a shock to us that you had even contemplated marriage; we had no idea that you were even interested in a particular girl. We sort of assumed that you were too carried away with your outdoor pursuits and that there was no time in your life for romance."

"There is a story behind this, and I owe it to you to tell it and let you know as much about it as possible."

Jenny sat by Raleigh as he began to reveal the circumstances that led to his signature on a marriage license. Richard and Jane sat together as they listened to the explanation.

"It all began..."

Raleigh told of his backpacking excursion into the Sipsey Canyon where he discovered the box and journal. He did not elaborate on the details as he wanted to get to the part of the story that led him to his chance meeting with Jenny.

"Looking for clues as to what might have happened to the family who took refuge in the wilderness to escape the Indian removal, I attended a tribal meeting at the Indian Mounds Park in Oakville where I met Jenny. She was there to do some running on the cross country track which winds through the park, and I thought that she might be a person who could give me some insight regarding old families of the Cherokees who had escaped the Trail of Tears and now live in Alabama. After meeting Jenny, I could get my mind on nothing else but her, and this resulted in my second contact with her. One thing led to another and..."

Jenny felt compelled to interrupt again to make a clarification, "I don't want Raleigh to give you the impression that we conducted ourselves in such a way that we had to marry to preserve our honor; shotgun style, as the old country folks might say. That certainly was not the case. I take pride in the fact that our marriage is based on love, not passion. Sooo—don't be expecting a grandchild anytime in the near future."

Raleigh grinned at Jenny's clarification. "I suppose that she doesn't want you to go out buying toys and infant seats thinking that they might be needed soon. We suppose that will come, but time will tell about that. Our wedding night was special for us both as we realized that we were destined to be lifetime companions in a pure and beautiful way. I am so fortunate to have her as my wife, and you can be proud to claim her as a daughter-in-law."

"You are a beautiful woman," Jane exclaimed. "If your actions are as becoming as your looks, I must say that Raleigh has done really well."

"I'm just plain ole Jenny," she said with a dismissive shake of the head. "There's not a lot to tell about me. I was raised as an ordinary country kid, and I, as did Raleigh, grew up as an only child under the tutelage of loving and responsible parents. That's just about it in a nutshell."

"Jenny is actually being quite modest," Raleigh spoke as he put an arm around her waist. "My lovely wife has qualities that she would never mention. I can say that for a fact because there are things about her that she never told me herself, but I had to learn about from others."

He grinned at her before continuing, "For instance, she told me that she worked at the Marshal Space Flight Center in Huntsville, working in a NASA program. But it wasn't until she took me on a tour there that I learned, when the guard at the gate greeted her as Dr. Riddle, that she has a PhD in Aerospace Engineering from Auburn. I also learned that she headed a group of other distinguished workers who were instrumental in designing components necessary for spacecraft.

"The claim of being a country girl cannot be disputed, but she has not told you that she was raised as a very rich country girl. I found this out only after my visit to her country home when we notified her parents of our marriage."

The conversation went on a little bit longer as Jane and Richard continued to get to know their new daughter-in-law, before they ended it temporarily to allow the two younger people to get settled in for their short stay. There was a lot to talk about and the weekend passed swiftly. The Walkers readily accepted their newest family member, and Jenny rapidly felt comfortable in their presence.

Before leaving on the last day of their visit, Raleigh was determined to gain additional insight on his own past family history. He had been negligent as a youngster in attempting to climb up the family tree. Events that had unfolded due to questions raised in the journal he had discovered, and a subsequent conversation with Mattie, Jenny's maternal grandmother, now prodded him to elicit as much family history from his parents as possible.

He began with a question to his father, which he hoped would provide insight into his ancestors, generations removed from the present.

"I recall a little saying which you occasionally quoted that had to do with our relationship with others and especially the unfortunate. You, at one time, and possibly still do, had it hand-printed, framed, and placed on the wall of your lab. I think I can quote it also. I'll try...

"Helpless we begin our life
Dependent on a man and wife
Nurtured then by love and care
We must each our burdens bear
Helpful then we must become
Troubles will surely fall on some
With the golden rule to guide
Help is always by your side
Always do unto others as you
Would have them do to you."

"How bad did I miss it?" Raleigh made the inquiry as he finished the quote.

"It's exactly right," Richard replied. "I'm surprised that you remembered that word for word. And yes, it still hangs on the wall in my lab."

"In the past I have heard you tell the story, as you know it, about that little quote, but it sort of went over my head because I was not paying as much attention as I should have been," Raleigh answered. "It would be interesting for you to recount to Jenny and me some of that history which you might recall."

Richard looked thoughtful as he responded, "I first heard that quote when I was just a boy. At that time I thought that it was a little silly and not very well worded, but as I grew up it became more significant to me. It may be true that it is poorly worded, but as the story began to come to light, I realized that the one who created it was not an educated person at that time—compassionate, but uneducated. Later he reportedly received a good education and became a doctor and perhaps let the saying which he had composed while young be his inspiration to do as much good as he possibly could."

Richard paused a moment, apparently in deep thought, before continuing. "Now when I say this you must understand that all this is tradition that has been passed down through generations and is not necessarily fact, although I am a firm believer that it is true. I base this on the knowledge that our ancestors have always been known as a compassionate family who took a special interest in helping others, especially underprivileged and infirmed children. As I grew up I was encouraged to carry on the family tradition of seeking help for the young who needed it; the way that I encouraged you to do the same," Richard glanced at Raleigh, pausing again with a smile on his face. "Unsuccessfully of course."

Raleigh returned the smile without a response as his father continued the story.

"Family tradition has it that about five generations ago, more or less, my great, great, great grandfather wrote that and quoted it throughout his lifetime. Back then there were those of our ancestors who were underprivileged and banished from society because they were Indians.

"Obviously, the Cherokee Tribe, our people, always got the short end of the stick, as did the slaves. He wrote that little quote when he was young and had been helped by people who cared. I understand that his sister had a saying also, which probably prompted him in writing his own. Sick and disabled Indians and black slaves also, no matter their age, lacked the care and medical help which they constantly needed.

"Consequently, many Cherokee, including our ancestors, were often in dire need of assistance from compassionate people. Because there were some who were willing to reach out to them and offer that help when it was needed, the good will of those people was not forgotten. With the passage of time, the descendants of those who had received that help, those being our forefathers, rose from the depth of poverty and were capable of practicing that golden rule."

"I was told when I was a small child and first heard the saying that the writer later became interested in a little slave boy who was handicapped. That boy's condition helped the writer, in some way, to avoid military service in the Civil War. As a result of that he dedicated his life's work to assisting handicapped children. That is the extent of what I know about that."

After his father's lengthy reply to his question, Raleigh felt compelled to clarify why he had asked it. "There is a story behind the reason I asked the question but not enough time to explain. I've recently uncovered some information about that quote, and I know you'll be really interested to hear it. I just might be able to fill in some blanks that have gone unanswered for a long time."

Raleigh was thinking back to just a few weeks ago, when Jenny's grandmother had been able to quote that very saying. Unknowingly, she had revealed much more regarding the family of her new son-in-law than she realized. She had, perhaps, provided a crucial piece of the puzzle needed to fill in the blanks to complete a picture of the Walker's family tree.

Was there indeed an ancient tie that would bring the Walker and the Riddle family together as being distantly related? If indeed that was the case, Raleigh thought it impossible that the connection could ever be made.

CHAPTER 3

◆

The marriage of Raleigh and Jenny had been an astonishment to both of their parents, but Raleigh was the one who would be the most surprised as to the drastic change that it would make in his life. He could never have envisioned that he would leave his employment with the State Board of Pardons and Paroles to be a dirt farmer. When he married Jenny, he had no idea that her father was a wealthy plantation owner who would persuade him to join in the operations of the farm.

Likewise, he was surprised that he would be able to enter an old cellar vault which was located on the farm to remove a box containing a journal which had been stored there for generations.

Raleigh and Jenny had met while he was in search of answers raised by a recorded chronicle of events in the life of a Cherokee woman named Eve. It had been written while she was hiding to escape the Indian removal to what was then the Oklahoma Territory.

Dutch Riddle, current owner of the plantation, had only infrequently entered the cellar vault which was cleverly concealed in a fenced location on his farm. The vault contained old wooden fruit crates in which millions of dollars' worth of gold and silver were stored. Additionally, there were bags spilling out on surrounding shelf space.

As the farm generated an excess of revenue needed to meet the expenses of the operation, there had been no need to remove the treasures stored there. The cellar vault was truly a motherlode of treasure: gold, silver, gems, and jewelry, which remained stored and securely hidden in the underground vault.

It was not these items, however, that had captured the interest of the Riddle Family. Over generations, the family history of the descendants of Joseph Stone and his Cherokee wife, Sunbeam, had been lost. The Indian removal had required that they keep quiet about the Native American blood that flowed in their veins. As they had claimed that Sunbeam was of a Black Dutch heritage, there was little talk about her pure Cherokee blood.

It was initially thought that the history of the family had been forever lost, but the historical treasures found in the boxes had begun to illuminate a long lost insight into the lives of their ancestors.

The details of the trip which Raleigh did not fully relate to his parents involved the backpacking trip he had taken into the Sipsey Canyon, a remote section of the Bankhead National Forest in Alabama. He had discovered the box containing a journal where it had been concealed in a rock shelter located in a hidden cove. This discovery had triggered an investigation, which had led him to Jenny.

The fate of the writer of the journal and her family had remained a mystery until Mattie Jackson, Jenny's grandmother, was able to provide the first small piece of the puzzle. While young, she had read a limited portion of a journal that her father had left lying on a table. She related to them that the writer of that journal had identified herself as being the daughter-in-law of a

Reverend Stone. She did not know the fate of the journal from which she read, but surmised that it could be stored in a cellar vault located somewhere on the farm.

After Mattie's death, Dutch Riddle had revealed to Raleigh the location of the cellar vault after declaring that Raleigh would succeed him as "keeper of the treasure." He took Raleigh to the vault and showed him the contents, where Raleigh recognized that two of the boxes stored there seemed to be identical to the one that he had brought out of the forest canyon.

After Dutch and Abigail had an opportunity to read the original journal, Dutch, for the first time, removed an item from the vault by bringing out one of the boxes. Along with additional items, it had contained not one, but two journals.

After those journals had been read, it was decided that the second identical box should come out for further inspection. The journals which had been stored in the other box that had been removed from the cellar vault were rich in family exploits and history. One journal had been written by Hannah (no last name was revealed) the sister of Eve, who was writer of the journal which Raleigh had found under the shelter in the Sipsey Wilderness.

The second journal that was in the box that Dutch had removed from the vault had briefly been used as a school tablet. It had also been owned by Eve, and in it she had continued writing of her family's exploits to avoid the troops who would have forced her removal to Oklahoma.

The journals that had been retrieved from the cellar vault had been of great interest to the Riddle and Walker families. They, however, had not contained information which the readers had expected to find. Grandmother Mattie had told of reading specific information written by the wife of Joseph Stone's son, but neither of the journals that had been stored in the first box had been written by her.

The foregone conclusion had been that Sarah, the daughter of Eve and Grey Fox, who was born while the couple was in hiding in the forest canyon, had been the writer of that journal. As Eve and her sister Hannah were responsible for the writings in the first two journals, it was then surmised that the second box, which remained in the vault, could contain the journal from which Mattie had read.

"It just might be time to use the keys to the cellar vault again," Dutch Riddle announced to the family.

Raleigh and Jenny were back at her family's home with her parents, and they were enjoying their Saturday afternoon meal which had been prepared by Angie, the cook for the household.

"As the box we left there appears to be identical to the one I brought out earlier, there is a good chance that it might contain the journal that Mattie referred to in her discussion with you. If it does indeed hold that journal, I think that it will be as interesting to us as the first three that we have already read."

"I promised Kurt and Cressy that I would let them know when we would read again. They want to keep up with this adventure from the journals," Raleigh mentioned, thinking of his old friend and his girlfriend.

Kurt Marshal had been with Raleigh when the first journal was read. Cressy Alexander had joined Raleigh and Jenny when the next two were read and had asked to be invited back should an additional journal be found.

"I will call them and see if they can come up this weekend," Jenny volunteered. "I'll do that now."

She had the number programmed in her phone and made the call.

"Well, I suppose we won't be having Kurt and Jenny with us if we locate another journal," Jenny announced a few minutes later as she hung up the phone. "Cressy said that Kurt is in Costa Rica working on a research project for his dissertation; he's close to getting his PhD. She said that she wouldn't feel right coming without him. I told her that she was welcome to come but she declined the invitation. If there is another journal, we will just have to read without them."

CHAPTER 4

◆

Dutch wasted little time before returning to the underground vault to retrieve the second box.

"When we opened the other box, we did it on a Sunday afternoon following church services. That worked out well, so I propose that we do the same with this box," Abigail suggested. "After we see what it contains, we can then decide our next plan of action."

There was work to do on the farm, but the weather had not cooperated. As the harvest had been completed, there was less to do in regard to crop work, but farming on the Riddle Plantation was consistently undergoing changes.

Winter wheat crops had recently been introduced to Alabama farmers and were proving to be a profitable venture. The farm already owned combines which were used to harvest soy beans and other crops; they had the basic machinery to cultivate and harvest wheat. Raleigh had convinced Dutch there was nothing to lose in giving the crop a try, so they had decided to sow as much acreage as possible in winter wheat. Rain, however, had hampered the effort, and the coming week promised to be a good time to rest and read if there was indeed anything in the boxes which would be of interest.

The rain continued on Sunday, and the family decided to eat at their favorite restaurant before returning home following church services. It was a place where other farmers in the area also met to eat, and there was generally an exchange of the latest farm news while there. It had become customary that a large table in the back section of the establishment served as a common gathering place for those farmers. The comradely conversations held there were often about farming but also other subjects such as sports and politics.

As the rain continued into the afternoon, there were an unusually large number who chose to eat at the "chitchat table" as it was called. Fortunately, the conversation was centered on farming activities, and there was no shortage of opinions regarding the pros and cons of growing crops that were profitable. Many farmers had developed a routine which they had followed for a lifetime, and they were not receptive to change by planting crops like wheat.

The Riddle and Walker families had heard it all before; they soon excused themselves and returned home. They were anxious to open the box to see what it had concealed for generations.

"I will venture a guess that there will be more cotton used for packing material like we found in the other box," Abigail speculated. "I also bet Dutch will be carding the seeds from the cotton, as he did from that box, to do his little experimental plantings; like he won't have silos full of expensive hybrid seed to plant."

"Since you mentioned it, the crop from the seeds that I carded from the other box did really well considering that they were probably over one hundred years old. The seal on that box did a good job in preserving them, as it did the other items which were stored there. I'll admit that the hybrid seeds which we now plant are superior to those, but I can understand how money was made by planting that variety of cotton. I saved seeds from that cotton and, for fun, I will try my hand at doing a little crossbreeding and see what I can come up with."

"Dad!" Jenny exclaimed, "I think that you would be better served to leave the crossbreeding to the agriculture department at Auburn, and you worry about making a profit from the seeds which you already have. They seem to be doing quite well."

Jenny put more faith in the ability of the agriculture department at her alma mater to be able to develop a superior species than what her father could do.

"Your whiz kids at Auburn have to use soil to grow their crops the same as I do. I will put the seeds in the ground and let nature do the rest. That is one of the many pleasures of farming."

"And, I must admit," Abigail added, "that is the reason you are successful at it." She smiled as she looked at the others. "I'm confident that Dutch won't lose enough money with his little seed project to put us in danger of going hungry."

The statement prompted a laugh from the group as Dutch picked up the box and cuddled it in his arms.

"Let's try to open this the way that we opened the other one." Dutch spoke to Raleigh. "That worked quite well."

With Dutch holding the box and Raleigh tugging on the lid, the box slowly opened.

There was no cotton visible as the contents came into view. There would be no additional seeds for Dutch to plant in his experimental farm plot.

"Newspapers!" Jenny was the first to identify the visible contents. Where cotton had been used for packing in the other box that they had opened, carefully folded newspapers were visible as Raleigh removed the lid. The entire edition of each date of the paper was not included, but pages that held an interest to someone had been cut to preserve the significant articles. It was obvious that there were many dated editions that had been saved. There was silence as the four looked down at the old newspapers in the box.

Jenny was the first to comment, "Won't be any crossbreeding coming from this box." The others chuckled as she continued, "Someone saved those old papers for their contents, not for packing material."

Lying on top of the newspapers was an envelope on which was written:

For Rebekah

On an impulse, Jenny reached and pulled it from the box. "For Rebekah," she read aloud. "The last box that we opened had two envelopes in it which we set aside and forgot about until Dad was repacking the box. We shouldn't make that mistake again."

After opening the unsealed envelope, Jenny pulled a sheet of folded paper from inside it. The front and back of the sheet were filled with writings. After unfolding it she held it so that everyone could read it.

Rebekah,

I am writing this while you are still very young for it is something that I wanted to put in writing while it is on my mind. Never forget your Cherokee heritage. It is something in which you should be proud. I am happy that you have not been forced to endure the difficult times me and your grandparents suffered when we were your age.

First there was the time when our ancestral lands were worth more to the white man than our people who were the rightful owners, dating back centuries before the intruders got here. The removal to Oklahoma was a dark time in our history. After that was the dreadful war between the southern and northern states. I am glad that it ended before you could remember the pain and hardships that it caused to many people who only wished to be left alone and stay out of the conflict. I pray that you can grow up in a peaceful country where all people will finally be treated as humans should be treated.

I was cleaning out the old schoolhouse and removed some old newspapers from a desk drawer. They contain a lot of history of those dismal days for our Cherokee people who once again suffered as did others during the war. Sadie and I used the newspapers to teach current events to our students who were isolated on the farm here. We wanted them to know what was going on in the world away from this place. I could not bring myself to destroy them so I want to pass them on to you to do with them whatever you may choose.

I do hope that you and our descendants will never forget the hardships that our Cherokee family endured to bring our people to where we are now. Never forget the importance of every person whether they be white or black or red skinned; it's what's inside a person that counts.

Sometimes in the future, maybe on a cold and rainy day, you may want to take these newspapers out of storage and read them. I think that they will help you to have a greater appreciation for the struggles our Indian people, and the black slaves had before and during the war that was fought in order that we might be treated with the respect that we deserve.

I am also leaving a journal which I wrote when things were bad and I did not know from one day to the next whether or not I would live long enough to bring you into the world. I remember that my mother wrote in one while we were hid out in the forest to escape the removal but she left it there because we could not bring it out with all the other things we had to carry out. The South lost the war but that was not bad. The oppressed Southerners; Indians, Negroes, and even some whites were the real winners. Sadly there were a lot of losers, those thousands who lost their lives in the bloody war.

I realize that the events chronicled in these old newspapers are now history and you know the outcome of those conflicts. History has a way of consuming the true facts and substituting whatever the conquerors wish to record. Consider that these newspapers represent history in the making and stand as a true permanent record. But even more significant is that their value lies not only in the events recorded in them but in the sentiments stirred by the weekly reports of the conflicts, the ebb and flow of emotions regarding good news and bad news.

Good news to some was bad news to others–such is the nature of a divided people which war breeds. Dancing in the street can soon retreat into a flight of terror-as happened in Florence. Euphoria can quickly be replaced by despair. Such is the uncertainty of life–which is a lesson that all should learn, that is, one must take one day at a time as we do not know what tomorrow may bring.

Always remember that I love you. I am confident that this love is mutual between us and will extend down through future generations.

Your Mother ~ Sarah Abston

Jenny refolded the sheet of paper, and placed it back into the envelope.

Abigail felt that it was her turn to speak. "We apparently have another generation being addressed in this message. Rebekah is obviously the daughter of Sunny and Sarah, and the papers were packed with her in mind, to open at a later date. I would guess that, for whatever reason, this was never read by Rebekah. From my experience, there are other things on young minds besides old newspapers. By the time one gets older those newspapers would be completely forgotten.

"Anyhow, it's amazing that these have been preserved down to this generation. Sarah told Rebekah to take time in the future to read them so that she would be reminded of her Cherokee heritage and the realities of life, encouraging her to remain strong. We, likewise, must never forget that this is our heritage also. These newspapers will possibly give us a refresher course on the trials and tribulations of the American Indians as well as the Negro slaves. Let's see what Sarah taught her students in her current events class during the Civil War and what she felt to be important for Rebekah and future generations to remember."

"After that we have a journal to read." Jenny added to her mother's comments. "I think that when we finish our inspection and readings from the box, we will have a stronger appreciation and respect for the sacrifices and hardships which our Cherokee people endured. Our family did it in such a way that they prospered through it all.

"And perhaps after reading this, we will have an incentive to stop more often and give thanks to those who endured adversity so that we can now live on easy street. It was a long and difficult journey for Sarah; from a rattlesnake infested rock shelter in a secluded cove where she was born, to one of the finest plantations in the state. You talk about a success story! But it was not easy. All this was accomplished by Cherokees who otherwise would be destined to eke out a meager existence in Oklahoma."

Dutch, remaining in charge of the box, lifted the top newspaper and examined it. "It looks like the big news when this was published was the status of the unrest that was brewing between the Northern and Southern states."

The old newspapers were printed in vertical columns which measured slightly over two inches wide. There were six columns spread over each page. Covering the front pages were the significant news articles. Most of the advertisements on additional pages had been discarded. It was immediately clear that the papers, as Sarah had written, were saved because of their content.

The top paper had the headlined article checked, apparently using an ink pen. Dutch held the paper so that it was visible for all to read. There was a check mark on one of the articles on the front page.

Florence Gazette

Florence, Alabama—May 9, 1860

Nine States Withdraw from the convention.

Our readers have doubtless, ere this learned, that nine of the 15 Southern States, withdrew from the Charleston Convention, Viz: Deleware, Texas, Alabama, Mississippi, Louisiana, Arkansas, South Carolina, Georgia, and Florida. This was a necessity, thrown upon them by a positive refusal on the part of the convention, to recognize their right of property in the Territories. Since the adaption of the Cincinnati Platform in 1856, the Supreme Court of the United States, in the Dred Scott decision, declared "it to be the duty of the General Government to protect slavery in the territories. On the assembling of the convention, at Charleston, a Committee of one from each State, was appointed with instructions to report a platform of principles. Seventeen states voted against sixteen, to embody the principle of the Dred Scott decision, guaranteeing *protection* to slave property in the territories. The convention refused to ratify the report of the majority of the committee by a vote of 2371/2 to 65!!! The nine Southern States had either to remain in the convention, and yield to the detestable doctrine of Squatter Sovereignty and thus give up their right to an equality in the Territories, acquired by their common blood and treasure or signify their dissent by peaceably withdrawing. The Delegates from Alabama, before leaving the Convention submitted a protest, (...) from which we make the following extract.

A lengthy summation of the protest made by the Alabama delegates followed, to which Raleigh made a comment.

"I have the feeling that these newspapers will have news of the Civil War as this article is the first stirring of discontent among the Democrats who controlled the Political South at that time."

The next paper that was removed from the box reinforced that assumption.

BALTIMORE CONVENTION
Baltimore, June 18

The Convention was called to order at 11 o'clock. Immediately upon the organization, at least fifty delegates arose at a time, endeavoring to be heard, A scene of indescribable confusion took place. The Douglas men had agreed among themselves to thrust the question of admitting the bogus delegates at once; but they were over-awed by the firm and decided resistance of the South. Every effort to gag and silence the Southern delegates was made. Mr. Russell however calmly notified the factionist that Virginia was prepared to meet the crisis and to lead the South in defenc of her rights. His remarks were received with vociferous cheers

If the Convention acts fairly, Douglas cannot be nominated under any circumstances, and excepting the enthusiasts and the legions of office seekers in prospective, there is a disposition to drop him and take up another man. Beckinridge is looming up, and many are firm in the belief that he will eventually be taken up. Guthrie will receive the vote of the entire South. Seymour is held in reserve for a while, when New York will bring him out. Dickerson would be the choice of the South if his nomination were possible. Pierce is mention in certain quarters. It is, however, almost certain that the Convention will break up

"Politics in the Democratic Party had already turned nasty in the first convention in Charleston when the delegates from the Southern states walked out, as we read in the first paper. It didn't get any better when they met again in Baltimore," Raleigh again spoke up as they finished their reading of the article. "In fact, the Southern Delegates had a separate convention in Richmond, Virginia, to nominate their choice for President, John C. Breckenridge and General Joseph Lane for Vice President. Of course, all this division in their party ensured a victory for the Republican candidate, Abraham Lincoln.

The next paper to be removed from the box had a leading article headed:

Disunion !!

Who has divided the Democratic party? Who is still endeavoring to divide the United States? Look over the country and see how easy it is to pick out the man whose every action, for three years past, has indicated such to be his hellist purpose. You see him first opposing that true patriot, James Buchanan, a Democratic President, and endeavoring to thwart his administration in all its aims , for the good of the country. You next see him opposing the admission of Kansas as a slave State. Although he had solemnly pledged himself to vote for it. Although he had told southern men, here now, you will get your rights, although not a human being of any party expected him to oppose it, yet he did so. Why? Because he has determined that no more slave states shall ever be added to this Union. He wanted to boast to the Black Republicans, that he has done more against slavery than they had, that he did what they could not do—defeated the admission of a State with a constitution recognizing slavery.-- Where do we see him since that time? Voting day after day with the abolitionist, never once casting a vote for a democratic measure, or for a democratic administration. His course was so obstinate, so false to all his pledges, that a Democratic Senate removed him from the chairmanship of the committee on territories. Follow him still further. His speeches are all made up of abuse for the Democratic President and Cabinet. Then what do you see? Hundreds of Know Nothings and weak-kneeds democratics, crowd around him , and urge him on. To do what! Well, this hungry and malevolent band have divided it, but thank God, it is not destroyed.

The old banner is afloat, with the names of Patriots on its folds, floating in the sunlight, and cheering the gaze of the great Democratic host. The arch traitor, S. A. Douglas, who has done all the mischief, who now seeks to rend the Union asunder; who has been allied with abolitionist for three years, will, if he succeeds in destroying the Democratic party, wear the blackest name that infamy ever stamped on the human race. But, will you allow it, freeman of America! Will you allow your dearest rights—the rights bequeathed you by an immortal ancestry; the rights guaranteed in your constitution—to be torn from your grasp, by this ambitious tyrant?

Choose you, between him and John C. Breckenridge, the true and tried----

"What a crock!" Jenny spontaneously uttered the words as she finished reading the article. "They write about the rights bequeathed to you by an immortal ancestry. The rights bequeathed to this land belonged to the original inhabitants of this land which were the Native Americans. They certainly did not honor those rights--and now they complain! Who is the ambitious tyrant in this picture? To whom did the immortal ancestry rightfully belong? Go back twelve years and who are the tyrants, and who raised a voice against the atrocities carried out against the Indians then?

"Those people from Georgia and the rest of the South showed no mercy on the Cherokee when they wanted their land and everything that they had. Now for the sake of keeping and oppressing the black man as slaves, they are doing the same thing over again.

"And I tell you something else about that article that hacked me off. When it reads, 'will you allow it, freeman of America?' the slave had no rights, just the freeman. We know that there would be a war fought so that the freeman could prosper while the slave would continue under bondage. This was all about keeping more people oppressed, not free. I'm happy that those who opposed slavery were the victor in the conflict which was soon to come."

The article concluded by heaping praise on John C. Breckenridge, the nominee of the Southern Democrats who had met in Richmond. Additional newspapers were removed from the box which had articles citing events which were intensifying hostilities between the Northern and Southern states. It was not all good news for the South as the following report showed.

Florence Gazette.
Florence, Ala---Oct. 17, 1860

For President.
JOHN C. BRECKENRIDGE
Of Kentucky,
For Vice President:
General Joseph Lane,
Of Oregon

"The constitution and the equality of the States, these are the symbols of everlasting Union."---Breckenridge.

After this endorsement by the editors of the *Florence Gazette*, the following article lamented the direction in which the Northern states were going in regard to their choosing sides in the developing conflict. Things were surely not going as they had hoped.

A Survey of the Battle Field

Pennsylvania, Ohio, and Indiana, have spoken. They are lost. As the smoke clears away, it shows that the enemies of the Constitution, and the South have swept the Old Keystone, by a majority estimated at 30,000,---and in the contest, all the elements of conservatism and opposition to abolitionism were marshaled in a solid phalanx, under their noble leader, Foster; but they went down overpowered by the deluge of Abolitionism which is sweeping, like the bosom of destruction , through the entire North. It was a deadly conflict, and our friends in the Old Keystone State, conscious that the eyes of the nation were upon them, fought nobly and well. They have fallen, but with their faces to the foe, battling for Truth, Justice, and the Constitution. Our surprise at the results in Pennsylvania, is as great as our sorrow. In Ohio and Indiana, we must say that we are not surprised. Notwithstanding, Mr. Douglas and his friends have said that he would carry the entire Northwest; yet we thought as the results shows, that he was as powerless there as he is everywhere else. Ohio and Indiana, counted by him as his certain and reliable States, have spoken against him in thousands. We truly and sincerely regret his inability to roll back the tide of Abolitionism in these States. Since the Baltimore Convention adjourned, State elections have been held in Maine, Vermont, Pennsylvania, Ohio, and Indiana, and the black Republicans have swept everything by increased majorities. Let us turn to the South, where, as Mr. Yancey eloquently said the other day, in Washington, "The Friends of the Constitution

> live." The Breckenridge Democrats have carried the States of North Carolina, Arkansas, Texas, Florida, Mississippi, and Delaware, by overwhelming majorities. In Missouri it is a drawn battle between the Breckenridge and Douglas forces—the former securing the U.S. Senator, and the latter the Governor. The tide that swells from the South, and rolls in an irresistible current towards the North, bears above the foam, the glorious mottoe of "The Constitution and the equality of the States."—All the indications, as evinced by the late elections, narrow down the contest to a fight between Black Republicanism, and the Constitutional forces, headed by Breckenridge and Lane.—How the contest will end, God, in his wisdom, alone can tell. As it now stands, it is between Lincoln on one hand, and Breckenridge on the other. The fairy spell, which the Douglas supporters in the South, believed hung around his name and fortunes, has now vanished.

A copy of the November 7th edition of the *Florence Gazette* included election returns for the Democrats in Lauderdale County. Douglas carried the vote by around 100 votes, another disappointment to the editor of the *Gazette*. With one or two precincts not yet reported the results were—Breckenridge-683, Douglas-774, and Bell-437.

The *Gazette*, dated November 14, 1860, however, gave complete election results which showed Breckenridge to be the winner statewide. Breckenridge carried the Southern slave holding counties by a large majority, while the counties in the Warrior Mountains where there were few slaves and opposition to secession, seemed to favor Douglas. Following the heading, the editors presented the following question:

How shall we meet the Crisis?

It is to be hoped that whatever we may resolve to do, will not be done by a partisan movement. As far as the editors of this paper are concerned, we shall do all in our power to allay party spirit. We are all beaten—badly beaten. It matters not which party got the highest vote; nor is it a suitable time to indulge in recrimination. But it is the duty of every patriot to law aside partisan prejudice and bitterness, and unite in council, irrespective of party, and consider what is best to be done. If our deliberations take a party turn, then madness will again rule the hour, and prudence will depart from our council chambers. We all know how utterly impossible it is for the different political parties to agree on any line of policy. Then let our first movement be to allay party bickering. The mere temporal success of this wing or that, is of paltry significance, when compared to the momentous questions that are now rising up before us, and which we cannot avoid. In fact they are upon us. Shall we meet and decide them as patriots? Our shall we, like cunning partisans, seek the strong, instead of the right side, and thus purchase partisan success at the cost of the best interest of the country? Shade of Washington hover over and around this people, and inspire their hearts with wisdom and forbearance, sobriety and patriotism.

Results of the Election

So far as heard from, Breckenridge has carried twelve states, all southern. Bell and Douglas, it is thought, have each, carried a State—not, however by a majority, but by a mere plurality. It is not certain; however, that Douglas has carried a single State. In many of the Southern States, Mr. Breckenridge will beat vote of Bell and Douglas combined. This will, doubtless, be the case in Alabama. The doctrine of squatter sovereignty, for years has been denounced by all parties of the South—when Mr. Fillmore ran, the contest was, who could denounce it loudest, and most unsparingly. (Sic) voters of the South were asked to select Mr. Douglas, as the only living man who stood a chance to beat Lincoln. It was urged that his popularity in the North, and North-west was unbounded. We knew it was not so. In the contest in 1858, with Lincoln for the Senate, the latter comparatively an obscure man, carried the popular vote of Illinois over Douglas, by from four to five thousand.—Although Douglas rode his popular sovereignty hobby, and assured the Black Republicans that it would secure to the freesoilers, all the Territories, more certainly and effective, than the Wilmot Proviso of Stewart and Lincoln. He appealed to the Black Republicans to support him, in preference to Lincoln, in the language:

"How following —said he—has the South lost her power as the majority section in the Union and how have the free States gained it, except under the operation of that principle which declares the right of the people of each State and each Territory, to form and regulate their domestic institutions in their own way." "It was—said he—under that principle that the number of free States increased, until from being one out of twelve States, we have grown to be the majority of States of the whole Union, with the power to control the House of Representatives and Senate, and the power, consequently, to elect a President by Northern votes, without the aid of a Southern State."

His doctrine of popular sovereignty, was denounced by Mr. Calhoun, by Mr. Crittenden, Mr. Denton and by the Democratic and southern whig, and southern know nothing parties, and by the Supreme Court of the United States, and yet we are asked to take him and his popular sovereignty doctrine! To abandon a *principle* for the *man* because he was strong at the North'—He has not carried a single northern or northwestern State, though in several of them, there was no Breckenridge ticket in his way. Mr. Douglas is particularly infuriated against the south, and threatens to aid Lincoln in whipping back, into the Union any southern State that dares, in the exercise of its sovereignty, to assume the power conferred upon its agent, the General Government. After that threat, the *Wide Awakes,* known to be Lincoln's body guard, welcomed Mr. Douglas back to the North, and escorted him with honors! Is the South then to be thus terrified into submission? Has she no rights but such as Lincoln, and Douglas, and a mere sectional, and now dominant majority, see proper to allow? Mr. Lincoln has long since announced the destruction of slavery—He says the States must be all slave, or all *free states.* Our fathers not only thought differently, but guaranteed to each State, the right to have slaves, or not as the pleased, and guaranteed to the slave States a return of fugitive slaves to their masters. Twelve of the Northern States have defied the Constitution, and nullified, by legislative enactments, the fugitive slave law.

"Abolitionism was certainly the hot issue in this election," Dutch made the comment after reading the article written in the last paper which they had read. "It seems that the focus of the newspapers stored in this box is on the slavery issue. Now we know that the ones who controlled the plantation from which this box originated were strongly opposed to slavery and sided with the North. Newspapers were their only way of getting the latest news regarding the events that were taking place in the country and Sarah saw fit to save those articles concerning that topic. For the sake of space, only the page on which the story was written was retained, and the remainder of the paper was discarded."

"It is taking longer to read this than I expected," Jenny said when everyone had finished reading the paper that was last removed from the box. "These papers have been well preserved due to the airtight fit of the lid onto the box, but the printing in those days left a lot to be desired. There were some words in that article which were hard to figure out and a couple that we have no clue as to what they were. The ink was smudged so badly that I couldn't decipher them."

"We have to consider the fact that those newspapers are over one hundred and fifty years old," Abigail responded. "Today, printing and publishing technology has advanced to such a high degree that it is easy for us to forget that there was a time when it was a difficult task to print and publish. Printing equipment was still in the primitive stages when these newspapers were published. There appears to be a lot of reading to be done from this box, and I suspect that some of it will be rather difficult to read—we shall see."

"Dutch re-entered the conversation by commenting on the many mistakes that were in the articles. "It is obvious that there was no proofreader in that newspaper organization. It apparently was a one-man operation, but I suppose that had it been us doing the work back then we would have done no better; probably a lot worse. The significant thing is that we still have them as they were printed, mistakes and all."

As Dutch removed another single page, he made an additional comment after glancing at it. "This is the *Florence Gazette* dated Nov. 28, 1860. It looks like the slavery controversy remains front page news. The focus is now on the President elect Abraham Lincoln."

The lead article was a print of a speech made by Charles Sumner on Lincoln's election, followed by the editor's short assessment of that speech.

A new Government.

On the second day after Lincoln's election, this noted abolitionist was serenaded by the "Wide Awakes." and among other things, made the following announcement.

Every four years we chose a new president, but it very rarely happens that we chose a new government. But yesterday we not only chose a new president but a new government. A new order of things were inaugurated by the vote of yesterday, which will put our country under a new direction and lift it up to the platform of principles on which it was originally placed by our fathers. Several things may be considered to be fairly established by the vote of yesterday, if we look at it in a practical light. First, the American people have declared, according to the very words of Madison, that it is wrong to admit into the constitution the idea that there can be property in man. They have declared that slavery, that if it exist anywhere, is sectional, and must derive all such life as it has from local laws, not from the constitution; in other words, that slavery is sectional and freedom national; in opposition to the idea which has been put forward so often, that freedom was sectional and slavery national. In the second place, the American people have declared by this vote that all the outlying territories of the government, so enormous in extent, and destined to be inhabited by an immense population, shall be concentrated to freedom; that the soil shall never be pressed by the footstep of the slave. In the third place, they have declared that the old original policy of the fathers of the administration of the national government shall be adopted in opposition to the slave policy which has been especially pursued for the last twelve years, and more or less during the last forty years. They have declared that the slave trade, which it is now proposed to open with increased activity, shall be in reality suppressed , and that all the force of the government shall be directed in that way. These things have been declared by that vote solemnly and in a way from which there can be no appeal.—Surely, this is a great action for our country, and forms a landmark in its history. It now remains that, having obtained this great victory, we should know how to use it with moderation, with prudence, with wisdom. I believe that Abraham Lincoln – (prolong cheers)—has those elements of character that will enable him to carry us through this crisis; that he is prudent, wise discreet, and also brave. I believe that bravery is necessary in directing the affairs of government, as much as prudence. I believe that he is the man especially to see that we are not in any way checked or set back by the menaces of disunion which sometimes come to us from the

South, and are repeated in Massachusetts. To these menaces we deem it necessary to make no other reply than to proceed with our work in the spirit of the constitution, wisely, prudently, answering their threats with "The Union shall be preserved," and made more precious by its consecration to human freedom. (Three cheers for the Union.)

This, now, is the programme—they have the numerical power, and the only way they can carry out their hellish purposes, is to keep us in the union. Out of the Union, they would have no power over us, and hence they now say that they will answer our threats with the boast that "The Union *shall* be preserved," and made more gracious by its consecration to human freedom, alias abolition of slavery. They may have a *new* government North, and we can have a new government South. We are beaten but not conquered.

Also on the same page was another article with the heading, *"Lincoln's Platform"* with the opening paragraph reading, "We hope every Southern man will read the proclamation of Lincoln's special organ. If the South is prepared for such doctrines, the sooner she decides it the better."

A third article is titled, *"Lincoln an Abolitionist Proof from his own lips."* This article from the New York *Weekly Express* covers a "Certain memorable occasion" when the "Ohio negroes saw fit to compliment Gov. Chase with a silver pitcher, as a testimony of their esteem for one who had so much affection for them."

The ceremony took place at Cincinnati with Mr. Abraham Lincoln present. In the course of an address to the Negroes, Mr. Lincoln expressed the conviction that "all the individuals of that class are members of the community, and in virtue of their manhood, entitled to *every original right enjoyed by any other member."*

He went on to say:

> "We feel, therefore, that all *legal distinction* between individuals of the same community, founded in any such circumstances as color, origin and the like, are hostile to the genus of our institutions, and incompatible with the true theory of American liberty. Slavery and oppression must cease or American Liberty must perish. I embrace with pleasure this opportunity of declaring my *disapprobation* that clause of the Constitution which denies to a portion of the *colored people,* the right of suffrage.
>
> True democracy makes no inquiry about the color of the skin, or place of nativity, or any other similar circumstances"---the article continued With Abraham Lincoln denouncing the practice of Slavery in the Union.

"I think we've got the message!" Jenny exclaimed. "The *Florence Gazette* has taken a stand against Abolitionism, Black Republicans, Douglas, Lincoln, and anything that has the word 'North' in it. I am also thinking that these papers were saved because they opposed slavery and all this was good news."

"I think that you probably hit the nail on the head with that assessment," Abigail replied.

Following the election of Abraham Lincoln as President of the United States, the Southern States could think of nothing but Secession. The *Florence Gazette* was filled with articles favoring a new government for the South as was evidenced by the following article which was printed in the edition dated Jan. 9, 1861. This article followed one covering three columns which discussed the *"great controversy between the Northern and Southern states"* where the Northern Confederates *"Desire to establish a despotism, not only omnipotent in Congress but omnipotent over the states; and as if to manifest the important necessity of our secession, they threaten us with a sword, to coerce submission to their rule."*

Progress of the Revolution.

Events are hastening on, and the great work of Deliverance and Liberty from northern wrongs and Northern oppression, progress to a glorious consummation. South Carolina has seceded, and her convention has appointed eight delegates to join the other southern States in a Southern Congress to adopt the Constitution of the United States, for the Southern Confederacy. The convention of the people of Florida, met on the third last, and there is no doubt that she, too, is has seceded. The convention of the people of Alabama and Mississippi met at their respective Capitals on the 7th last, and before we serve another paper, both of these States will each have re-sumed thepowers delegated by them to the General Government, and will have declared their independence.

In the meantime, the Governors of the southern States have seized on the forts and arsenals in their respective States—to prevent them from falling into the hands of our enemies. A wise step, and deserving of all praise. Georgia voted on the 2nd January, and has given an overwhelming majority for immediate secession. The legislatures of Virginia, Tennessee, and Missouri, met on the first Monday in January, and no doubt, each will call Conventions to determine

> on *the mode and measure of regress;* and what the mode and measure of regress will be—none can doubt. The mode will be a convention of the people in their *Sovereign* capacity—and the measure of redress—secession, immediate, absolute, and forever. Louisiana, Texas, and Arkansas have already called Conventions, and before the Abolitionists can inaugurate Mr. Lincoln, and the "irrepressible conflict" on the 4th of March—the southern states will have formed and established a Government, amply able to protect their people and their liberties and institutions—so deeply imperiled by a remorseless northern, sectional disposition. Let all lovers of free institutions, rejoice. Let co-operation men, and resistance men cease their bickering—for the end for which all aimed—namely—a united south—is rapidly being accomplished.

Abigail spoke up after reading this article, "If the editors of the *Gazette* could have gotten a glimpse of the carnage that lay ahead, the optimism and prediction of a glowing future for the South would have been silenced. As we now know, the Southern states at that time were taking action that would lead to devastating results. They were picking a fight which would leave battlefields covered with the bodies of their brave young men and their cities laid in ruin. In everything that we have read, at this time the South was confident that the action that they were taking in seceding from the Union would be '*everlasting*'."

Abigail was much too late in her remark to warn the Southerners that they were making a grave mistake.

A subsequent article in another edition of the *Gazette*, quoting an article from the *Memphis Avalanche*, dated January 30, continued to paint a rosy picture for the future of the South after seceding from the Union.

THE SOUTH UNITING—PUSH ON THE COLUMN.

The South is fast consolidating her forces. In less than sixty days we believe her people will be grappled together with "hooks of steel" in the great cause of Southern Deliverence—joined in the tender ties of nativity and kin—and each brother, hand in hand, resolve with one heart to defend, and die if need be, in defenc of the right. A few—actuated by some unaccountable hate for the community in which they move and breathe and have an unworthy existence—are fostering petty feuds, engendering animosities, and wrangling and disputing about trifles but the great masses of the Southern people, as if by an irresistible attraction, are gradually meeting and moving together toward a common centre. Eminent statesmen of the South—Chieftains of the old parties—veterans, marked with the scars of mutual contest—forgetting and forgiving the past, at length are uniting their efforts to cement our union—to hush our dissensions and to spread the broad banner of peace and love over all our people.

The frothy demagogies—the sputtering partisan—the scheming tricksters, whose souls are absorbed inself—whose patriotism consist in the acquisition of place, and the hope of pay—men whom no change can (sic), and to whom notoriety is fame—will continue to plot, as they always done, to foment disputes, and stir up heart-burnings amongst us. The coward's heart and traitor's wile, which blast-alike the counsels of the brave, will seek to "sickly o'er the native hue" of manly resolution, and to unnerve, by whisperings of distrust and dismay, the strong arms of the South's noblest champions. But, we trust the virtuous indignation of our proverbially chivalrous but injured people, awakened at last to their true interest, condemning the artful whispering by which they have heretofore been denuded, conscious of their rights and resolved to maintain them, will now sweep in to (sic), and cover with contempt those vile deceivers by whom the South has, so long been weakened and embroiled. Let every high-souled true-hearted Southron, no matter of what political faith or party, lend a helping hand in the consummation of the glorious work of bringing the whole South together in the maintainence of our rights and the dignity of our position as equals in the confederacy, or in dissolving a compact under which we are to become slaves. Speed on the calumet among all our hitherto hostile tribes until bickering and jealousies and strifes shall be heard no

more throughout all our borders. When this time shall arrive, then, indeed, will the South come forth, "as a bridegroom from his chamber, rejoicing as a strong man to run a race," invested with a power, a dignity, and a splender, which will elicit the envy, as it will attract the admiration of the whole world.

The edition of the *Gazette* dated February 6, 1861, which Dutch next removed from the box, consumed four complete columns to report the speech which Governor Moore made to the two houses of the General Assembly of the Senate and House of Representatives on January 14, 1861.

After its removal, Dutch was compelled to comment, "These newspapers are more than I bargained for when

I opened this box, but they are interesting reading. Do you want to read these as we remove them, or should we set them aside to read at a later date?"

"They obviously were put in this box for a purpose," Jenny answered. "As the articles are marked which were of interest to the one doing the packing, I feel that if there is another journal at the bottom of the box, as was found in the first two, that these papers might be pertinent to the messages written in it.

"And on top of that, I find them quite interesting. I have just scanned the message of the governor and he is reporting to the General Assembly the status of the Secession movement in the Southern states and the action he has taken to separate the state of Alabama from the Union and seize control of anything which might belong to the Federal government.

"He seized control of the banks and prepared to get the finances needed to carry on the business of the state as it prepared for the conflict with the North. He reported that he had made plans for the qualified voters, to elect delegates to a convention of the state."

"Very well," Dutch responded. "We will keep reading what looks like could well be a history of the action which led up to the Civil War, and from the looks of these newspapers, perhaps the war itself." Dutch reached deep into the box and lifted one end of the stack of papers. "Yeah, just as I suspected. There is another journal beneath these papers. It looks like that there is some kind of box beneath these papers with a journal at the bottom."

After reading the governor's message, Abigail suggested that they take a break from their reading and eat some dessert which had been prepared by Angie.

"It appears that there is another long article in this paper," Dutch commented as he removed another paper after their short recess from their readings. He removed a paper with an article copied from the *Montgomery Advertiser* dated Feb. 1861. It was headed:

INAUGURAL ADDRESS
Of
PRESIDENT DAVIS
Delivered at THE CAPITOL, on
Monday, 1 o'clock, pm, Feb. 18, 61
Gentlemen of the Confederate States
Of America; Friends and fellow
Citizens:

"The entire Inaugural Address which was given by Jefferson Davis after his election to the Presidency of the newly established Confederate States of America is printed in this edition," Dutch reported. "I propose that we just shuffle through some of these or else I could miss a crop while we read newspapers that are over one hundred years old.

"I am sure that President Davis delivered a stellar presentation to his friends and fellow citizens of the Confederacy, but I think that we just won't read that at the present time. Whatever he hoped for, we now know that the outcome was not what he envisioned at that time."

After the others agreed, Dutch placed the paper on the stack that had already been read. He removed more from the box and was granted permission to also forgo the reading of them. However, one paper from the *Avalanche*, April 13th, caught his attention.

The War Has Begun
FIRING SINCE 4 O'CLOCK A.M., FRIDAY

> TWO OF THE SUMTER GUNS SILENCED!
> ## A Breach Made!
> Only seven Confederate Batteries in
> Action out of Nineteen!
> NO CASUALTIES IN THE S.C. RANKS
> Great excitement in Charleston

"It looks like the bell has just sounded for round one!" Raleigh exclaimed after reading the headline and the dispatches that followed of "Beauregard and Anderson, etc. etc." After looking at the following edition of the *Gazette* dated Wednesday Morning April 17, 1861, Dutch made a follow-up response to the comment made by Raleigh.

"Round one goes to the Rebels of the South," he announced as if he was the ring announcer.

The news of the outcome of the first battle of the Civil War at Fort Sumter, South Carolina, brought the citizens of Florence into the streets to celebrate. The *Gazette* reported the celebration.

> Florence, Ala.,
> Saturday Night, April 18, 1861.
> GLORIOUS NEWS RECEIVED
> Fort Sumter Surrendered
> Flag of the Southern Confederacy
> Hoisted on its Walls.
>
> ## GLORIOUS DEMONSTRATION!!
> Enthusiasm Unequaled
> ## BONFIRES IN THE STREETS!
> Burning of Fire-Crackers, Rockets,
> etc., etc.

Houses illuminated.
Military Parading!
SPEECHES!
Volunteers Called for, etc., etc., etc.

On Saturday night, last about dark, the news was received here, that Fort Sumter had been surrendered to the Confederate State troops, and that the **flag of the Southern Confederacy had been hoisted on its walls. And then,** reader, commenced a scene. The flame of rejoicing was small, at first, but, like fire in the stubble, it gathered strength as it went, and very soon, our streets were thronged with people, all of whom were rejoicing in the strongest manner, as if they were wild with delight. The masses were in commotion. The streets were soon lit up with bonfires, around which the people clustered, shouting hurras for the Southern Confederacy, its beautiful flag—the flag of the *free,* under the folds of which the *true* southern men are determined to conquer, or fall. Cheers for General Beauregard; cheers for Jeff Davis and cheers for the South. Soon the houses, shops, and offices, were more brilliantly illuminated, which gave our town a truly cheerful aspect.—The sounds of the Drum and fife we soon heard, the notes of which seemed to inspire the assembly with a double degree of enthusiasm. The musicians marched up Main Street, followed by a large crowd, and as they passed the residence of Dr. Mitchell, cheers—heartily cheers—were given for the noble and gallant Yancey, (whose son was then a guest of the Doctor's) proving that though he was far away, yet he was not forgotten by his friends. These were answered by the ladies with wavings of handkerchiefs. On the return of music to the square, the "college Grays" were formed, and marched to and fro, in the streets, halting occasionally in front of a house, and giving the inmates three hearty cheers. Finally, they marched around by the seminary, which was beautifully illuminated, and here they gave three cheers for the young ladies, they answered by waving their handkerchiefs, which, with the ladies mean a great deal. The beauty of Florence not only cheered with the waving of their handkerchiefs, but they congregated on the corners, in front of their doors, and looked on with an interest and feeling that the sterner sex knew not of. The following are the houses that were illuminated, that we noticed, others might have been illuminated, but we do not remember of seeing any other:

Campbell's Hotel,
Stewart and Hays Doctor shop,
Farmers' livery Stable,
Mr. Hodgkins residence,
Mr. Podigger's residence,
G.W.Fosters residence,
Mrs. Stewart' residence,
Mr. Porrtlock's residence,
Female Seminary,

The list continued with the writer determined not to leave off the list anyone who went to the effort of illuminating their house.

It was surely a grand celebration, but in a short period of time it became hard for the Southerners to find reason to do any celebrating. The reality of war soon became a sobering experience.

CHAPTER 5

◆

The South had cut their ties with the Union and optimism was rampant as was displayed by the article in the next newspaper which was removed from the box. It was again the *FLORENCE GAZETTE*, dated March 20, 1861.

The Southern Confederacy.

The Southern Confederacy is now an established fact. The convention at Montgomery have ordained and established a constitution, and named the Republic "the Confederate States of America." Hon. Jefferson Davis of Mississippi, has been chosen President, and Hon. Alex. H. Stephens, of Georgia, Vice President. The constitution is substantially the same as that of the United States. Great care, however, is taken in the preamable to recognize the complete sovereignty of the several States. Were we to venture a prediction, we would say that we here have. The germ of a Republic which history, at no far distant day, will record as the most powerful and wealthy of ancient and modern times. It will grow and that, too rapidly, by additions from the North, from the South, and from the West. Its Government.

Purged of every notion of consolidation no State will hesitate to take shelter under its wings from any fear of losing its sovereignty. The burdens of that government will be light. It will be ministered according to the Southern idea. In the exercise of its powers it will be confined within the legitimate sphere of the Constitution.It will not be used as an engine of corruption.—it will not be used as an instrument of executing those projects which belong only to State governments or individual enterprise. It will build no railroads and canals. It will undertake to build up no manufacturing interest at the expense of other interest.---Hence its burdens will be light, and consequently trade will be nearly or quite free. Capital which has for the last three quarters of a century has been aggregating in northern cities, will begin to turn Southwards. By dedress the trade of Boston, New York, and Philadelphia will decrease, whilst that of Charleston, Savannah, Mobile, and New Orleans will proportionately increase--- Immigration will also turn thither ward. The North has lost, irrevocably lost, we fear, her largest and best customer. Our future we may read in the past of Canada. Negro sympathy which has of late been so active with us, will in a few months more, be like a tale told. We shall hear no more of slavery in the South, than we now hear of it in Cuba, and Russia. From New England, at least, the scepire of Empire has departed forever, and that through the folly of her own sons.---Banger Daily Union.

"Some of that I can relate to," Dutch commented after reading the article. "The burden of the government will be light; it will be confined to the legitimate sphere of the Constitution; it will not be used as an engine of corruption; it will not be used as an instrument of executing those projects which belong only to the state government or individual enterprise; it will build no railroads or canals; it will undertake to build up no manufacturing interest at the expense of other interest; its burdens will be light and trade will be nearly or quite free. Now that I can go along with, but in the next sentence it says that slavery should remain as it is; that I cannot go along with."

"Remember, they had politicians in the Confederacy just as we have today. If you don't understand that all those promises are nothing but political rhetoric, then you don't have a good understanding of politics," Raleigh weighed in on the statement made by Dutch. "Promises made by politicians or that are reported in a newspaper one day are irrelevant the next."

"You certainly have a valid point there," Jenny echoed.

"There is no longer dancing in the streets in Florence!" Dutch exclaimed as he held up the next paper from the stack in the box. "These battle reports seem to be taking more and more of a local slant as the losses of the homegrown fighters take a greater toll on the families in the Tennessee Valley area."

He held a copy of The *Florence Gazette* dated July 31, 1861, with S. G. Barr & Brother as the editors.

To the voters of Lauderdale COUNTY

Yesterday we received the painful intelligence of the killed and wounded of Capt. McFarland's company. My son is among the wounded at Manassas, and I feel it to be my imperative duty to go there to attend to his wants. This will deprive me of the opportunity of attending the appointments of the Candidates, as was my intention. In this canvass, I shall take it for granted there can be no party issues; that the one great common object with us all, will be to conquer an honorable peace, by a vigorous prosecution of the war. It is a war of aggression on the part of the north; of self defence, of resistance to tyranny and oppression on the part of the south. I am for a liberal appropriation of men and money for our defence. After this, I would save every dollar, by a strict economy in all the departments of the Government. To shrink from liberal contributions of necessary taxation at a time like this, when all the property of the country, and the dearest rights of freeman are staked upon our success, in this war, would certainly prolong the war, if it did not lead to our ultimate defeat and subjugation. In this great hourof our country's need, we must not be "penny wise and pound foolish." We are well able to defend ourselves, our resources are ample—our soldiers are invincible. The great victory at Manassas, is also a great grief, to many families in this county. In McFarland's company, alone, we hear of ten killed and twenty one or two wounded.

The names of the killed and wounded filled the remainder of the column.

"So much for the burdens of government being light," Raleigh stated after reading the article. "Just as I said, don't trust what a politician might say or a newspaper might print. The person who printed it in the last edition has now changed his tune when his son gets wounded in battle. He is now for a liberal appropriation of men and money and liberal contributions of necessary taxation. 'The burden of the government cannot be light now because this war is getting personal and my son is wounded.' I wonder what he expected when they started a war and the shooting started? People get hurt and killed in wars; that is the nature of the beast, and it cost a lot of money. It shouldn't have come as a surprise!"

Then they saw in the third column, in the same edition, on the front page, filling the entire column was an "Account of Eye Witness!" Richmond, July 22, 1861.

"At 8 o'clock on Sunday morning the enemy commenced operations at Mclane's Ford on Bull Runn, by opening their batteries of rifled cannon and heavy light field pieces..." A lengthy, colorful account of the battle followed. General Beauregard and Johnston were highly praised after they *"heroically threw themselves into the thick of the fight, and their words, presence and example of reckless personal daring infused new life and spirit into the brave soldiery."* The account of the battle continues:

"General Beauregard covered himself with glory. Lient. Col. Johnson of the "Hampton Legion" of South Carolinians, being killed, and Col Hampton wounded, Gen Beauregard assumed command of the Legion, and in person led it into action in the most gallant style.

In leading the charge the head of Gen. Beauregard's horse was struck off by a shell which also killed the horses of two of his aids, messrs Howard and Ferguson of South Carolina at the same moment.

Reinforcements of the Confederates having come up just at the critical moment, the tide of battle began to turn in our favor, the enemy falling back, though in good order.

Col. Bartow, of Georgia, was struck dead from his horse, while leading a magnificent charge of his regiment with its colors in his hand.

Beauregard commanded throughout the day, bearing himself in the most gallant style and utter disregard of personal danger. He was everywhere, directing maneuvers small and great. He was several hours under heavy fire, escaping many shells and rifled shot evidently aimed at him. I myself saw a shell burst not twenty yards from him.

General Johnson "aided" him; it is said, though entitled to command by superior rank. They appeared to be mutual in command, acting with perfect unison and accordance.

The panorama of the field was magnificent, beyond description. The line of battle extended seven miles, with its columns of charging infantry, its dashing squadrons of cavalry and flying artillery, its batteries thundering and sending up clouds of smoke.

The battalion of Washington Artillery of New Orleans, Col. Walton, managed their battery with wonderful judgment and dexterity, doing great execution in the enemy's rank. Sergeant Johna Reynolds was the only man belonging to the battalion who was killed. He was struck in the forehead while given the word of command to his gunners. Privates John Payne and Crutcher were wounded. The artillery had their position within close range of the Michigan Regiment."

And so the account of the battle continued filling the page.

The next paper removed from the box was dated Wednesday morning, Nov. 13, 1961. It contained "Election

Returns from All Quarters," showing the results of the Presidential and Congressional election for the Confederacy. The list showed that Davis and Stephens were the clear winners for the position of President and Vice President, to which they had earlier been appointed.

Abigail chuckled when she spotted a short written comment in the next column over from the news of the election. She was compelled to read it aloud to the others. "Check this out," she prefaced her reading of the article.

> "The Bible says, "let your light so shine." Etc., but nara time does it say to pay fifty cents per pound for candles, and from two to four dollars per gallon for Coal Oil, which are the ruling prices in this neck of the woods, and no oil to be had at that.

"Thank goodness for TVA," Jenny laughed at the thought of life before Edison. "Maybe I am a tad weird, but I enjoy reading the short articles and local news stories which would have nothing to do with the reasons those newspapers were saved," she commented. "They have nothing to do with the war which was the major story at that time. When we continue reading, I may want to verbally read one or two of them just to lighten the horrors of the printed accounts of the bloody conflicts."

"Everybody ready to read?" Dutch questioned the others. "There are additional articles in this edition which were of interest to the individual who preserved these newspapers."

Two additional articles found in the *Florence Gazette*, dated Wednesday morning, Nov 13, 1861, had been checked. The first one was a denunciation of the "Tories" in their midst.

Bridge Burning

We learned by the Memphis Appeal, of Friday last, that the tories in EastTennessee, and Georgia, have burnt the railroad bridges, up to with in five or six miles of Chatanooga. One or tow bridges on the Memphis and Charlston road have been burnt, and one or two on the road leading to Richmond. We were inhopes that this was not the case, but have since been assured that such is the fact. We were slow to believe that there were any persons so far lost to any sense of honor, and so deeply steeped in sin, and hatred to the south, and ardently attached to the old Union, as to be guilty of such an uncalled for act of traitorism as to burn the bridges refered to. All bridges of any importance, on railways, should have good and efficient guards placed at them, in times like the present, either by the Government, or the railroad companies, to protect them against the torch of the incendiary, or the vile touch of the tory.

Tories in our midst, can and will do us more injury than an open enemy. They can profess loyalty to the Southern Confederacy, and at the same time be engaged in their hellish plots for its overthrow, and utter destruction; they are giving our enemies all the information they can; giving them the plans of our defences; the number of our men, and instructing them in different ways, as to the best way of attacking us.

We are no alarmist , far from it, but would it not be a good plan to have an increased guard put upon our bridge, to protect it from the torch of the incendiary? One man cannot guard it as it should be guarded at a time like the present. Who knows

> but that we may have some tories among us, only
> waiting for an opportunity to apply the torch to the
> bridge that now spans our river, and if that it be
> destroyed, how or on what will we cross the river?
> We throw out these hints, that those in authority
> may set on them, if they see proper.

"There is another marked article on this page, but before we read it, I want to comment on the first one," Raleigh interrupted. "Wesley S. Thompson wrote a very good book in 1960 titled *Tories of the Hills*. It has been some time since I read it; the book is no longer in print and copies are almost impossible to find, but I still remember some of what I read from it. The book gives an interesting account of the Tories which were condemned in the article we have just read.

"Many of the hill people in North Alabama, especially in Winston County and surrounding areas, were strongly opposed to Secession and the war that followed. These people were branded as Tories, reviving the terminology of 1776 which was given those who opposed the War of Revolution. A statewide election was held the day before Christmas on December 24, 1860, with Dr. Andrew Kaeiser being the candidate to represent Winston County in a Secessionist Convention.

Raleigh stopped his recall of the story to add, "By the way, the author spells this doctor's name differently than how Kaeiser's relatives always spelled it in their correspondence with him. Thompson spells it K-a-i-s-e-r, and his relatives spelled it with an extra 'e' in it, so I'm not sure which way is actually correct."

"Anyway," Raleigh continued with the main part of his story. "The convention was scheduled to meet in Montgomery on January 7, 1861. Chris Sheets, who opposed Secession, was selected as his opponent in the election. Although Dr. Kaeiser campaigned hard all over Winston County, Chris defeated him by almost a four to one margin."

"I was in Winston County on State Road 195 a few weeks ago, and near a little place called Ash Ridge, there was a barn that had 'THE FREE STATE OF WINSTON' painted on the front and side of the building. What is that all about?" Dutch inquired, "I know that it had something to do with the county's opposition to the Secessionist movement, but I don't remember the details."

"The best that I can recall," Raleigh responded to the question, "and that is covered in Wesley Thompson's book and some more accounts that I have read, that handle was given to the county after a meeting at Looney's Tavern on the Fourth of July 1861. The meeting was called by those who were in opposition to the State of Alabama seceding from the Union. Bill Looney, the owner of the tavern was strongly opposed to Secession and consented to make his tavern, which was a large building made of logs, available for the meeting. A number of individuals in favor of Secession showed up also, making it a somewhat contentious gathering. A free feast of barbecued wild hog, deer, cows, turkeys, bread, and an ample supply of beer, moonshine, and cider was served.

"Afterwards, the crowd was summoned by a large farm bell at Bill Looney's cabin. After the meeting came to order, Chris Sheets, who was the convention chairman, addressed the crowd of nearly three thousand people who had gathered there."

Raleigh paused and looked at Dutch, "I realize I am going the long way around to answer your question, but bear with me because I want to give you some background as to the reason for the proposed title that you asked about.

"Well anyway, Chris Sheets had appointed a committee to draw up resolutions for the meeting; he appointed a man named Tom Pink Curtis, the Winston County Probate Judge, to be the chairman. After Chris Sheets made a fiery speech condemning the Secessionists, the Committee on Resolutions was called on to submit their proposals. The first one commended Christopher C. Sheets and other representatives for their work and loyalty to the Union.

"The second one stated that if a state can lawfully and legally secede or withdraw, being only a part of the Union, then a county could. Being a part of the state by the same process of reasoning, a county could cease to be a part of the state.

"The third one stated that it was their beliefs that their neighbors in the South bolted and nominated a ticket which resulted in the election of Republican Abraham Lincoln; they made another, and even greater, mistake when they attempted to withdraw from the Union and set up a new government.

"The resolution read that they did not want their neighbors in the South mistreated; they would not take up arms against them, but on the other hand, they were not going to shoot at the flag of their fathers— the flag of Washington, Jefferson and Jackson. They asked the Confederates on one hand and the Union on the other hand to leave them alone, unmolested. That their political and financial differences might be worked out here in the hills and mountains of North Alabama. In other words, they were saying, 'Just leave us alone!'

"After the reading of the second proposal, a large man with long whiskers and wearing homespun jeans known as Uncle Dick Payne, a Confederate sympathizer, who was sitting on the edge of the table burst out in

a deep coarse voice and a sarcastic laugh, 'Ho! Ho!
Winston secedes! The Free State of Winston! The Free
State of Winston!'

"After a resounding 'Aye' vote had reverberated
through the hills approving the proposals, another old
man named J. L. Meeks, with long white hair and short,
pointed chin-whiskers, arose to address the crowd.
He started his little speech by saying that he felt that
not a whole lot of organization or preparation had
gone into the submitted proposal. He pointed out that
should they secede from the state, they would lose their
representation in the state legislature, and thereby, they
would have no voice to express the sentiments and
wishes of the people. To secede would mean that they
would have no way of sending representatives to either
the state or to the Union with claims of representing
them as a lawful and organized people.

"He added that to withdraw would make them to be
enemies, cut off from the rest of the Union, completely
surrounded by the seceded states, and left to the mercies
of the Rebel armies. He suggested that they instead,
approve a resolution asking that their rights as neutral
citizens be recognized, without seceding.

"Tom Pink Curtis promptly declared that, in view
of the facts just presented, it would be a wise thing for
them to postpone the act of secession and insert in the
resolutions a statement to both sides asking the Union
and the Confederacy to respect their neutrality. After
taking a vote to include this resolution that they be
allowed to remain neutral in the conflict and receiving
an even louder 'Aye' the resolution was adopted.

"Winston County never seceded from the state, and
it was never the Free State of Winston. It did, however,
result in their being branded as Tories. The newspaper
article that we have just read condemned the actions

of the Tories in East Tennessee and Georgia, but the Warrior Mountains and surrounding areas were filled with 'Tories of The Hills.' Considering what we learned from the first two journals we read from the cellar vault, I suspect that this place here may have been a Tory haven. Maybe we will find out about that!"

"That was an informative bit of history and very interesting," Dutch spoke when Raleigh had finished his history lesson. "We have interrupted the girls from their newspaper readings, but maybe they will forgive us. We will go to the next article which is circled on this page and see what it has to say."

"It appears that God was getting it from both sides," Abigail laughed as she started reading the next article. "Preacher Elliot asked the blessings of God upon all who sought peace and deliverance from the ravages of war and that they be spared the awful conflict, and then Jefferson Davis asked that God side with the Confederacy and be a shield and aid them in being victorious in their conflict."

There were actually two articles with headlines that dealt with the same subject.

They read:

Fasting and Prayer.

The president of the Confederate States, has issued a proclamation, setting apart Friday, the 15th inst, as a day of fasting and prayer. He requests both Ministers and people, to hold divine worship at their respective churches on that day. We are confident that our Ministers will do so, and we hope to see a general turnout on next Friday. Let all the stores, shops, and offices, be closed at the proper hour, and all repair to the house of worship, and there humble

> ourselves before the Ruler of the Universe, for his kind protection over us, since the commencement of the struggle now going on.

At the top of the next column over, the headlines read:

By the President-Proclamation

Whereas, it has pleased Almighty God, the Sovereign Dispenser of events to protect and defend the Confederate States hitherto, in the conflict with their enemies, and to be unto them a shield:

And, whereas, with grateful thanks we recognize His hand, and acknowledge that not unto us, but unto him belongeth the victory; and in humble dependence upon His Almight strength and trusting in his justness of our cause, we appeal to him that He may set at naught the efforts of our enemies, and put them to confusion and shame:

Now, therefore, I JEFFERSON DAVIS, President of the Confederate States, in view of the impending conflict, do hereby set apart Friday, the 15th day of November, as a day of fasting humiliation, and prayer: and I do hereby invite the Reverend Clergy and the people of these Confederate States, to repair on that day to their usual places of public worship, and to implore the blessing of Almighty God upon our arms, that He may give us victory over our enemies, preserve our homes and alters from pollution, and secure to us the restoration of peace and prosperity.

Given under my hand and the seal of the Confederate { SEAL} States at Richmond, this thirty first of October, in the year of our Lord one thousand eight hundred and sixty one.

JEFFERSON DAVIS
The President,
R M T HUNTER,
Secretary of State

"Times sure have changed," Abigail declared when she had finished reading the article. "I suppose that someone has learned the lesson that calling on God to choose sides doesn't win the battles. When there are prayers offered by opposing sides, it pays to have good weapons and ammunition to go with them. God is not going to deal with strategy and direct the attacks just because a proclamation or prayer is offered for him to intervene in the hostilities."

"Today that proclamation would immediately be declared unconstitutional and an injunction issued to prevent its enforcement," Jenny added.

"Since the Confederacy was no longer under the Constitution of the United States, things were apparently different under their new laws," Raleigh joined the conversation. "Of course, at that time, the same proclamation could most likely have been made by President Lincoln with no objections. The big ruckus about the Separation of Church and State has gained momentum within the last fifty years and was hardly an issue during the Civil War era.

"The proclamation was of interest to the person who outlined it and placed it in the box. I fully suspect that the article about the Tories was the primary reason the issue was saved. I suspect, considering the attitude that the family had against slavery, that they would have been classified in the Tory category. The journals that we have already read made it plain that Reverend Stone was adamantly opposed to slavery and did not consider the blacks who worked on his farm to be slaves, allowing them to leave if they wished."

Abigail reentered the conversation, "Of course none of them did, because they could find no better place to live than here on the farm."

After glancing at the next article which he had removed from the box, Dutch commented, "It looks like the Yankees have emptied those streets where the dancing took place about ten months ago. Instead of doing a dance, it appears that they are now running a marathon to get out of town! The war is not going the way that they had envisioned when they set those bonfires in the streets and illuminated their buildings. Of course, we know that it gets worse, much worse."

THE GAZETTE

FLORENCE:

WEDNESDAY MORNING—FEB. 12. 1862.

The headlines read:

Great Excitement in Florence!

Citizens Leaving!

THREE STEAM BOATS BURNT

TWO OTHERS SUNK

TWO YANKEE GUN BOATS AT
OUR LANDING!

Three or four shots fired, but "nobody hurt."

"I see the reason that issue of The *Gazette* was saved," Raleigh reasoned. "It was a report of the Civil War conflict as it reached down into the Florence area of Alabama."

As they began to read, it was understandable why there was created "GREAT EXCITEMENT IN FLORENCE" as the headline proclaimed.

On Saturday last, our citizens were thrown into the utmost state of excitement, by the appearance of two Yankee Gun Boats, which were seen from an eminent position overlooking the river for many miles down its nearly strait current. The black, ugly things, wraped, as they were, in the habiliments of death, and mourning, well represent the principle upon which this unholy war is waged, for the destruction of southern rights and lawful interest.

Three beautiful steamers, one well laden with valuable freight, lying at our wharf, had been hotly chased by these Gun Boats for hundredsof miles. They had arrived in safety at our landing, but was placed in a condition that the more agreeable if not less destructive element of fire couldplace them in thirty minutes, beyond the reach of the destroying foe. Instantly that the approach of these black agents of destruction was discovered, the torch was applied to the combustible material, previously arranged, and soon one of the most sublime scenes that has ever been witnessed by our cizes was exhibited, the three steames were now wrapped in curling flames, and were as useless to the hungry vultures, whose appetites had been whetted doubly keen, by having, for many hours, been in close pursuit, constantly expecting to grasp in their expanded talons, the dainty prey. A fire was then kindled upon the holy alter of patriotism, that found a hearty response in every heart, except the disappointed pursuers. Soon the destructive element had done its work, and the burning wrecks were drifted along by the surging flood. Our landing was made, and the soil of North Alabama was desecrated by the tread into the hands of the invading foe. One of the warehouses was opened without a key, and such articles as were suppose to belong to the Confederate States were taken, private property, we were informed, was respected. A courteous interview took place between the commander of the expedition and a deputation of our citizens, in which the citizens of the town were assured that violence was not intended to person or property of peaceful citizens. We believe that pledge was kept, and soon after the sable shades of night were drawn over this sad spectacle, the cables were loosed, and the demons of an abused power, went steaming down the river. We were honestly told that we might expect them again. Ought not we, in the meantime, to be up and doing? every possible means of defence ought, at once, to put in requisition, and every man who is a friend to his country, ought now to step forward into the breach and help to build the wall, if necessary, with his lifeless corpse---Let those who have a right, take the thing into their hands, and do what the time and circumstances allow. If God is with us, it does not matter who is against us. We believe our cause is just, and if so, He will not forsake us, in this, the hour of danger.

As above stated, three steamboats were burned by their commanding officers, when the Gun Boats hove in sight of our landing. The steamer Julia H. Smith, was on the south side of the river, below the bridge and when fired, her engines were set to work. backwards. and she floated down the river, a burning mass, causing one of the Gun Boats to change her position in "double quick time" The Kirkman and Time were on this side of the river and were nearly consumed when the federals landed below them and then cut them loose and all three of the steamers floated down the river. The Captain of the Time informed us that he had on board near one hundred thousand dollars worth of Government stores, destined to Fort Henry, all of which was consigned to the fort and it fell into the hands of the marauders.

The Gun Boats fired three or four shots, but at what they fired, we do not know. We were a quarter or a half mile of them when they fired, but could. not see any signs of where their shots struck. We suppose that they were firing at the burning wreck of the Smith, as she was passing them at the time. Some say one shot struck the Bridge, but how true it is, we can't say, as rumors of all sorts are abundant, just now...The Steamer Dunbar, a large, fine, side wheel steamer, was chased to out landing, by the Gun Boat; from Fort Henry, but succeeded in getting away, and ran up ma little creek not a thousand miles from Florence, and is now lying at the "Gundle Ford," in fifteen or tweenty feet water. She was scuttled and settled down nicely. The Robb, or Samuel Orr was also scuttled and sunk, (so we have been informed) below here a few miles. When it was certainly known that the Gun Boats were coming, a good many of our citizens took their moveable goods, and went to the country for safety. Some reported that 10.000 yankees were in town some 20.000 and that they were destroying every thing before them. One fellow affirmed that he saw *twenty seven* gun boats land here, on Sunday evening, with his own eyes. That is the way such rumors get afloat. Suffice it to say, the Gun Boats lay at our wharf about three hours, and then retired, since which time, we have seen nothing of them, but heard a great deal.

We hope the noble example of masters and owners of the burnt steamers will be followed by our planters, and rather than a bale of cotton should fall into the hands of the foe, that they, themselves, will apply the torch to the last bale of cotton in the Tennessee Valley.

When everyone had finished their reading of the top newspaper there was silence. Their eyes remained focused on the old paper, but it seemed as though they were contented to allow the article which they had just finished reading to speak for itself.

Finally Jenny broke the silence. "Well, I suppose that was worth saving. Mr. Barr, the editor of The *Gazette*, must have written the piece, and he certainly went heavy on the colorful, maybe descriptive is a better way to put it, account of the event.

"He was liberal with his punctuation, with writing and printing mistakes abundant, but maybe that was the accepted way to write back then. As I read it, I could imagine him, in his excitement, pounding out the story to be printed on the old printing press. The enemy at the city's dock was surely a cause of concern to the populace of Florence and Tuscumbia."

"When I was reading it, I thought of the journal which we read that Eve had written while on the Stone's Plantation." Raleigh spoke up next. "A number of times she mentioned that the Reverend Stone frequently brought in newspapers when he went into Florence to buy supplies. It appears that it was an established practice to buy, read, and use them in the classroom and save them to be read later. We are so dependent upon the electronic media that it is hard to imagine a time when the only way that one could keep abreast of events happening throughout the country and world was to read it from a newspaper.

"Today, we know election results many times before the polls close. At that time, it sometimes took days before the results of an election were known. Another thing that strikes me while I read these old papers, is the great difference that time has made in assisting those who now write articles. Modern computers correct the spelling and other errors in composition. I am struck by the amount of mistakes that were printed in many of these articles."

Jenny added to her husband's comment, "In getting my degrees at the university, I would have probably flunked out if hadn't had spellcheck to help me on my papers. We are fortunate to have the modern tools that we have to assist us in so many ways."

Another page of a newspaper was the next one removed. Beneath the heading of 'By Telegraph,' a short article had been circled. It read:

From the Avalance, Jan 18.

Nashville, january 17—private dispatches report federals landing in force this morning below Fort Henry, Tennessee river There was some firing, but

---

> the federals' balls did not reach the fort. Advice from fort Donelson says Gen. Tilghman feels confident of his ability to defend forts Donelson and Henry.

"There are a couple more interesting things on that page," Raleigh said as he moved to stop Dutch from placing it on the stack that had already been read. He pointed to two short articles, one above the other, both above the one that was circled. They read:

> Dead Colt—Quite a famous colt died at Hartford Conn., On the 10th inst. His name was Samuel Colt, and he had made a great name by inventing 'Colt's Repeating pistol'.

The article directly beneath this one was a river and weather report.

> The river at this point has been rising for the last few days. The steamer Muscle, has been making regular trips between this place and Eastport, carrying a good many "contrabands,' and a number of others of a whiter hue. If the Yankees want to know what they are, or where they are going let them come and see.

"The weather report at this point in time may have some significance." Raleigh placed his hand on his forehead as if in deep thought. "As I recall, during this period of time there was a lot of rain which resulted in the flooding of the rivers. If I remember correctly, at the time that the Yankees captured Fort Henry, the river was flooded to the point where it was over the walls of the fort, and all the Yankee gunboats had to do was just to steam inside and cause their havoc. In fact, the commander of the fort, General Lloyd Tilghman, surrendered the fort before the Yankee army even got there. Maybe we will learn more about this later."

"How could that happen?" Jenny inquired.

"The way that I understand it," Raleigh answered her, "was that those in the know advised that the fort not be built on the location where it stood as it was in a flood plain. Not wanting it in Kentucky, which was then neutral in the war, the wiser ones were overruled and the site in Tennessee was chosen. That was one of many mistakes the South made during the war."

The next articles contained battle reports of the war which was raging at that time, some expressing optimism, others with names of the local soldiers who were killed or injured in a losing battle. The edition dated March 12, 1862, broke the bad news that the war was not going well for the South. The first article announced:

Federals in Tennessee

Fort Henry Captured.

Destruction of Tennessee River Bridge

Danville. (Tennessee River Bridge.) Feb 6. 2 p m—Firing commenced at Fort Henry about 12; m today. About one hundred and fifty guns have been fired. The result is not known. The firing has ceased.   J G T

LATER

Special to the Avalanche.

Paris Tenn., Feb 6, 1862---Captain Houston, with his cavalry company has just arrived from Fort Henry. Reports that Fort Henry was captured by the federals to day. The fight lasted about two hours. It is reported that the federal gunboats were seen in the vicinity of Danville (Tennessee river bridge) by the telegraphic operator. when he closed his office and went to Paris. He said that he witnessed the destruction of the bridge over Tennessee river before leaving.   J. W. M.

STILL LATER

Special to the Avalance

Paris, Feb 6.---I saw the conflict at fort Harris. And witnessed the defeat of our forces at that place with the deepest regret. After our forces gave up the fort, I learned that the enemy had landed a large force of cavalry on this side of the river. They advanced on two sides to cut off our retreat, but we managed our escape by swimming a creek and arrived at Paris safe.
The enemy now occupy our position.

C.P.T. HUBBARD.
of Houston Cavalry

"It appears that the *Gazette* did a lot of reprints from other papers published during that time," Raleigh observed. "Some of those articles were from *The Avalance* which was a newspaper published in Memphis, Tennessee. The larger cities had more resources to gather the news and some of the smaller towns, which Florence was at that time, used their material, always giving them credit as the source."

Turning to the next newspaper from the bundle, Dutch glanced over it before speaking. "There are two articles marked here. One has to do with a militia force to protect the gulf area, and the other one looks like we have a proclamation from Governor Shorter which deals with agriculture. It is rather lengthy, but let's read both articles before we go to the next paper."

The March twentieth edition of the *Gazette* printed a speech made by Governor Shorter, given on March 1st and a proclamation he made on March 6th in which he ordered out a large militia force.

> "for the protection of our Gulf Coast and to repel invasion, and to place Mobile in a state of security. The militia will be taken from the counties of Mobile, Washington, Clark, Baldwin, Marengo, Choctaw, Greene, Sumter, Perry, Wilcox, Monroe, Pickens, Dallas, Tuscaloosa, Bibb, Shelby, Covington, and Autauga, for the term of ninety days." He said "I will accept in advance of the militia, and for the same term—sixty volunteer companies from the same counties, who must arm, clothe, and equip themselves; each company to consist of one Captain, one first Lieutenant, two second Lieutenants, five Sergeants, four Corporals, and not less than sixty four, and not more than one hundred privates."

The proclamation further read that:

> "All companies raised under this proclamation, will be held as *minute men,* and must be prepared to proceed immediately to Mobile. Each company must provide at least six axes, four hatchets, and four shovels, or spades, and at least *ten days* rations, to commence the march.

It is not probable that the services of these troops will be required for the full term; and they will not encumber themselves with any useless or unnecessary clothing; and no more baggage than is allowed by the Regulations, will be transported.

It is desirable that each man should—if possible, provide himself with at least, twenty rounds of ammunition—suitable for the gun he is armed with, before marching; and take with him his bullet mold and powder flask.—Each company will furnish its own transportation to the nearest point on the river or railroad, and transportation will be furnished from such points to Mobile. As Time is of importance, the Captain of each company, so soon as it is organized, with the full number of officers, non commissioned officers, and privates, and provided with the rations and implements specified, will report his muster roll to the Adjutant and Inspector General of the State, and proceed *immediately* with his company, to Mobile, reporting on his arrival, to the officer in command at that place."

The proclamation was signed by Jno Gill Shorter—Governor of the State of Alabama.

"What a way to fight a war! I hope that I have this straight in my mind," Dutch exclaimed after reading the proclamation from Governor Shorter. "Six of you in each of sixty companies find axes, somebody get four hatchets and four shovels. If you have guns and ammo bring that too, and we are going down to Mobile to show them that we mean business. We don't play around when it comes to fighting a war!"

"You have it figured out, Dutch," Raleigh responded, "When those sixty detachments show up with their three hundred and sixty axes, those Yankees will be running scared. I can certainly understand why the Governor said that it would not be probable that the services of those troops would be required for the full term. They could go down to Mobile and make short work of scaring those Yankees back up North where they belong, and then they could be back home in no time a'tall."

Abigail chuckled at Raleigh's statement. "I can visualize it now," she added to his comment, "When those Yankees see the Minutemen headed that way with the front line of three hundred and sixty fearless men, each in his one pair of overalls and brogans, waving their axes, followed by two hundred and forty men in the same outfits of clothing, raising their hatchets. Backing them up are two hundred and forty more with their shovels and spades upright on their shoulders, and throw in whatever muskets they may have come up with; that would be enough to make anybody run scared."

This prompted a laugh from the others, and Jenny felt that it was time for her to enter the conversation. "The smoke is beginning to clear as to why the Southern armies were defeated. The South secedes from the Union and starts a war when they have no troops, no guns or ammo, no supplies, and depend on volunteers to jump in and do the fighting.

"If that were to be the case today, I'm afraid that it would be hard to get one company of volunteers to show up to get shot at. The younger generation would much prefer to fight their battles on electronic games; it is much easier and safer that way. It makes me wonder what the Southern leaders were thinking when they picked that fight."

"There is another article from the Governor in this edition." Dutch turned his attention back to the newspapers. "Let's see what he had to say in that address to the people."

BY THE GOVERNOR OF ALABAMA
Executive Department
Montgomery, Ala., March 1st, 62

The recent disasters which have befallen armies, instead of depressing, should nerve the unconquerable purpose and arouse the mighty power of these Confederate States. Seven millions of people resolutely determined to maintain their right of self government and not bow their necks to the oppressors yoke, can never be subjugated. They will rise in their majesty and strength, and with the blessing of God upon their righteous cause, will drive back the invader from their land and country.

The reverses to our arms have imposed new duties upon Alabama and her sister Confederate States. The first is, to bury the love of Gold, and quence out that sordid spirit which values property above liberty, and to piously cultivate that martyr spirit which will sacrifice every material interest rather than peril the priceless inheritance of freedom.

Cut off, as their supplies may be from the northwest, the Cotton States should rely solely upon their own granaries and products to furnish subsistence for the armies within their borders. With their ports closed against the markets of the world, without remuneration for the labor of its production and without even the material for covering the staple, the growing of cotton to any considerable extent will not only endanger the organization of the great armies which must be fed, but will serve to increase the energy and stimulate the avarice of our foes. The people of Alabama are requested, and the military officers of the State will be directed to burn every lock of cotton within the State, if it be necessary, to prevent it from falling into the hands of the public enemy, and if the people of these cotton producing States are a wise people they will raise not another crop of cotton beyond the demands of home consumption, until this unholy and cruel war shall cease. Let the States of the North, which have fattened upon your toil, and which now seek your subjugation, and to impose upon you the burthens of untold millions of war expenditures, and let the Nations of Europe which behold your struggle for deliverance, while their suffering people are clamoring for your great staple; see, and learn, that you value liberty and free government far above all earthly considerations. Plant not, then, one seed of cotton, beyond your home wants, but put down your lands in grain and every other kind and description of farm product, and raise every kind of live stock which may contribute to the support of your own families and the needy families of your brave defenders, and which are for the grand armies which shall march to achieve your independence.

It was Raleigh who interrupted the reading this time. "The proclamation, if you may call it that, was dated March 6th, 1862. The battle of Fort Sumter which caused dancing in the streets was on April 18, 1861, less than a year earlier. The losses on the Tennessee River, as well as the blockades which President Lincoln had imposed on all Southern ports, were having a great adverse effect on the economy of the South.

"I realize that I am interrupting our reading, but I noticed an article in an edition which we have already read, the one where Jefferson Davis called for prayer and fasting, I think that it was dated Nov. 13, 1861."

Raleigh picked up the stack of papers they had already read, speaking as he turned through them, "I just want to take a few minutes to check this out as it has relevance to the article we are now reading. Yeah, here it is!" he exclaimed as he found what he was looking for.

He started reading.

> "There is hardly a port, of any importance, on our southern coast, but that some vessel has either passed out of, or into, Since Lincoln declared the southern ports blockaded. Over five hundred vessels have run the paper blockade, at different ports on our coast. A Spanish brig ran the blockade recently, and came into a southern port, and in fact they are passing both in and out constantly.
>
> As the powers of Europe have entered into an agreement not to recognize the blockading of the ports of any nation, unless it be effectual, it may well be supposed, that when the European powers do recognize the independence of the Southern Confederacy, they will not long submit to the paper blockade, that the Northern despot has established about the southern ports, and which is, and has been broken by over five hundred vessels, since its establishment."

Raleigh paused from his reading and looked at the others. "The next paragraph, and also the last one, is what caught my eye when I was reading from this page. It is certainly evident that the Southerners did not think too highly of Abraham Lincoln. I'm afraid that any newspaper writer would lose his job if he wrote in such words today. Political correctness was not high on the agenda when this article was penned."

He continued reading the remainder of the article he had returned to.

> "It seems from all accounts, as if the despot at Washington, is not respected very much, by foreign powers, just now. He has shown himself such a nincompoop by his proceedings, that the foreign powers, and a large number of his own people at home, are becoming sorely disgusted with his actions, and even a great number of his own people are determined to have as little to do with him as possible. He has transcended the powers delegated to him by the Constitution of the old United States; and set at naught plain and unmistakable points of law governing civilized warfare; and been guilty of such gross outrages upon humanity, that he is held up as an object of contempt and scorn, by all honest and christian people.
>
> The rump government at the north, in selecting a ruling despot, utterly disregarded brains and common sense, or refined manners, when they selected the nincompoop that now desecrates the chair once occupied by a Washington, a Jackson, and a Polk."

Putting the paper back in the order in which it had been packed, Raleigh had one last comment. "That little paper blockade was having a much greater adverse effect on the Southern economy than the writer would attest, but Governor Shorter realized that the state was feeling the pain, which is the reason that he imposed the ban on goods that might fall into the hands of the enemy and be of value to them." Raleigh smiled as he concluded his brief interruption. "You got that little tidbit of information whether you wanted it or not."

Satisfied that he had the papers back in their original order, Raleigh turned his attention back to the others. "Now I suppose we can get back to the ban on cotton farming. This restriction surely had a great negative effect on the farm here."

The reading of the plea from Governor Shorter was continued.

Men, brave and gallant men, responding to the call of their bleeding country, are rushing, by thousands, to the field. Their cry is for arms with which to engage the foe. People of Alabama! will you not commit your arms into their hands? People of Alabama! will you not send the shot guns and rifles, rusting in your houses, that I may place them in the hands of your own sons to defend your alters and your homes? Agents are appointed all over the State to collect arms. If they do not find you, I beg you to find them. Let every Sheriff and Judge of Probate, and all State officers, civil and military, receive and forward arms---expenses will be promptly paid by the State.

Let every man do something towards arming our troops if he cannot go to the battle field. Turn your shops into laboratories for manufacture of arms and munitions of war. Send me thousands of shot guns and rifles, bowie knives and pikes. Send powder, and lead, and ball. What you cannot afford to give, the State will buy. Let the entire resources of the people be devoted to the one great purpose of war---war stern and unrelenting---war to the knife---such a war as, in the providence of God, we may be compelled to wage in order to vindicate the inalienable right of self-government.

As vile extortion is an abominable sin against humanity, all good men are earnestly urged to denounce its practice and crush out its spirit. Creditors are counseled to exercise moderation and forbearance, and all classes and conditions of people invited to cultivate a spirit of mutual confidence, of loyalty and devotion to their State and Confederate government. With a true appreciation of the dangers which surround us, and of our duty to God and our country, let us all live and labor, and if need be die, for the advancement of the glorious cause for which we are contending.

In testimony whereof, I have hereunto set my hand and caused the great seal of the State to be affixed, at the city of Montgomery, this first day of March, 1862, and of the independence of the Confederate State of America, the second year.

JNO. GILL SHORTER

By the Governor

P.H.Brittan, secretary of State.

———

N B—All papers in the State please copy twice and sends account to Exective office

March 12, 1862. bw

CHAPTER 6

———◆———

The Sunday afternoon had stretched into Sunday evening, and there were still more newspapers in the box.

Dutch looked at his watch and made the suggestion, "Normally, I would say that we should continue our reading at a later date; time is getting away from us. The weatherman, however, warns that there is a hundred percent chance of rain and possible thunderstorms tomorrow, and there will be no farm work done in that kind of weather. I will not be getting out of bed early, and there are only a few more newspapers left in the box, so I make a motion that we just keep reading until we empty the box."

"Motion seconded," Raleigh immediately voted.

"All in favor say, Aye", Dutch grinned as he spoke.

After the women had voted in the affirmative, another paper was taken from the box. In it there was an article which had been marked with the notation written in the margin—"*GOOD TO KNOW!*"

> **Flux**---As the flux is now raging to a considerable extent among our soldiers at different points, we give the following as a remedy for the disease. It is a simple remedy and within the reach of all, who may be afflicted by this dreadful disease. We have tested

> it, and seen it tried, with entire success, when the disease baffled the skill of one of the best physicians in the State. Here it is:
>
> "Take the inside bark of a white oak tree, (remove the rough or outside bark) steep it in water till it is strong enough to suit the taste, then use it freely; drink no other water." If a cure is not effected in 48 hours, it must be an exceeding aggravated case.
>
> An old lady told us of this remedy years ago, and since then we have seen It tried, she said, take the bark from the north side of the tree, but we can't say whether or not there is any more efficacy in the bark from the north side of the tree, than there is in the bark from the south side, she might be somewhat superstitious about that. But be that as it may, the remedy is a good one.

"*What is this?*" Dutch mumbled, more to himself than to the others.

Pulling out a small bundle of newspapers that had a length of small brown jute cord tied around them; he soon answered his own question.

"*Oh, I see!*" he said with a slightly louder mumble. "Some papers have apparently been separated here that deal with agriculture."

While pulling out the pack, the others could read the two large words that had been written on a sheet of paper that had been torn from a ringed binder and wrapped around the bundle. It simply read: Farm News.

The top newspaper had a short article circled with a handwritten notation in the margin which read: *NOT ON THIS FARM!* It was a spring edition of the paper with a plea for food to feed the troops.

Navy Beans for the Army

We would earnestly (sic) cultivation of this important source of food to the attention of farmers. Now is the time to plant. It has always been found to be one of the most convenient, healthy, and nutritious articles for the army and navy. When roasted (which with a simple apparatus for the purpose it can be easily be done and in large quantities) and ground into meal. It can be made into soup in five minutes. Being already cooked, it is only necessary to cut the pork into thin slices, put in water, into which, when brought to a boil, the meal is to be stirred until it attains the proper consistency, when the soup is made and ready for use. The whole process, with a good fire, will not require more than five minutes---and will be found to be not only nutritious in the highest degree, but exceedingly pleasant to the palate, far better than eating the fat meat without any other accompaniment than bread, which now constitutes almost half of the sole staple of a soldiers food. The earth yields nothing more abundantly and with less labor and pains to the husbandmand than this bean. Its cultivation, therefore, in large quantities, is more earnestly involked. As this is a matter of such vast importance, we suggest that the papers generally call for the attention of the farmers to the hint we have thrown out.{--Richmond Whig.

"I take it that the Reverend was not interested in providing beans for the army," Raleigh made the assessment after reading the article where he had made the notation that navy beans would not be grown on his farm. "He was surely a compassionate individual, but it is clear that he did not want to get involved in the military conflict in any way."

"I understand where he was coming from!" Jenny commented. "He just wanted the Confederacy to leave him alone, seeing as to how he was so opposed to the underlying factor of their fight." She paused before adding, "Which was to maintain slavery."

"He was opposed to aiding and abetting the unjust cause for which they were fighting." Raleigh reached back into his law enforcement vocabulary to describe the reason for the refusal of Reverend Stone to provide assistance to the war effort.

After reading through several papers which had to do with farming news, most of which promoted the war effort, Dutch laid the bundle containing farm news aside and changed the subject. "These old newspapers certainly have a different look than what is published today. The columns appear to be slightly over two inches wide and they line the page, completing the story. Today on the front page of a newspaper there are several articles started but not completed, continued on another page inside the paper.

"That has been one thing that has always irked me! I hate to start a story and then have to turn to page A7 to finish reading it. It took a lot of labor to publish a newspaper on those old printing presses," Dutch spoke as he lifted the next newspaper from the box.

There were two short articles, checked, which were of interest to the citizens in the Tennessee Valley. It was another copy of the *Florence Gazette*, dated Wednesday Morning on March 19, 1862.

Fight at Chickasaw, Ala.—On Wednesday last, two federal gun-boats came up the Tennessee to Chickasaw, 30 miles below here and engaged a battery that has lately been erected there. Over one hundred shots were exchanged, when one of the gun-boats was disabled and had to be towed off. We did not have a man hurt altho' the yankee shot and shell fell fast and thick around and in our battery. As the boats came up they threw several shells in the town of Eastport. without hurting anything, however---Tuscumbia 'North Alabamian,' March 14 1862.

The cannonading at Chickasaw was very distinctly heard at this place. It was also heard at Rogersville, in this county, a distance of about 54 miles from the scene of action. The reports were heard at Pulaski, Tenn., not less, we suppose, than 80 miles from Chickasaw.

Following this bit of news was an article regarding the weather.

HEAVY RAINS AND HIGH WATERS---

Last week there was a tremendous fall of rain in this section of the country, which we suppose was general. The smaller water courses near here were swelled higher than they have been for years. There was considerable damage done. The bridge across Cypress creek near here, was swept away, the bridge over Shoal Creek, on the Nashville road was swept off and one pillar washed from under the bridge over the same creek on the Huntsville road, and another pillar damaged. Two bridges over Blue Water, one on the Lexington, the other on the Huntsville road, were also swept off. Two hundred and fifteen or twenty bales of cotton, belonging to Baugh, Kennedy & Co. were

> swept away from their Factory on Shoal creek, part of which, robably, has gone to the yankees, as it was seen passing this place floating in the river. Some of the bales were caught. The Gist Mill belonging to Martin, Weakley, & Co, on Cypress, was washed away, and we learned that one or two of their Factory buildings, or the water machinery, or something else, was damaged—The Tennessee river was very high.

Shortly following the publication of this issue, which was March 19, the printing of the *Florence Gazette* was suspended. Publication did not resume until Wednesday morning—Dec. 10, 1862, with I.S. BARR::::::Editor, no brother listed. It was smaller than the earlier editions had been. Instead of the usual six columns that had filled the pages, the smaller sheets allowed only space to hold three, cutting the size in half. In the first edition, the first column, an explanation was given regarding the reason for the suspension of the paper and the impetus to begin publishing it again.

> ### To the patrons of the Gazette
>
> The occupation of this county, by the Federal army, suspended, temporarily, the publication of the Florence Gazette. We wish to re-produce, to the people of Lauderdale County, that old and useful Journal, and we trust its long and faithful services, will be kindly remembered and rewarded.
>
> We have been solicited to do so, by men of business, who suffer greatly, for the lack of a public medium, thr'o which to make known, or obtain information, on current, events, events of a local nature.

A few friends have promised to assist us, occasionally, in the editorial department, and with their aid, we shall endeavor to make the paper as useful and entertaining as circumstances will allow.

A newspaper, however humble may be its pretensions, is a public benefit, and should receive the support, and countenance of every member of society, who desires the general good. It is in fact, the common property of the community, and should be cared for and patronized as such.

A village which cannot, or does not support a newspaper, must be deplorably wanting in energy and vitality, and nothing so much indicates the intensity and prosperity of a country town, as an independent, well conducted, and well- patronized newspaper. With these few remarks, we shall go to work, trusting in your kindness to favor and befriend us.

There were a couple of short notations with further information and request in the second column. At the bottom of the page and continuing on the third and last column an explanation was given as to the reason for the smaller size.

Our size

The size of our paper is a great deal smaller than we like, but it is the best that we can do at the present, and it is unnecessary to make any apologies in reference to it. Surrounded by circumstances over which we have no control, these war times, make it more of a matter of necessity than of choice with us, in publishing this size sheet. We have no assistance in the mechanical department of our business, our brother having gone to the army before the late exemption law was circulated through this part of the country, with his assistance, we could have published a paper as large again, and would gladly do so, in preference to the present size, although our raw material cost two or three; or maybe four times the amount it did prior to the war. If we can succeed in getting more aid, we will publish a larger paper, but until we do so, we will be compelled to remain as we are, although much against our will or desires.

Up and Going----We would say, to Administrators, Guardians, and Executors, and all persons wanting advertising or job work done, in this or adjorning counties, that we are "up and going" again, (on a small scale) after a suspension of seven long months; a calamity that we hope that never again may befall us, especially under the same circumstancies.

Behind time----Our paper is dated Wednesday the 10th , the day that it should be published, but we were delayed for the want of wood. While speaking of wood, we will say to our wood hauling friends, who live in the country, or town either, that if they wish to subscribe to the little Gazette and pay for it in wood, they can now do so, as wood is the same as money to us.

In the next edition there was another note that was written regarding the paper being "up and going" again.

Notice,----Last week we sent the Gazette, (our little Gazette) to a good many of our old subscribers, who were in arrears, with us, for subscription, when we suspended the publication of our paper last spring, we send the paper to them again this week, and if they wish to subscribe, they can do so, if not, we will not send it to them, as paper cost too much to give it away.

Those receiving the Gazette this week with a cros mark, beside their name, may know that they are indebted to us for subscription, on the old score, and would be glad they wol'd liquicate, as we are just as needy as ever for 'material aid' Remember the cross mark. We will continue to send the paper to those who had paid us in advance and beyond the time of our suspension last spring.

The December 10th issue had a short article in it which was of interest to the readers.

We will try and get up a price current list next week, if our merchants have got 'conscience' enough left to give us the figures at which theyhold their goods and chattles. But we say to the people not to be frightened at the high prices, for we do not intend to exaggerate at all.

The next paper in the stack was The *Gazette* dated Dec. 17, 1862. The article of interest to the person who packed the box was:

THE CONSCRIPT LAW AND STATE MILITIA

By the "Act to further provide for the public defense," passed by the Confederate Congress, on the sixteenth day of April last, all the twelvemonth's men then in the service, over eighteen and under thirty-five years of age, were continued in the army for two years beyond the period of their enlistment, and all male citizens of the respective States, within the same ages, who had not previously enlisted, were, by the act, declared subject to military duty, for three years, or during the war, and provisions were contained in it for their enrollment and muster into service.

The power of congress to pass this law, I think should be conceded by the states. The several States, as sovereignties, had the power to declare war, and to levy armies to wage war. These powers they have delegated, in the constitution, to the Confederate Congress for the common protection, reserving the right to call out troops to suppress insurrection or impel invasion. Under this delegation and grant of powers, Congress has declared war against the Lincoln Government, for the common protection, and, in the passage of the Conscript Act, has only used a power which the States, as sovereignties, unquestionably possessed, to raise armies with which to wage the war.

But whatever doubts may have risen as to the powers of Congress, all agree that the public exigency demanded the adoption of the most stringent measures to preserve the efficiency and increase the strength of the army. It was a severe disappointment to thousands of our brave troops, to be retained in service beyond the period when they fondly hoped to return to their loved ones at home; and the willing obedience rendered by them to the hard requirements of congress, and their continued unsparing sacrifices in the field, excite the admiration and claim the undying gratitude of their country.

The third section of the conscript law directs the employment of the enrolling officers of the States, whenever they can be obtained, to enroll the persons subject to the operations of the act. Accordingly, the superintendent and commandant of the camps in Alabama, applied to the Executive for a detail of the enrolling officers of the State, to perform this work, but as, by his instruction from the Secretary of War, the compensation to such officers was limited to such allowances as were made by the laws of the State for like services, in enrolling the militia of the State, and as the Military Code of Al-

[Concluded next Week]

Dutch made a brief search through the remaining papers, but the concluded article was not saved. Turning back inside the same paper there was another small article that had only a check mark beside it. It had no heading but simply read:

Last week we promised our readers that we would try and get up a price current list this week, but we have not been able to get up a regular table as yet; we will give the figures at which a few things are selling by way of a sample. Salt..$150.00 per barrel, or 50 cts per pound by retail, but a little below these figures if paid in gold or silver, or yankee green back. Calice $1.50 per yard; Ladies shoes $10 per pair; Shoethread $2 per ball; hats from 20 to 25 dollars apiece, worth not exceeding 5 dollars; boots $25; shoes in proportion; snuff $5 per pound, or $2 per bottle, real worth, nothing at all; plug tobacco $1.50 per pound; old prices 20 to 30 cts a plug; country jeans from $3 to $4 per yard; flower from $12 to $14 per hundred; meal 75cts per bushel, cheap enough, that.

> PORK---We wish to buy a few hundred pounds of pork. Who will accommodate us?

"Are you tired of reading?" Dutch asked as he looked back into the box. "It looks like we are near the bottom of the stack, but we still have a few more newspapers to read."

Jenny answered, "I'm enjoying the readings and am learning a lot that I did not know." She paused before speaking again, "I am amazed at the history of this area, and that much of it took place on the river between here and the Quad Cities, especially Florence and Tuscumbia. We refer to the area now as the Quad Cities, with Florence located on the northern side of the river and Tuscumbia, Sheffield and Muscle Shoals on the southern. The area along the river has grown a lot since the days that these papers were printed.

"The articles that we have read are certainly an interesting bit of history regarding the importance of the Tennessee River in these parts as the war was raging. I can certainly understand the concern of the people living in towns along its banks when the Union gunboats started showing up and firing their heavy weapons."

Looking at the others, Dutch suggested, "We voted earlier to continue our reading; I am now proposing that we pick up in the morning where we leave off today. It is late and time for bed," Dutch yawned as he spoke. "If it is raining tomorrow we will see what else this box might hold."

They all agreed and the box was closed. Raleigh and Jenny left for home after making arrangements to return the following day.

CHAPTER 7

◆

The rain had stopped sometime during the night, which prompted Jenny to call her mother.

"I was just looking at the weather and wondering if Dad is planning to do some farm work outside today?"

"Give me just a minute and I will ask him," Abigail replied. "I think everything is still on for us to resume our reading."

Jenny could hear her mom as she forwarded the query to Dutch. She was back in the minute that she had promised. "Dutch says that it's too wet to do anything on the farm today, so y'all come on over when you get ready. He watched the weather forecast, and he says that the rain is not over. Another front is moving in, and there are flash flood warnings in some places. We still need to finish reading the newspapers, and then we have a whole journal to read. With what we have left in the box, it might take two days to complete our reading, but that is okay because of the rain."

It was after ten o'clock before Raleigh and Jenny finished eating breakfast and taking care of their morning household work. When they arrived back at the plantation, Dutch and Abigail were waiting for them.

Abigail initiated the morning's conversation when they assembled around the box which contained the old newspapers. "I am not completely convinced that we are still in our right mind, reading newspapers about one hundred and fifty years old. Last night I lay in bed and asked myself, *What in tarnation are we doing, spending all this time reading these old things? People would think that we have collected bats in our belfry if they knew what we were doing.* But it's giving me pleasure, and I think that's reason enough to continue."

"Strange that you made that comment," Raleigh added. "I had similar thoughts last night. I remembered that note that was left for Rebekah, which has more meaning now. The initial jubilation of victory in one battle has certainly given way to the realities of war. Prompted by that note to Rebekah, I have tried to follow that ebb and flow of emotions which the war generated. Sarah was very clever to pick up on the underlying messages contained in those old newspapers where there is that jubilation one day and lamentations the next.

"And another thing impressed me. I now better understand the rationale of those who opposed the war. Many remained loyal to the Stars and Stripes and felt that the South was not prepared to win the conflict, which history proved to be correct. Also many opposed the very principles which stirred the conflict, that being slavery and the oppression of fellow humans because of their skin color. Our Native American people had already been forced to endure this during the removal to Oklahoma, and it was time to rectify that injustice.

"Perhaps the Tories were the true patriots when one considers these circumstances. All they asked for was that they be allowed to remain neutral, but their wishes were ignored," Raleigh said before pausing. "Nuff said."

"I must admit that I too am enjoying reading those old newspapers," Dutch added. "This one is dated Dec. 24, 1862," he announced as he continued to go through the remaining papers. "It was the day before Christmas but it appears that salt was the issue that was of concern in this paper. I suppose that no one was in the Christmas spirit on this holiday with the war raging all around them."

The article read:

Salt

We have reason to believe that Gov Shorter has done everything in his power to procure, and send us this most valuable and vital necessary. He has long since bought the salt and had it sacked, and ready for transportation, but we fear impediments, beyond his control, may delay its delivery at this point, until it is too late for us to use it in saving our pork, still we entertain good hope that it will come. We understand that the Court of County Commissioners have sent B.F.Ellis home a man every way qualified as Special agent, to confer with the Governor, and to assist in hastening forward the salt, which may be due this county. Farmers who lack salt had better feed for a while longer. Mr C.will be heard from soon. The commissioners court deserve much credit for energy and forethought in thus making timely and judicious efforts to bring to our doors an article we need so much.

Dutch laid the next paper out so that all could view it. The front page was completely filled with a continuation of the Governor's message regarding salt, or the lack thereof. He felt that it was time that he made a suggestion.

"I am not going to read this whole message that Governor Shorter felt to be so crucial at the time it was written. Today we buy a little round container of salt and it lasts us for months; it is only natural that we should question why all the hoopla about salt. We forget that today when an animal is slaughtered the meat is immediately put into coolers for preservation. Back when this was written there were no such conveniences for those people. Salt, and a lot of it, was used to place on pork to prevent spoilage. It drew the moisture from the meat, helping to cure and preserve it. It was a vital staple for the people who wanted to preserve their meat supply.

"Alabama was at a great disadvantage in getting the needed supply of salt as it was not a great natural resource for the area, and the ports were under a blockade, preventing the importation of the necessary commodity."

1862 had not been a good year for the Southern armies. They were victorious in a few battles, but the outcome of the war was going against them. The losses of troops were heavy on both sides but the North had more resources to fight their battles. The next paper announced a new year but all was not well! The editor of the *Florence Gazette*, I.S.Barr, reflected back to the bonfires and acclamations, the dances in the streets, when the South was victorious in their first battle at Fort Sumter, but as the year ended and a new year began, the celebrations became a thing of the past. He had hopes that the tide would turn in the favor of the South in 1863, but perhaps he knew that would not likely happen.

The article was an interesting one.

The Florence Gazette
I.S. Barr:::::Editor.
FLORENCE, ALA.---DEC. 31,1862
New Years Day

To-morrow is New Year. What a merry and hopeful day it used to be to young and old. Bonfires and acclamations ushered it on the great stage of time. Hope attended its entrance, and joy was its handmaiden. Not so at present, shattered and heart-broken, the old year goes to its grave, and leaves as an inheritance to its offspring, war, care, crime and wo; 1862 has left to history a mournful duty. Well may its pages be clothed in habiliments of sadness and shame; but we of the South cannot be charged with wanton and cruel misdeeds. The sin and punishment must fall upon our enemies of the North; already has the day of humiliation and retribution overtaken them; distracted, derided, bankrupted & demoralized at home, despised and mocked at abroad, chastised and rebuked by the stern foe, who they so proudly threatened to crush, The old United States is this moment the most contemptable nation on the globe. It staggers under the burdens of its enormities; is bloated by corruption and wickedness, and before long it must expire in a great heave, which will shake the world. Proudly stands the South in contrast with this deformed and loathsome picture; a child amongst nations, she has already earned, for herself, a name and a place, which, in after years, will be a theme for poets and orators. She has reneected the heroism of Greece and Rome. Many a blood-stained field will vie in renown with Themopola or Marathon. With countless odds against her, she has baffled and beaten back her ruthless foe. What nation has ever exhibited equal courage, patience and determination? Let us hope on, the morning star of our deliverence begins to gleam in the east. If true to ourselves, our cause and our country, the year 1863 will bear us on its great bosom to victory, glory and independence. Let us increase in energy, and may every man and women hyme forth, on New Years morn, joyful songs of gratitude and love to our Heavenly Father for his wonderful goodness to us in our time of trouble and distress. Let us also resolve to do good and discharge our duty in the coming year.

In the third column on the same page, there was an article that does not paint such a rosy picture of the combatants in the conflict.

Absenteeism.

The worse symptoms which we can see, in the condition of our army and country, is the bold and impudent feeling exhibited by two many of our soldiers, on absenting themselves from the army. It has become a pestilence, hail and stout young men, often in uniforms, and in the pay of the government, can be seen hanging around villages, crossroads and country taverns, and oftimes sponging on private families, if this were occasional it might not attract attention, but it has grown into a huge magnitude; until, as we are informed, not much less than forty thousand are at this time, absent from their colors in the two armies of Bragg and Price. This, if true, is a startling and ominous fact. It portends evils too serious to be disregarded. What has become of the patriotism, pride and principle of a young man, who can, and will abandon his command, his country and himself?---Will not his friends, when this war is over, feel justly ashamed of him? How can he stalk the streets with composure, when he must know and feel that the finger of contempt is pointed at him. Surely his conscience must smite him keenly when he remembers that his comrades are doing double duty, and fighting battles at fearful odds, owing to the absence of many from their post of duty. Such conduct is infamous and scandalous in an officer whose pay, position and respectability require of him constant presence and attention at the post which has been assigned to him. To whom can his men look for example, protection and comfort? For the sick or wounded soldier, every house and heart should be thrown wide open, but never to truant or cowardly absentees, a furlough at this crisis is no excuse---a brave and good man would not have one, his soul would pant for his colors.

"Well, well!" Jenny exclaimed, with tongue in cheek. "After the first article, I thought that the South might win the war after all, learning that she had baffled and beaten back her ruthless foe and was expecting the new year of 1863 to bear the South on it's great bosom to victory, glory, and independence. But after reading the second one, I have my doubts. Forty thousand troops absent from the ranks of only two commanders was a serious problem for the South if they wanted to beat those Yankees. And another observation! Just who had abandoned his country? I think that all that abandoning occurred during the Secession."

The papers from the year 1863 began to paint a gloomier picture of the tide of war as it raged throughout the South. Local citizens of the Tennessee Valley were being lost to enemy fire and some of their names were printed in articles regarding the different conflicts. In the January 17, 1863, issue of the *Florence Gazette*, an article appeared which had been circled with the handwritten notation in the margin which read: "*We have lost another good and faithful Christian to this senseless war. May God give his soul an eternal rest in Heaven!*"

We are again called upon to announce, with sadness, the death of another one of our citizens, who fell mortally wounded in the late battle near Marfreesboro. Mr. James Sotherlin, is no more, he died on the second of this month, from a wound received in the abdomen, from the deadly missils of our unscrupulous foe. A young man of high morel character and religious habits, beloved and respected by all, his untimely death will be mourned and lamented by all! His friends were many, his enemys few. Our Sunday School has lost a faithful teacher, no more will he be with his faithful class in that school, nor will they be permitted to listen to his words of instruction. The church has lost a faithful member; the army an honorable and brave soldier. We understand that his sufferings were great, but that he bore up under them with christian fortitude, and when death claimed him as his own, he yielded up his spirit to the God who gave it, and died in the triumphs of a christian faith. Thus another heatstone is made desolate in our midst, by the revages of war. We feel confident that the bereaved family and widowed mother has the sympathy of the community, in which her unfortunate son was so much respected—we say to his stricken mother, be faithful unto death, and you will meet your much loved son, beyond this world of sorrow, pain and death, where war's devastating hand is never laid, and sorrows never come.

A portion of a Speech by General Payne, a Union officer, addressed to his soldiers and delivered at Tuscumbia, Alabama, under the date of October 8th 1862, and reported in the January 17th Edition of the *Florence Gazette,* was *"faithfully reported by Col. Thornton, one of our most distinguished lawyers and a gentleman of high standing."*

I give you this as a specimen of the kind of enemy we have to contend with."
THOMAS J FOSTER.

Soldiers!---This country is yours---these people have unwittingly planted everything we need in this beautiful valley, and it shall be dealt to you with a lavish hand, and not stingily. If you want corn, these waving fields will supply your wants, take it. If you want fruit, vegetables, chickens, or potatoes, take them, they are yours. If the cows need milking, milk them yourselves, or make the milk maids do it for you. Every thing here in this rich and beautiful valley is yours and for your use---enjoy it, you deserve it all, you are in arms, exposing yourselves in defense of your country against Rebels and Traitors, who have no rights. They own no property except through the Government. They are outlaws.

But remember soldiers, we are not done yet, there is yet work to do---The idea of a restoration of the Union as it was, is now a humbug—it has passed away. It is now a war to the knife, and to the hilt, hilt and all---Yes soldiers, It is a war of extermination. Then I say to you take everything you want, it is yours--but remember to preserve discipline.

The above is a part of a speech delivered by Gen. Payne to some of his regiments at Tuscumbia, Ala., in August, 1862, and they acted according to its spirit and letter.

L B THORNTON.

The last paper to be removed from the box was *The Florence Gazette*, dated January 17, 1863. The person who had preserved the papers had marked certain sections, evidently the ones considered important at that time. On the entire page there was a printed new law which had been enacted by the Senate and House of Representatives of the State of Alabama. In the first paragraph there were several sections which dealt with the money to be used by the Confederacy. A line had been drawn down the left side of the article with another handwritten notation. It read:

WORTHLESS! GET ONLY GOLD OR SILVER IF POSSIBLE. SHINPLASTER IS ALL THAT IT IS!

After reading the notation that had been written on the margin of the newspaper, Raleigh made an observation regarding it. "That word 'shinplaster' is a new one to me, but the effort to get only gold and silver is certainly understandable," he said. "The family has never put any trust in anything the Federal Government put into print, including money, as they always demanded to be paid in the gold and silver standard, and they surely put no trust in anything the Confederacy, or others, circulated.

"From the last journal, we learned that Reverend Stone strongly opposed slavery and the Secession of

the Southern states from the Union, and he had no
confidence that any currency that was issued by the
Confederacy would have been of any more value than
the paper on which it was written. Of course, time
would prove him absolutely right in that assessment."

Although the article dealing with money was not
the only one for which the newspaper had been saved,
a portion of it caught the attention of Jenny and she
read a little of it, from section 4 of the act, to the
others.

> *"Be it further enacted. That any person, private
> corporation or association, or any individual member
> thereof, who circulates, passes off, or pays out any
> paper or instrument commonly called shinplaster,
> issued without the authority of law, and to answer
> the purpose of money, or for general circulation,
> shall be deemed and held the maker of such paper
> or shinplaster is passed or paid may bring suit on
> the same against the person passing the same as
> maker thereof, and recover judgment upon his own
> oath, upon one days' notice, before any justice of the
> peace in any county in the State without regard to the
> county in which said paper was passed or paid out..."*

Jenny paused from her reading and looked at the
others. "Excuse me for the interruption," she begged.
"I didn't realize that would be so lengthy. That section
goes on and on, covering everything imaginable without
a period or stopping place. That word 'shinplaster' is
used again in the article. I'm like Raleigh; I don't ever
remember hearing or reading the word."

"Neither have I!" Abigail said, also revealing her
ignorance of the word. "I suppose the article defines it,
but I think that I will look it up in the dictionary. I keep a

large paperback copy of the *Merriam Webster Dictionary* here by my chair."

She picked up a red covered book and searched it for the word. "Well," she declared after closing the book, "it appears that Merriam Webster hadn't heard the word either, leastwise I couldn't find the word in this book." She paused for a moment before speaking again. "In the library we have an old volume of the *Webster's New Collegiate Dictionary*, which would probably define it for us. Let me get it."

Abigail left the room and came back in a short time, carrying a large grey hardback book. "If it is not in this one, we are out of luck," she voiced as she started her search in the book.

As she turned pages she mumbled to herself, *"Let's see now, shinplaster, shinplaster,"* spelling the word as she searched.

"Oh, here it is!" she suddenly exclaimed. *"Success!"* She began to read; "1: a piece of privately-issued paper currency; *esp:* one poorly secured and depreciated in value. 2: a piece of fractional currency." She closed the book with a slam. "Now you have it! We are now familiar with the word *shinplaster*. That article defines it quite well."

"I suppose that those people back then who were familiar with the token were also knowledgeable about the shinplaster," Dutch gave his assessment of the currency. "It sounds like, to me, that whereas a token was a coin, shinplaster was paper."

"I apologize again for getting us off track with our readings," Jenny again proclaimed. "Let's read the article which is marked as being of significance."

After scanning the article she added, "It's a good thing that we rested our eyes a while. There are two complete columns that have been highlighted. It looks as if it had to do with corn, which would have been important information for a farmer, especially one on a farm as large as this one was at that time."

An Act

To regulate the sale and exportation of Corn

Section 1. Be it enacted by the Senate and House of Representatives of the State of Alabama in General Assembly convened, that from and after this act..

"Wait a minute!" Dutch interrupted the reading almost before it got started. "That is a lot of reading on that page. If we want to get to bed tonight, we need to decide how much of it we want to read."

After scanning the entire document, Jenny made the suggestion. "I see what you mean. There are eight sections to that act and most of it would be of no interest to us. A lot of it is repetition and I think that the first two sections will give us a general idea of why the article was saved. Let's read only the first two sections."

That from and after this act becomes of force, no person, except the producer or the miller, shall sell corn without first obtaining a license from the Judge of Probate of the county in which the corn is to be sold, which license shall, authorize the person, or partnership to whom the same is granted, to sell corn in such county, and no other, for one year from the date of such license, and at a profit of not more than twenty per cent. on the price paid to the producer and charges exclusives of the license, fees and taxes on the same; but no license shall be granted, unless the applicant first make and subscribe an affidavit written before said Judge, that he will not sell any

---

corn within one year from the date of the license, should this act remain in force for that period, at a greater rate of profit than twenty percent, on the price paid the producer and charges, exclusive of the fees and taxes in the license, and I will sell only in the county in which said license shall be granted, which affidavit shall be filed in the office of the Judge of Probate granting the same.

Sec. 2   Be it further enacted, That no miller shall sell any corn, except the corn received by him as toll for grinding, unless he be the producer of the same, without first obtaining a license under the preceding section, nor shall he sell any toll at a higher rate than the usual market price in the city, town or neighborhood in which the mill is located.

The additional sections set out regulations and penalties for violation of these restrictions, even the Judge of Probate who would fail to comply with the provisions which were set forth by the act. Another section expanded the jurisdiction to include a penalty for unlawfully exporting corn outside the limits of this state. Penalties, on a misdemeanor conviction, would be a fine of not less than five hundred dollars and imprisonment in the common jail not less than six months. This section did not apply to the exportation of any corn owned by the Confederate Government or any of the Confederate states.

The rain that had been forecast had arrived, and Dutch felt that he needed to check on a cow that was due to deliver a calf at any time.

"I need to check to make sure that the cow is out of the rain when she delivers that calf safely. She is prized stock, and I would hate for something to go wrong when she delivers. It's supposed to rain all night and into tomorrow, so I think we should wait until then to check out that journal. We have read all the newspapers, so it's a good place to quit for the day."

CHAPTER 8

◆

An early morning telephone call made by Abigail summoned Jenny and Raleigh to the plantation house for breakfast.

"The weatherman was right on mark when he forecast that this would be a rainy day. Angie is cooking a big breakfast this morning; if you'll come over and eat, we can get an early start on finding out what else that box might hold. It appears that we will have all day to check out its contents. Of course, we may be disappointed as there might not be anything else in there that would be of interest to us today."

An invitation to eat Angie's cooking seldom was turned down. With a box that still contained unknown items, the Walkers were at the Riddles' house shortly after the call was ended.

"We didn't want to let the biscuits get cold," Raleigh joked as they entered the house.

"That rain is really coming down in buckets out there. It'll be a good day to stay inside and hopefully find out more about the history of the farm and family," Jenny added.

"This heavy rain will mess up farming for a few days until the fields dry out."

Dutch always had his mind on farming.

"I suppose that the Lord sends these rainy days occasionally to give us a little rest. Then again, we need the moisture to water the plants." He paused a second before continuing, "Maybe not this much, but we take what he sends."

After eating breakfast and clearing the table of the remaining food and the dirty dishes, Dutch brought out the box and set it on the table.

"Dum-de-dum-dum!" Raleigh exclaimed in a rhythmic tone as Dutch removed the lid. "The box is about to reveal the remainder of its secrets!"

The bundle of newspapers had filled most of the box. As Dutch removed them again it was obvious that there was not much room left for anything of any size.

Jenny was the first to comment on what she saw. "It looks like an old cigar box," she judged from its appearance as she glanced into the box.

"And an old spyglass," her mother added, looking at the second item found stored in the box.

"That does look like an old one!" Raleigh intoned. "If I were a betting man, I would lay money on the fact that it dates back and was used in the Civil War."

No one took his bet as it was evident that the box was filled when the war was the concern of those who were responsible for packing it.

"I failed to see that spyglass when I lifted those newspapers to see what remained in the box," Dutch commented as he picked it up, examined it, and then placed it on the table. "Looks like something Blackbeard might have used as he sailed the Atlantic," he quipped. "Maybe he tired of sailing the oceans and took a side trip up the Tennessee River in his *Queen Anne's Revenge* and hid a treasure chest right here on the farm."

He smiled as he mumbled to himself, "I loved those old pirate tales when I was young. I even envisioned myself as Blackbeard or Captain Hook, sailing the oceans with a parrot on my shoulder and a spy glass in my hand, inquiring as to *'what's up matey?"*

After the brief encounter with his boyhood fantasies, Dutch collected his thoughts and turned his attention back to the box he was emptying.

Commenting to the others, he said, "Guess I got sidetracked there for a moment; excuse me. I'm quite sure this was used for spying purposes during the Civil War and has never been touched by a pirate."

He laughed to himself as he reached and removed the cigar box from the larger box.

He also examined it closely before making an additional comment. "This is an old nailed wooden box, the most common kind made during the Civil War era. Cigar boxes, after the cigars were removed, were frequently used to store items for safe keeping. I never was one to use tobacco, but I do know that there were a lot of cigars smoked and boxes manufactured to hold them.

"I recently read an article written about cigar boxes. I was surprised to learn that every year, for a century before 1940, there were over one hundred million nailed wooden cigar boxes manufactured to hold over one trillion cigars made in the United States. Over ten billion nailed wooden boxes were used during that time, so the article said. There are still a lot of cigar boxes out there. There are a lot of collectors holding them, but there are many that are still being used for storage like this one. There's a whole big interesting cigar box story, but we don't have time to go there, so let's see what this one holds, if anything."

Dutch reached into the cigar box and pulled out a round, disk-shaped piece of metal that had two concentric disks attached and the English alphabet printed clockwise on each. The outer disk measured about 2 ¼ inches and the inner disk 1 ½ inches. In the middle was the inscription "CSA" stamped with the letters "S.S." underneath. On the rear was the inscription "F Labarre Richmond VA." The two concentric disks shared a central axle which allowed each to be turned to the desired position.

"What is that?" Abigail inquired.

"Beats me!" Jenny responded.

"I'm sure that it has something to do with the Civil War," Dutch said. "I'm almost certain that the 'CSA' inscribed in the center stands for Confederate States of America."

They passed the strange device, taking turns looking at it more closely.

"We'll find out more about this gadget later," Dutch informed the others. "There are several folded sheets of paper in the cigar box," he said as he pulled one out and examined it. "This makes absolutely no sense," he mumbled. "I can't make heads or tails out of what this is all about."

"Let me see," Jenny requested, reaching for the paper. "It looks like a message written in some sort of code. I smell a little espionage here."

"And this device was probably used to decode the messages," Abigail said as she turned the disk around in her hands.

"I'll make another assumption," Raleigh spoke up as he too observed the codes. "I bet that this fell into the hands of Northern spies and was used by them to decipher messages sent in code by the Southern army. It could have been made available by a turncoat who was secretly a spy for the North. There were a good many Tories who were forced to join the Confederate cause but were adamantly opposed to the war. Some joined, knowing that they would be forced to do so, making it appear that they were dedicated to the Confederacy but were secretly working with the Yankees."

Dutch nodded in agreement before adding, "Reverend Stone and all the people on the plantation were lying low but were secretly working with the North. This, undoubtedly, was a spy sanctuary, and I think that the hidden shelter which had earlier been used as a hideaway, was being used during the war to conceal Yankee spies. It seems they even left a few items behind."

Part Two

———————◆———————

THE JOURNAL

Sarah was a school teacher in the classroom which had been built by Reverend Stone in order to provide an education to the children who lived on the plantation. She recorded in her journal an account of her use of the newspapers in keeping her students informed of current events. She was obviously aware of the history that was being played out in this tumultuous period in the nation. Sarah was teaching black, white, and Indian students, and the history that was being made had a profound effect on the future of all of them.

As she was using the same newspaper articles which she later saved and stored in the box, her journal contains some repetition as to what has been recorded by the reading of the articles as written in the newspapers. The Riddles and Walkers frequently made comments about the articles which they were reading from the old newspapers long after history had been written about the bloody conflict. They read, knowing what the outcome would be. On the other hand, as Sarah wrote in her journal, the ebb and flow of the newspaper accounts painted a glowing description of the South's battleground successes, only to lament over their losses in the next edition. The final outcome of the conflict was not to be known until after four years of bloody battles. She, however, shared with those who might later read her writings in the journal her feelings as to what she rightly considered to be a huge mistake on the part of the South to undertake such an endeavor. Much of her writings regarding the war were written with foresight as to what she expected to be the outcome, which were echoed by the comments made in hindsight by the Riddles and Walkers, as to the futility of the South to consider that their cause could be victorious.

The resulting massacres are history. Sarah lived during that agonizing period and recorded it for future generations. Possibly she was wishing that a lesson could be learned and there would be no repeat of such carnage in our nation. Her desire, as a mother, was for her children to live in a united nation where they could live in peace.

CHAPTER 9

◆

Dutch laid the cigar box to the side and made the announcement that they all were waiting to hear, "It looks like we are back down to the journal. The cover is a little different from the other ones, but it is similar in size to those that we have already read. It seems to be in remarkably good shape considering its probable age," he commented as he removed it from the container.

"Could this possibly be the one that we have been looking for?" Jenny wondered aloud to the others. "By that I mean could it be the one that Grandmother Mattie mentioned? The one that she had sneaked and read a small portion from?"

"The only way we can answer your question is to open it up and start reading," her mother advised.

Utilizing the limited available space in the notebook, the author of the journal's handwriting was small and neat.

May 6, 1860

I am Sarah Abston and I am a Cherokee. My husband is Sunny Abston whose mother is a Cherokee too. My daddy is Grey Fox and my mother is Eve. They are Cherokee but we don't let that be known or they might get sent off to the Indian's new lands in the Oklahoma Territory. Sunny's dad is Joseph Stone. He says to just call him Joe, but people call him Reverend Stone as he at one time was a Methodist preacher who worked with the Cherokee people before they got sent off to that Indian Territory in Oklahoma. A lot of the people who work on the farm here call him Master Stone or Reverend Stone but he don't really care what people call him. I just call him Papa Joe and Sunny calls him dad. Sunny's mother is called Sunbeam and she is a Cherokee, but we don't let anybody know that either. We just call ourselves Black Dutch and since nobody round here can rightly say what a Black Dutch looks like then they have left us alone so far. Since Sunny's mother and dad were not married when he was born his mother gave him the last name of Abston. She said that she decided to do that cause she did not want to give him a Cherokee name that might get him sent off to Oklahoma. She said that she just took the first two letters of the English alphabet, Ab, and added stone to it cause that is the last name of his dad and dropped off the last e and came up with Abston. So his name is Sunny Abston.

Raleigh interrupted the reading, "Well, we don't have to speculate who was writing in this journal. In the first journal, the only name we got from the writer was Eve, and her sister never gave her name in the account she recorded as she traveled on the Trail of Tears. We knew who she was only because she talked about her sister, Eve. Eve gave very little information about her family in her second journal other than revealing the name of her sister, Hannah, when she returned from Oklahoma. It appears that Sarah wanted to let the reader know who she is, and who her family is from the get-go."

"Good for her!" Abigail declared.

"Let's see what she had to say," Dutch directed their attention back to the journal.

My mother wrote in a book like this when I was a little girl and in another one when I was a growing up and I thought that I would do that too. She wrote on Sundays most of the time so I am going to try to write some on Sundays too. Now I know that I can't write every Sunday cause we get real busy around here but I am glad to get this paper to write down some of the stuff that I've got on my mind. I would not be writing this if'n I didn't have a good place to hide it so that nobody could find it. When we came to live on this farm, we lived in a secret place where nobody knew where it was. We still use it today but for a different purpose. There is a secret place there where I can hide this so nobody can find it and then know what I write about us being Cherokee and that we was supposed to go to Indian Territory. We have it good now to what I first remember when I was little. My mom and dad were hid out in a secret place in the Warrior Mountains across the river over there whenever I was born and we stayed hid out until I was about five years old. I don't exactly know my birthdate cause there was nothing in the place we were hiding out in when I was born to tell what time it was or what date it was either so I don't know how old I really was when we got out of there. I remember that I had a little brother named Buck but he got bit by a rattlesnake and died while we were still hid out. My mother told me that she and my dad got married by Reverend Stone who is my husband's daddy. They married before the government made all the Indians that lived in these parts go out west to Indian Territory. Reverend Stone was a Methodist circuit riding preacher who preached to a young Cherokee woman named Sunbeam at Pinhook which was one of the places he stopped on his preaching circuit. It seems that Reverend Stone went to teach the Gospel of

Christ to Sunbeam but she was a very pretty woman with a good nature and he ended up making a baby by her before they were married. They named the baby Sunny and he is now my husband. Seeing as to how Reverend Stone was a preacher of the Gospel and he had sinned and took Sunbeam and made her to have a baby, he made like something had happened to him and he disappeared. The people that he had preached to on his circuit counted him to be dead but he took Sunbeam and came to this place where we are living now and started farming. He married Sunbeam after Sunny was born and after that they had another baby boy they named Flash. They did the naming of their children in the Cherokee way and did not leave a record at the courthouse which would have caused problems as the Cherokees were all supposed to be in Oklahoma. All this time that my brother Woody was a baby we were still hid out in that canyon in the mountains. When my mother was going to have another baby after it was that little Buck died from that snakebite my daddy was gone a lot of the time and we thought that we would die in that place. My mother even taught me an old proverb which I think is good and it has helped me when it seems that times are bad. I know that things now could never get as bad as whenever we was in hiding and when we didn't have nothing. I still say it to myself sometimes. I remember it so well because mother use to make me write it down in a journal she use to have. She was using it to write down whatever it was that she had on her mind and she used it too to teach me how to write. I will write it down here so as not to let it get lost. It goes like this:

WALK WITH THE WIND AT YOUR BACK
WHENEVER YOU CAN.
FACE IT WHENEVER YOU MUST.
BE BRAVE AND STRONG

HARD TIMES WILL SOON BE GONE.
TOMORROW IS THE BEGINNING
OF A WHOLE NEW DAY.
WE CANNOT KNOW
WHAT THIS DAY MIGHT BRING
BUT THE SKY IS NOT ALWAYS GRAY.
ENDURE THE STORMS
AND SOOTHE THE PAINS.
ENJOY THE SUNSHINE
THAT FOLLOWS THE RAINS.

What mother didn't know was that whenever dad was gone a lot of the time that he was here at this farm helping Reverend Stone and his workers to build a secret hideaway for us to get out of the mountains and go to so as not to get caught by the bounty hunters who were still rounding up Indians to take them out west. He came back just before my little brother was born. My dad got to name him because he had named Buck but he died and daddy named him Woody. My mother helped Woody write his own saying whenever she was teaching him how to write like she did me. I have learned it too so I will put it down like I did mine:

"Helpless we begin our life
Dependent on a man and wife
Nurtured then by love and care
We must each our burdens bear
Helpful then we must become
Troubles will surely fall on some
With the golden rule to guide
Help is always by your side
Always do unto others as you
Would have them do to you."

Mother taught Woody that proverb that she had me to write down and she also had him to write down that other one. I know that the one she gave to me to write down has done me a lot of good and I think that it has helped Woody too. We had it real hard whenever we was younger but I believe that whenever Woody got older it made him think about how he might be able to help other people and he has been good at taking an interest in other people who need help. He is all the time helping out the crippled and sick folks who need help. There are some young children on the farm here who have had a hard time and he helps them out whenever he can. There is also a story that has been passed down by our family members about a cripple who would have been killed if his mom and dad hadn't hid him out in a secret hideout. It is said that there is a cave there where he hid out a lot of valuable jewelry and maybe later where a lot of things were hid whenever the Cherokees saw that they were going to have to leave Alabama and they wanted to hide out their valuables so as not to let the white men get them. I think that story may have got him to thinking that the cripple's family needed to have someone to help them out. This is a good place to live here cause everybody wants to help out whenever somebody needs something. I have wrote a whole lot today and it is time for me to do something else but I am a going to write in this book ever chance I get like my mother did hers and aunt Hannah did whenever she was made to walk all the way to Oklahoma. I asked Sunny if he could get me a book to write in and he got me this one. His dad has some that he always keeps for whenever he needs them to keep up the records that he needs to run the farm the way that it oughta be run. He said that he had let mother and Aunt Hannah have one and he was glad that I wanted to write and put down on paper whatever I had on my mind.

♦

"Finally we have the journal that Grandmother Mattie sneaked and read from when she was little. This has to be the same one because she related to us a lot of what we have just read. She probably had time to read only this first part as she was sneaking around and doing it, but it was enough to clue us in on what happened to the family following the abrupt ending of the first journal which was left in the canyon. I am amazed that she remembered so much of it so vividly, yet the only name she could recall was that of Reverend Stone." Jenny made the comment following her reading of the first entry that Sarah had made in the journal on May 6, 1860.

"It does look like that she only got through with reading the first account before her father almost caught her with it, after she had been instructed not to do so," Raleigh said, agreeing with the assessment that Jenny had made. "I suppose that the remainder of what Sarah had to say in this book will be all new to us. This is a thick notebook. If it is filled to the last page with her writings, then we will have a lot of reading ahead of us. Since it looks as if it is going to rain all day, I suggest that we read as long as possible, and we will see how far into the day that will take. Of course, if we don't keep our mouths shut, I suppose we won't get very far into it. I'll be quiet so we continue reading."

"You are right, and I should keep my mouth shut too," Dutch spoke this time, "but something just occurred to me which I will mention. Grandmother Mattie was almost one hundred years old when she died. We don't know her age exactly because she was Cherokee and they didn't run to the courthouse and record things like they do today. Now you say that she said she was young when she read from this book, but she obviously was old enough to read, so that would probably place her at least in her pre-teens. There were not a whole lot of Cherokee children who learned to read so she was one of the fortunate ones. Having said this, I would suppose that she was somewhere around being a teenager when the incident occurred. Now, I am saying this in order to get an idea as to how long it has been since this box was last opened. The newspapers which we have already read are dated, so we can probably say that the box was first packed during the days of the Civil War, or shortly afterwards. Since then, probably around eighty or eighty-five years ago, it was opened and the journal removed and read by those men Mattie mentioned, so Sarah was not the last one to close this box. And another thing! Since the journal was in the bottom of the box, the newspapers and other items would have to have been removed also. When it was closed at that time the contents were probably replaced just as they had been initially packed. Considering this, I would say that it was more than eighty years ago when this box was last opened."

"Grandmother Mattie said that the reason it was brought out was because the men found things of interest written in it. I suggest we find out what that was all about!" Jenny was anxious to continue reading.

May 13, 1860

Sometime it is real hard to understand what it is that is going on around here seeing as to how there is so much talk about the South breaking away from the Union and if'n Lincoln is elected to be the president of the country there is going to be war. There is all this talk about a convention in Charleston and the word is that there aint nobody that can agree as to what this country should be like. Sunny's dad says that the South don't want nobody a messing with their slaves but the North wants the negroes to be able to go wherever they want to and work for whoever will be good to them and pay them the most and they not be required to do slave labor.. He tells us all about these things because he thinks that black people should be treated just as good as the white man is. They done ran the red men out of their lands and treated them like they were animals and they is doing the same things to the blacks, cept they won't let them go nowhere but to go to work in the fields. I don't know a whole lot about all this political stuff that is a going on but Papa Joe is a keeping up with it all and he gets a newspaper named the Florence Gazette and it has a lot to say about what is going on. The best I can get in my mind about what it is all about is that the Democrats had a convention in Charleston, South Carolina from April 23rd to May 3rd where they were spose to have nominated somebody to run as a Democrat for president. It has been ten days since it was over and the word is getting to us that there wasn't nothing settled about who would be the Democrat to run for President. The people from the North and them from the South got crossways with one another and about fifty people from the South walked out of Institute Hall where they were having their meeting and went over to Saint Andrews Hall on Broad Street and finished their meeting. They didn't get nobody nominated and the Northern Democrats are going to meet again in Baltimore and the Southern Democrats will meet in Richmond to pick whoever they want to run. Now all this is too much for me to understand what is going on but Papa Joe says that this country is in real bad shape and he said that it won't be long before we are fighting one another. He says that he is on the Republican side and he hopes that their candidate named Abraham Lincoln gets elected. He says that with the way that the Democrats are fighting one another that he is almost sure that the Republicans will win. He says that then the slaves will be freed and he is all for that. There aint nothing that a person like me can do cept just wait and see what happens.

♦

May 20, 1860

Another week has passed and Papa Joe got another newspaper and he says that the news is not getting no better. He brought in a newspaper that talked about what it was that I was writing about last week about all the turmoil that is a happening in our country. It is a newspaper that is dated May 9, 1860 and the headline is nine states withdraw from the convention. It says that nine states out of the fifteen southern states withdrew from the Charleston Convention, They are Deleware, Texas, Alabama, Mississippi, Louisiana, Arkansas, South Carolina, Georgia and Florida. The paper says that this was a necessity thrown upon them by a positive refusal on the part of the convention, to recognize their right of property in the territories. It says that since the adoption of the Cincinnati Platform in 1856, the Supreme Court of the United States in the Dred Scott decision declared it to be the duties of the General Governors to protect slavery in the territories. It says that when the convention assembled that a committee, one from each state, was appointed to report a platform of principles. Seventeen states voted against sixteen, to embody the principle of the Dred Scott decision, guaranteeing protection to slave property in the territories. The convention refused to ratify the report of the majority of the committee, by a vote of 237 1/2 to 65!!! It says that the nine southern states had either to remain in the convention and yield to the detestable doctrine of

Squatter Sovereignty and thus give up their right to equality in the territories, acquired by their common blood and treasure or signify their dissent by peacefully withdrawing. Now I am copying this straight from the newspaper which I have in front of me and the articles go on to talk about the injustice that was being done to the southern states and the points of difference between them but what it all means is that the North is getting crossways with the south and there is going to be a lot of trouble between them. Papa Joe said that after the northern Democrats couldn't get a majority to nominate any one candidate because the south had walked out, that they will meet again in Baltimore on June 18 to pick somebody to run for president. He says that he is sure that it will be a Senator from Illinois named Stephen A. Douglas and he says that the southern Democrats don't like him and that the Democrats don't have no chance of getting anybody elected. The big thing that they don't agree on is what should be the law about keeping slaves. The south says that issue was decided in 1857 when the Supreme Court ruled in the Dred Scott case that the newspaper talked about and that the Constitution protected slavery in all territories. The northern states refused to accept that decision and want to abolish slavery in the whole country. Papa Joe has always said that the slaves ought to be free and he is on the side of the north. He says that Chief Justice Taney's decision that slaves were so far inferior that they had no right which the white man was bound to respect is what's wrong with this country. He said that a lot of white man thinks that the Indians and black people in this country can be treated any way they want cause they are second class people who have no rights. He says that God created all men equal and that is the way that they ought to be treated. He say that in the Bible it says that we are all of one blood. The black man's blood and the red man's blood and the white man's blood ain't different in no way. There's a lot of people around here that says they don't want to take sides cause they don't own no slaves anyhow and they just want to be left alone. The talk is that there is going to be war before this thing is settled and a lot of people don't want to get into no gunfight with other people when they don't want no part of the conflict. The newspaper is stirring up people by saying that the southern states shouldn't let the politicians from up north tell us what to do even though the Supreme Court has already decided what is right under the Constitution. I am just a gonna stay right here on this farm and hope that it don't come down to them trying to make Sunny or anybody else that lives here have to join up with any army. Papa Joe and Sunny says that right now what they is worried about is that the crops do good and we get the right amount of rain for the cotton and corn to grow good this year. Sunny says that he is scared that if the south gets into a fight with the north that there won't be no way to sell the corn and cotton cause a lot of what we grow here is sent off in boats up north and to places across the ocean. There aint nothing that we can do about it cause them people what runs everything in Montgomery are a going to do what they want to do and they don't care who gets hurt or killed a doing it. There is talk that Governor Moore is all for war if things don't go his way in the election that will be held in November. Papa Joe says that there was a joint session of the legislature in February and they passed a resolution where they advised Governor Moore that if'n the Democrat Stephen A. Douglas is nominated or if a Black Republican is, that he is to call for an election for representatives to a State Secession Convention in Montgomery. He says that there is a man named William Lowndes Yancey that is stirring everything up to try to get us into war with the North. I just try and not think about it and hope that everything settles down and there aint gonna be no war.

♦

"It looks a lot like we are about to get a replay of the newspaper material we have just spent a couple of days reading," Abigail said. "Do we really want to do this?"

"I don't think we can make that judgement until we read a little more than what we have already covered. And yes, we want to read this journal to see what Sarah wants someone to know in later years," Jenny responded.

"Let's read!" Raleigh ended the brief exchange between Abigail and Jenny.

May 27, 1860

I don't like to think about all this bad stuff that is happening in our country because of all that I already been put through that was caused by government people. I get to thinking back to when I was a little girl whenever we was a hiding out and how bad it was and now I think about how good we have everything . When I started writing in this book I told a lot about our family but I will write some more about what is on my mind. I was born in a snake den and didn't get to leave it until I was about five years old. My mother didn't think that we would ever get out of that hiding place alive but she didn't have no choice but to stay there because she didn't want to have to walk all the way to Oklahoma what they would make her do if they caught her. Whenever my daddy came and told mother that we was finally going to leave that place I believe that it was the happiest day of her life. She had been holed up in there for nigh on six years with nobody else around to talk to but me and daddy was gone a lot of the time. Momma was carrying another baby and she was having a hard time of it. She thought that she might die while birthing it and she was worried what would happen to me if'n she died and left me there by myself cause daddy was gone so much. We was real happy to see daddy come back right before the baby was born and he said that we would be leaving the hiding place whenever momma was strong enough after the baby got here. After the baby was born momma was ready to get out but daddy said that she would have to wait about two weeks so she would be strong enough to make the trip to wherever it was that we was a going to. Daddy named the baby Woody cause he said that his little Indian would be a good woodsman. He had got to name Buck but whenever that snake killed him he wanted another boy so that he could do manly things with while he was growing up. We did not know why daddy was gone a lot while we was in hiding but when we was waiting for momma to get strong enough after Woody was born he told us what he had been doing. He said that he had been working on building a place for us to go to where we would be safe from the Federal men and bounty hunters who was trying to round up all the Indians who was still hiding to keep from being made to go to the Oklahoma territory. Daddy brought us here to the hideaway that he had help Reverend Stone build to hide out Indians and slaves and we have been here ever since then. I got to go to school with a teacher named Sadie who is still teaching in the schoolhouse here that Sunny's dad had built to have school classes in and to go to church in. While I was growing up Miss Sadie was the teacher for all the children who grew up here on the farm and she married one of the boys who grew up here. I did not realize that it is getting so late so I will write more later when I have the time to do it.

♦

June 3, 1860

It is Sunday again and I am a going to write some more until I run out of time cause I have got a lot of other things to do before dark. I was a saying when I quit writing the last time that Sadie married one of the boys that lives here on the farm. When people here want to get married they have to pick out somebody that lives here on the farm too cause we don't go nowhere to find somebody else. Me and Reverend Stone's boy, Sunny, grew up together and so last year we got married. His dad married us and he said that he was happy to have me to be married to his boy. Reverend Stone had married my mother and daddy at Kinlock whenever he was a preaching on that circuit through the Warrior Mountains and he said that he considered it an honor to be able to perform the marriage ceremony for Sunny and me. He said that he knew me real well because I had growed up on the farm and me and Sunny had worked together and played together almost all of our lives. Sunny was always so good to me while we was a growing up and we never had no cross words so I never did think about marring nobody else but him. His mother, Sunbeam, is full Cherokee and she was all for her boy to marry another Cherokee. I love Sunny and know that he will make a good husband and father to children if we have some. Papa Joe says that one of these days this farm will be ours so Sunny needs to learn how to do everything that has to be done to keep the farm a running and making money. He says that all the workers that he has here on the farm has got to be treated good and they are to have a good place to live and plenty to eat. They've got to have a place where they can go to church and a schoolhouse and a good teacher so the kids can learn to read and write and do numbers. Papa Joe says that I am a right smart girl and he has had me learning how to teach and to help Sadie at the schoolhouse cause we are having to get more workers here a lot since Papa Joe is getting more land all of the time. Now me and Sadie ain't never been to no college and Papa Joe has been our only teacher and he is real smart but there are a lot of things that I still need to learn. That is one of the reasons I wanted to write in this book so as to practice my writing. I know that I will make a lot of mistakes and I will put in here some things that I have already wrote about but I am just going to put down what is heavy on my mind whenever I am writing it. I ain't a going to try to put in no paragraphs and I will write longer sentences because I want to make use of all the space that I have in this book. There are too many children here now for Sadie to be able to teach them all so she needs some help. Papa Joe has always said that the black children needs to learn just like the white ones do and he don't want no children here to not to be able to read and write and do numbers. He has never called the black workers slaves cause that word makes it sound like he is forcing them to work whenever they don't want to and he says that he don't drive nobody to do things that they are not able to do. He says that everybody has got to do their part so that we can grow things to sell and have plenty to eat but he don't want nobody to be unhappy here on the farm. He says that ifn they are here and don't want to do their part of the work then they are free to go somewhere else but there ain't nobody who wants to leave here because he is so good to them.

♦

"She is certainly doing a better job in her writings than her mother did in her journals." Jenny said. "That first journal that Eve wrote was so full of mistakes that it was hard for me to read. I think that Reverend Stone was a pretty good teacher. It's obvious that Sarah was not polished in her writings and still made some mistakes, but that is to be expected considering that her education was limited by the isolated circumstances in which she lived. She was teaching others and perhaps that was not the perfect situation for the children. But hey, from what I have observed, she may have been able to give her students a better education than some of our young people are getting today." She paused before adding, "And we are not yet getting that replay of those newspaper articles as you expected, Mother, but I suspect that will come."

June 17, 1860

I didn't write none last Sunday because after I went to church. Me and Sunny decided that we would go swim in the river like we did when we was a growing up. The days are getting warm and the water sure does feel good whenever you go in and get cooled off. There are a lot of sandbars that we can sit on so we packed a picnic lunch and we had a real good day. I like to go to the shoals and listen to the water as it rushes downstream. Some of the Indians call it the singing river cause of the sounds it makes as it flows over the rapids on the river. It is a good way to spend the day and get your mind off all the work that needs to be done on the farm. I have extra time to do some writing now that I am helping Sadie teach the kids that are here on the farm. Papa Joe said now that we got most of the cotton chopped and the corn hoed where the grown-ups can finish it that the children can go to school till it is cotton picking time. We are all scared of what is going to happen next cause there is a whole lot of things going on in this country that aint good. Papa Joe goes into Florence which is on this side of the river about once a week and he brings back copies of the Florence Gazette for us to read and talk to our students about what is going on in the country. He said that he would like for us to have a class once a week on what he called current events so the students know about things that happen away from the farm here. Here of late there aint nothing in them papers but what the Democrats are a doing to try to keep the slaves from getting their freedom. Papa Joe says that this whole talk about war with the Yankees is nothing more than the rich plantation owners down south of here not wanting to give their slaves the freedom that they ought to have. He says that the black people in a lot of places are not being treated any better than the horses and mules and oxen that they have on the farms with them. He says that a lot of slaves has to take beatings and made to do more work than what they are able to do and the slaves aint got no other choice than to take all of this bad treatment cause they are not free to go nowhere else. A lot of the young girls, Papa Joe says, are made to give the white men whatever they want and some of them are having the white man's babies but they don't have no choice but to lay down and let them take whatever they want. Now I am looking at the latest paper here and most of whatever is wrote in it is how the southern Democrats are getting ready to show them Yankees that they don't have to answer to them no more and they are going to secede from the Union if they don't get their way and don't get the people elected who they want to be elected. The big news today is about the convention that the Democrats are a holding in Baltimore cause they didn't get nothing settle whenever they met in Charleston. Papa Joe says that there is going to be war and the southern political leaders had better think twice before they start shooting cause they are about to bite off more than they can chew. He says that there are a lot of people around here in the valley and in the Warrior Mountains where we was hid out who don't want no part of war. He says that it don't make no sense that we here in Northwest Alabama be made to send our men to get killed for fighting the war for the rich farmers in South Alabama who won't even get close to no battle lines. He says that the Democrats expect that everybody ought to get their guns and go out and kill the very people who want to make this country a place where all men are free. He says that we need to teach the children that the freedom of all people is one thing that the founding fathers made sure to include when they wrote the constitution for this country. Papa Joe says that now it has got to where only the white man is free and the colored people have had all their rights taken away from them and even though the land belonged to the Indians before the white man got here it was took away when they wanted it. The red man has been run out of their homelands and they won't let them come back and the blacks have been brought in and they won't let them go nowhere but to the fields to do hard work. He wants for me and Sadie to let the children know about the things needed to make this a great country and he wants us to let the children know that we are not on the side of them people who wants to fight and we want everybody to be safe and free. I have been writing this in the classroom and it is time for class to start and I have a roomful of children. Today we are going to do some reading from some newspapers that I brought with me. The children have to learn to read and we don't have many primer books to read from so I get them close together on the benches and we read about what is the latest that is going on in this country. I am saving some of the articles in the newspapers so as to be able to come back later to review what all has been going on. I cut out the pages that have the news about what is happening in our country and save the rest for to use for paper in the toilets. Most people like to use paper more than the corn cobs that they use most of the time.

◆

CHAPTER 10

———————◆———————

As war clouds accumulated over the Southland, Sarah faithfully documented her apprehensions that there would be difficult days ahead. She continued to make entries in her writings almost every Sunday, often lamenting that Southern politicians were leading the country toward a civil conflict between the Northern and Southern states. She continued to teach at the schoolhouse and continued to use newspapers as a tool for teaching her students, assisting Sadie in educating the children that lived on the farm.

The dates of the entries into her journal moved closer and closer to the beginning of the war. The focus of her writings shifted to her concerns as to what role the farm workers would be expected to fill as they had expressed the desire to remain neutral in any conflict which might occur. Recruitment of troops needed to fight the Yankees had begun, and there was a plea for all able bodied men to get their guns and enlist to fight for the Confederacy.

The foursome took their time as they read the weekly entries which Sarah had recorded in the journal. The developing news of the deteriorating relationships between the North and the South was her greatest concern. However, on some days she described the activities in which she was involved on the farm, especially regarding the school.

October 7, 1860

    The crops did real good this year and we are not having school until all the cotton is picked and the corn is pulled and put in the barn. Papa Joe had the young children stripping the corn stalks for fodder to be used in the winter time to help feed the pasture animals. There is a lot for everybody to do this time of the year and the kids keep real busy doing things that they are able to do. There is the sorghum cane to strip and the syrup to make where the young ones feed the stalks through the crusher where the juice is squeeze out and tote wood for the fire under the pan where the molasses is made. There is corn to pull and put in the crib and the cotton to pick. The older men cut the firewood and stove wood that is needed in the wintertime and the younger children help tote it and stack it up. There is so much to do that there is not time to have school but we will get started back whenever we finish doing all that. My mother and dad no longer live in the secret hideaway where we lived when we came here to stay hid from the bounty hunters that was catching Indians and sending them to Oklahoma. Now a days the government is thinking about fighting a war and they are not interested in hunting down Indians to ship them to Oklahoma. Mother and dad still work at the secret place so as to keep the animals fed, the cows milked and the eggs gathered. They kept real busy for a while a hiding out slaves that were traveling what I have heard called the Underground Railroad but what with all the unrest in this country there are not as many who come through as they once were. This whole war thing is mostly about what to do with the slaves and the north says to free them and the southern land owners say that they were bought and paid for and they have the right to keep them as workers. Papa Joe says that you can keep them as workers if you treat them right and they don't have to belong to nobody but themselves and people ain't made to be bought and sold like animals are. He is right cause there are a lot of blacks here on the farm that could leave if they were so aimed to do but they don't go nowhere cause they got it good here. He says that if there is war that he will do what he can to help the slaves get their freedom and he shore aint going to send nobody from the farm to go to shoot at Yankees who want to set the slaves free. I have wrote about this before but it keeps bearing on my mind as to just what we will do here on the farm if there is a war. I guess that the best thing to do is to keep on praying that the two sides can get together and work out their differences without going to war.

◆

October 21, 1860

I am looking at the Florence Gazette dated Oct. 17, 1860 and they are telling people how they think that they should vote. The editors are JOHN S. KENNEDY and S. A. M. WOOD and they got it that you should vote for JOHN C. BRECKENRIDGE of Kentucky for president and GENERAL JOSEPH LANE of Oregon for vice president. Under that they have the candidates they are backing for the Democratic Electoral Ticket and for the state at large. The first name that they have is David Hubbard of Lawrence County. That caught my eye because David Hubbard lives at Kinlock close to where we was hid out when I was born. He is the one who had a plantation there and ran a mill at the falls where we passed by when we got out of the place where we had been hid out. His brother, Greene, was the one who built the mill but David bought it from him and is running it now. There was a long list of names from all over the state that they said to vote for on the Democratic Electoral tickets in each district and the alternate candidates, and for the Democratic Executive Committee. For the districts they have the name of J. S. Kennedy on the Democratic Electoral Ticket and he is the editor who is endorsing hisself. For the Democratic Executive Committee he says to vote for E. A. O'neal, of Lauderdale county. The election is not far off and Papa Joe says that the Democrats are so crossways with each other that there is no way that a Democrat can be elected. I am already good and tired of reading about all that I have wrote about. I am just a going to stop writing today and get busy with something else to take my mind off all this that is going on.

◆

November 4, 1860

Just about what I wrote about the last time all the talk now a day is still about the election that will be held Tuesday for president and vice president of the United States. I have a Florence Gazette newspaper I have been reading from that came out last Wednesday. Papa Joe picked it up Saturday in Florence and it has nothing of news other than the election. Papa Joe said that is what all the talk was about when he was in town and most people are for the Democrats but there are some that are for Lincoln cause they are afraid of what might happen if the Democrats win. He says that everybody is expecting that there will be war no matter who wins the election cause neither side is going to stand for what the other side wants to do. In the paper he brought back and gave to me for to keep there is that big headline again for Breckenridge and Lane and for all the ones who are running on the Democratic ticket. There is a little article in the first paragraph under all them endorsement that says "Go early to the polls on Tuesday the 6th day of November, and vote for Breckenridge, the friend of the Constitution and the south" After that they printed an address by a Prof. Holcombe–"The Election of Lincoln an overt act of aggression" and says that "The election of a Black Republican President is an overt act of aggression on the right of property in slaves". He says "That event, there is too much reason to fear, must be regarded as a fixed fact. The late elections in Pennsylvania, Ohio, and Indiana, are generally considered as having virtually decided the election in favor of Lincoln." There was a lot more written on that front page about the election and one headline read "SHAME ON DOUGLAS" which talked about the strife and bitterness within the Democratic party which handed the election over to the "Black Republican, Lincoln." I suppose that we do not have to wait until after Tuesday to know who our next President will be because everybody says that the Democrats don't have a chance to beat Abraham Lincoln. After that they say that there is going to be war.

♦

"How right she was," Abigail muttered as Dutch turned a page in the journal.

November 11, 1860

The election for President of the United States was held last Tuesday but Papa Joe brought in the Wednesday Newspaper that came out the day after the election and they didn't have the news yet about who the winner was but Papa Joe says that the word in Florence Saturday was that Lincoln was the big winner and he will be the next President. The newspaper that I have from Wednesday still has the headlines endorsing Breckenridge and Lane and the other Democrats even though it came out on November 7, the day after the election was over. It did carry the results of the election in Lauderdale County which showed that Douglas got 205 votes, Breckenridge got 161 and Bell got 158 with more votes for Douglas to be counted. In this county Douglas got about 100 more votes than Breckenridge which just goes to show how much influence that newspaper and its editors have on the people in the county since they heavily promoted Breckenridge. Papa Joe says that he talks to a lot of people in town who don't agree with all the anti-abolition stuff, and the people who wants to keep the blacks as slaves that the Gazette keeps writing about, and it is not worth fighting a war and getting people killed just so those rich farmers in South Alabama can keep their slave labor.

◆

November 18, 1860

I always write on Sunday after I go to church cause that is the only time that I have enough time to stop and do some writing. The children have not been in school cause of cotton picking and corn pulling but Papa Joe said that he wants for me and Sadie to get ready to get school started back up because they need to be learning from books. The first picking of cotton is getting close to being done but there is always a second picking for to get whatever is left in the field after it has been picked the first time. This will take on into the wintertime to get it all done but Papa Joe says that the older people can do the rest of it cause the young ones need to be in school. Some farmers just burn their fields after the first picking and a lot of cotton is burned without being picked. Papa Joe says that is just a waste and he wants to get as much as he can from the fields before he burns them and start plowing them up again for next year. The children can still do their chores after school every day so they will be busy with everything that we got going. Papa Joe went back to Florence last Saturday and got another newspaper from Wednesday, November 14 that had the results of the presidential election which it did not have the day after the election. It says that Breckenridge has carried twelve states, all Southern. It says that it is not certain that Douglas has carried a single state and in many southern states, Mr. Breckenridge will beat the vote of Bell and Douglas combined. This has gotta be the case in Alabama. The paper gave the total vote for each county in Alabama. The headline is "How shall we meet the Crisis" and says that the New York Herald of the 5th inst. (the day before the election), contends very clearly that the North would not submit to Southern aggression and domination. Quoting Steward it says "There is an irrepressible conflict existing between freedom and slavery, which must go on until all the States are free of slaves." Gidding says that "Congress has a right, in case of a rupture between the North and South, to free the slaves." Lincoln, the candidate for the presidency, declares "that slavery and freedom cannot exist together. The paper then ask the question, now what does all this mean? It reads; Steward, the great leader, if he means anything, means that slavery must be abolished in the south; for he says that the conflict must go on until all the States become slave or free. The northern states, having abolished slavery by disposing of their slaves to the south, will again readapt it; therefore the southern states must become free. The article is a long one but what caught my eye as I read it is what it says down toward the end. "Now, what is to be the result of this irrepressible conflict? Nothing more nor less than the freedom of the slaves, destruction of commerce, frightful massacres, and the ruin of the union–Lincoln tells us that slavery and freedom cannot exist together. Either the slaves must rise upon their masters, or the master be reduced to an equality with the slave. And as the two races cannot exist together, a war of extermination must follow. And as it is believed that the Negro South cannot support himself in a state of freedom, hundreds of thousands will congregate to their friends–the Republicans–North, and be placed by them side by side in competition with white men–are you ready to divide your money with the negro? Are you ready to work with him in competition–to work more than you do now for less pay? If you are, vote for the Republican candidate, who, if honest, must break up the present relations between the north and south." Now that is not all that article says but it is enough for me to not like what is a fixen to happen now that the Republicans done won the election. Papa Joe says that there is about to be some mighty hard times ahead cause some people in the south wants to fight the Yankees and some say to go ahead and free the slaves and there is going to be a war. I have wrote this over and over in this note book about a war a coming and it looks like it is about to get here. I have wrote a lot today but with this new president we got it makes me scared as to what is going to happen to us here on the farm. Sunny and some more men here are at the age where they say they will have to join up and fight if war breaks out. Papa Joe says that the word is out that they are going to try to get it so that slave holders will not have to leave their farms but I don't know just how that will work out. I will just keep on writing on the Sundays that I have time to and hope and pray that things are not going to be as bad as the papers say they will be.

♦

December 2, 1860

I didn't write none last Sunday cause we got school back going again and I have been real busy getting all the lessons ready for the students and getting everything ready in the schoolhouse to get started back teaching. Sadie has been working real hard too and we are happy that we can get the children out of the fields and into the classroom. When I was working with Sadie getting everything ready for school to start back we talked some about what is going on with a new president being elected. Sadie says that she is glad that she is here on this farm where blacks are not considered to be slaves but that she can understand what the Republicans are saying that all the slaves should be set free. We had a lot of them who we hid out for the underground railroad and some of them had been treated so bad that they had rather die if they got caught running away than having to go back to their masters who they knew would beat them so bad that they would wish that they were dead. Sadie says that she is just going to stay here on the farm and do her job and hope that it don't come to somebody coming and taking everything that we got and burning down our buildings. We have saved all them newspapers that Papa Joe got over the summer and fall and we have said that about every day we will take about an hour and talk with the students about all this that is happening. We will use the newspapers to teach them how to read and this will help us to get them interested in reading things for themselves so nobody will have to read to them. I have the latest copy of the Florence Gazette which talks about the United States not only having a new president but also a new government. I hadn't got time to put down what it says but it says that the election put our country going in a new direction and there are going to be a lot of changes made and especially when it comes to slavery. It says that Abraham Lincoln is an abolitionist and will free the slaves. That is about all that is in the news now as the south says that they will not allow the abolitionist to tell them how to run their states. I think that it will be good to talk about all this in the classroom with the students so they can keep up with what is going on. I have some real smart students and I am glad that Papa Joe wants them to get an education so they will be able to do something beside farm work if the slaves are freed and from what I read in the paper they will be if the President and northern states have anything to do about it.

♦

"Sarah not only saved those old papers for school purposes but also for posterity. I know that she had no idea who might want to read them in future generations, but I am happy that she had the foresight to use them as packing for the box; she apparently vetoed the use of cotton." Jenny smiled as she glanced at her father. "Sorry, that you didn't get more seeds to plant in your little patch, Dad, but that is the way that the ball bounces."

This brought a laugh from the others and a request from Dutch. "We have been reading for a while now, and I would really like to have a glass of iced tea."

"Angie made a big pitcher full, and it's in the refrigerator. I'll get us all a glass and a piece of that pecan pie she made yesterday. We need to take a little break and rest our eyes. I know that it's not too hard for you two young'uns," Abigail said with a smile while looking at Raleigh and Jenny. "But for me and Dutch, our eyesight is not what it once was."

CHAPTER 11

◆

January 13, 1861

We have a new year, 1861, and it is already starting off in a bad way. The newspaper says that South Carolina has seceded and it is almost certain that most, if not all, of the southern states will do the same thing. This is not a good way to start the year but the way that I see it is that it is just going to get worse and there will be a war. I have a hard time trying to understand why the south wants to keep having negroes as slaves and are treated them no better than they do some of the farm animals. As I done wrote about what papa Joe said, people are not supposed to be bought and sold like horses and cows and pigs and other farm animals. I am just a looking now at the Gazette dated Jan 9, 1861 and on the right side of all the big news is a line of advertisement. The one that caught my eye says: TRUSTEE'S SALE OF NINE Valuable Negroes!! By virtue of a Deed of Trust executed to me by N. H. Rice, and recorded in Deed Book A No. 10 P. 419–420, I will offer for sale, to the highest bidder, for cash, before the door of the court house, in the town of Florence on MONDAY 4TH FEB. 1861. The following slaves, viz: Sylvester, age 42 years. Abram, age 40 years, Cynthia, 4 years of age, Ms. Ida, about 32 years, Little Ann, about 9 years of age, Nancy, about

35 years of age, Lizzy, about 10 years of age, Ed, about eight years of age, Amanda, about 6 years of age, Said slaves are very likely and will be so without reserve. The title is believed to be unquestionable. ALLEN W. HOWELL, Truststee. Jan. 2 1861, 5w qb. I think it is shameful that these people cannot be treated like people should be just because of the color of their skin. Them names that were in that advertisement are real people but are treated like they are farm animals or merchandise that is bought and sold. In the paper all the time are advertisement where mules and horses are sold just like those people are. Now that just ain't right. Just like the advertisement underneath that one that says: fresh Arrivals. 250 pairs Negro Brogans. Dry Goods! Etc., etc., Large lot of Negro Blankets, Brown and Bleached Domestics, prints, Delanes and ladies dress goods of every variety just received and for sale very low by TAPP, JONES & co. Now I am wondering just what is a Negro Brogan? From every Negro foot that I have seen the only thing different is the color of the skin. I am asking myself, now if it is a Negro Brogan can a white person wear it, to my thinking a boot is a boot. And what is a Negro blanket? Will it not keep a white person warm? There are advertisements for saddles and harnesses and horse collars and things like that in the same newspaper for horses and mules and I understand that those things are made for those animals but why single out Negros when they are human just like the rest of us. I can understand why there are people who say that slavery should be abolished.

♦

January 27, 1861

I did not write any last Sunday because we had a picnic and fun day for all the school children in the afternoon after church was over. Sunny and Papa Joe went to town and bought a lot of food that the kids would like and it was dark before we did everything that we wanted to do. Sunny said that with school starting back that the children should have some activities outside the classroom and I think it will help the children to get settled down and do their schoolwork. We told them that if they studied real hard and did good in their bookwork that we would do it again later on. According to what the talk is and what the paper says, the southern states are uniting and that secession from the north is all but done. I read in the paper that in less than sixty days, the southern states would have everything completed to be delivered from northern rule. I just try not to think about it. The last time that I wrote I had read about a slave auction where nine Negroes would be sold to the highest bidder. I showed that advertisement to Sunny and told him that I had heard him and Papa Joe talking about needing more help here on the farm. I asked him why he and Papa Joe could not go and get those Negroes and bring them back here to the farm. I told him that we probably had more money than anybody else around that could use slaves and that at least they should go and see what they could do about getting them. He looked at the advertisement and said that there were a terribly lot of young children in the nine Negroes listed and he said that what they needed most here on the farm was big strong men who could do a lot of plowing and heavy lifting and there weren't but two men whose name was listed and he would have to look them over to see if they looked like that they might be of help doing the farm work. I said to him that to me it was just not what those Negroes might be able to do for us but what we could do for them. I said that we are plenty able to feed and supply those nine people with their needs and that we will be able to get work out of all of them except the least ones. I said to him that I know what it is like not to have anything because the first years of my life when we were hiding out from the people who wanted us to go to Oklahoma that I never saw nobody but our family that was there. I have compassion for people who are being mistreated like the Indians were and the Negroes are today. He said that he was going to talk with Papa Joe and they would decide what is best. I told him that I would appreciate it if he would do that.

◆

February 3, 1861

The last time I wrote about me asking Sunny about going to Florence and see if he and Papa Joe might could get those nine slaves that will be sold to the highest bidder which will be tomorrow. Papa Joe didn't take too well to the idea at first because he said that we did not have housing here on the farm to bring them here. I reminded him that we still had that secret hideout that we used for to hide out Cherokees and Slaves when I was little and we used it for the Underground Railroad but we don't do much of that anymore and they could stay there until we could build them a place to live. I said that the way it sounds that there are two families with their children and I know that in the past we have just built houses for our workers as needed and since the farm is getting so big that we are going to have to get more workers anyway and that now might be the time to do it. I also told him that he had always wanted to be of help to those people in need like he was to us to give us a place to live to get out of that canyon that we were hid out in and that this sounded like some people who could use somebody to help them. He thought about that for a few minutes before he said that he would go tomorrow and see what he could do but said that he would not promise anything. I told him that I thought that was all that he could do so we will see what will happen tomorrow.

♦

February 5, 1861

I am writing this on Tuesday because I am so excited. Yesterday Papa Joe and Sunny went to Florence to the slave auction that I wrote about Sunday. When they came back they had nine Negroes with them that they had bought at the auction. When they left to go to Florence early yesterday morning Papa Joe went to the vault where he keeps his money and got some to take with him. When he left he said that he was taking a certain amount but did not tell me how much it was. He said that if the bidding got any higher than what he had in his pocket that he would not get the Negroes but he was prepared to spend the amount that he had to get them if it looked like they could be of help to him on the farm. He was smiling when he came back with them because he said that he was able to buy them and bring a lot of the money back with him. He said there was not many people there bidding for them. He talked to one man that told him that most people are uncertain now that the Black Republicans and Abraham Lincoln got elected and they have said that they want to abolish slavery. With the talk that the Confederates will be changing up the money to Confederate dollars everybody wants to hang on to what little gold and greenbacks they have because nobody seems to trust the new Confederate government. Nobody wants to spend a lot of money on slaves just to have them set free in two or three years and this was probably the reason that they were up for auction in the first place. The man said that another reason people

did not want to bid too much was because only four of
the nine were of the age where they could do a lot of work
and there wasn't but two men. There would be five more
mouths to feed and when they did get old enough to be
of any help they might be set free and that would be a big
wasted expense. Four of the children are girls and most
slave holders are looking for men who can do the hard
work. Sunny said that when the bidding started and they
saw that Papa Joe was going to go higher than what they
wanted to pay that everybody stopped bidding against him
so he got them real cheap. When they came in I got to talk
to them and we all let them know that they would not be
mistreated on this farm like some are on other farms. They
are very likeable like the advertisement said that they were.
There are two families of them just like I thought that there
would be and the children are very sweet and I told them
that I was anxious to get them in school. There is Sylvester
and his wife, Nancy with their children Ann (they call her
little Ann), Amanda, and Cynthia. Abram and his wife Ida
have two children, a girl named Lizzy and a boy named
Edward (He is called Ed). Ann is 9, Amanda is about 6, and
Cynthia is 4. Abrams children, Lizzy is about 10 and Ed is 8.
Sunny says that the adults look like they are healthy and will
be able to be a big help on the farm. My mother and dad
had the other side of the hideaway from where they once
lived all ready for them to move into when they got here
so that they could begin to feel at home on the farm. Papa
Joe let them know that they would not be called slaves and
they would not be treated like slaves. The first thing that
he told them was that he did not own a single person who
lives on the farm and he was not going to start with them.
He told them that he had bought and paid for them and
got a clear title to them and he handed them the title and
told them that he was giving them back to themselves and

that they owned themselves and were free to do whatever they thought was best for them but told them that as long as they stayed on the farm that they would have a place to live and be well cared for. He told them that they would start soon to build each family a house to live in and that he wanted the children to go to the school on the farm so they could get an education and maybe not have to do farm work all of their lives. I am all excited about the good way that all this turned out and that is why I took this time on Tuesday to write. I let the students out a few minutes early today because I wanted to write this while it is fresh on my mind.

◆

"When we were reading the newspapers, I saw that advertisement," Abigail stated. "And I had the same thoughts that Sarah expressed in her entry. It is disgraceful that a civilized society could make merchandise out of other members of the same society when the only difference was their skin color. That is the same way that they treated the red skinned people." She paused for a moment then added thoughtfully, "It never crossed my mind, however, that those Negroes would find a home on the farm with Papa Joe and Sunny."

"It's clear that Reverend Stone and Sunny bought them for humanitarian reasons as much or more than for the work that they would be able to provide," Jenny replied. "It appears that many people back then were like those in today's age; they were interested only in making money and didn't care whom they had to run over to do it. It's refreshing to know that there were those like Reverend Stone who cared about all people no matter the color of their skin. Of course this was shown in his work while preaching to the Cherokee. We need more people like him today."

While his wife and mother-in-law were talking, Raleigh was getting a head start on reading the next entry in the journal.

February 17, 1861

The reason that I didn't write none in this notebook last Sunday was because I had just wrote that on Tuesday and I took Sunday afternoon to help the new Negroes which Papa Joe bought to get to know something about the farm here where they will be living. They are now living in the other side of the hiding place where my mom and dad lived when we first got here but Sunny has already made plans to get houses built for both families. The first thing that Sylvester and Abram was told to do was for them to get with Sampson who is the one who helps run the farm and to go cut down some big pine trees that is a growing down by the river and take them to be sawed into lumber. Sunny told them that if they had a hand in building their houses that they would appreciate them more and he wanted them to feel like this is home to them. Whenever they get their houses built then they can move out from where they are staying now. After that Papa Joe says that he is going to have Abram and Sylvester work with Sampson to get the fields plowed and everything ready to plant after the last frost is on the ground. He has Nancy helping mother milk the cows and gather eggs and get things to the workers that they need. Ida is helping Sunny's mother, Sunbeam, by carrying water from the spring and doing the clothes washing and house cleaning. The children are already started in school and they need to be there because they were never taught nothing about reading or writing where they were before they came here. Little Cynthia is just 4 years old so she is not old enough to be in school but

Amanda is six years old and I says to let her come to school because she needs to start learning while she is little. Sadie is a teaching Ann and Lizzy and Ed and she said that they are way behind the children their age that has been going to school but she says that they are smart and she thinks that they will be able to catch up with the other ones if she spends a little extra time with them. I try to keep my mind on what I am doing here and not worry about what is happening between the North and South. I am still getting the newspapers and talking about what is in them with the students and it is not only helping them learn how to read but it lets them keep up with what is going on away from the farm here. When I quit writing today I am going to see my mom and dad and check to see how the new families are doing because Papa Joe gives everybody Sundays off who does not have daily chores that has got to be done.

♦

February 30, 1861

Things are getting so busy what with March almost here and everybody is working real hard to be able to plant just as soon as the warm weather gets here. Sunny likes to put seed in the ground as early as he can after the winter weather is over so that he can have the plants a coming up and growing before it gets to hot and dry. If he waits too long to do the planting a drought can really hurt getting a good crop. I keep not wanting to think about what is going on in our country but the last newspaper we got told about a Provisional Government being created in the South now that the South has seceded from the Union. On Feb 18, 1861, at 1 pm in Montgomery the paper printed the Inaugural address of President Jefferson Davis of what they are calling The Confederate States of America. He says that he is looking forward to the speedy establishment of a permanent Government to take the place of the Provisional Government. Now he says something at the start of his speech that makes me wonder if the Southern States really know what they are getting into. Sunny and Papa Joe says that there is no way that the South can just say that we will not be a part of the Union any longer and the Northern States just accept that without there being a heap of trouble. But Jefferson Davis says in his speech that he enters into the duties of the office of President of the Confederate States of America with the hope that the beginning of our career, as a Confederacy, may not be obstructed by hostile opposition to our enjoyment of the separate existence and independence which we have asserted, and with the blessing of Providence, intend to maintain. He says that our present condition, achieved in a manner unprecedented in the history of nations illustrates the American Idea that Governments rest upon the consent of the governed, and that it is the right of the people to alter or abolish Governments whenever they become destructive of the ends for which they were established. He goes on and gives a long speech but when I read all that he said I wonder why they think that they can just make a speech and say that they are free from the government of the United States and consider that will be all they have to do to be a separate Government. When me and Sunny read that speech, Sunny says that the reason that their present condition was achieved in a manner that is unprecedented in the history of Nations, like Jefferson Davis says, is because everybody has had enough sense to know that there is going to be war before everything is settled. He says that as the new Confederate States don't even have no government and no army to do no fighting that he don't see no way that they can win no war. The union has already had to fight a war against England and won it and how does the south think that they can win a war when they don't even have no army. Sunny says that somebody should think this all out before they start shooting. I am afraid of what is going to happen but there aint nothing that we can do about it cept just stay here and do what we have always done. Papa Joe says that we need to say a lot of prayers and I am a doing just that but I am not sure that God is going to take sides on this thing, and if he does, I suspect that he might lean toward siding with the people who says that people should all be treated right and not be judged by their skin color and that sure would not be on the Confederate side. The Bible says that God is no respecter of persons and you sure can't say that about the South, course then I think about what the Federal Government did to the Indians who owned this land first and they weren't treated no better. That is why we had to stay hid out when I was born so I just really think that God is going to stay out of this and let the people here settle their own differences.

♦

Following this entry, there were only a few additional short ones made by Sarah. She wrote that with spring's arrival she was busy in her work, and the teaching of her students was requiring a lot of her time. She felt it to be more important to do her writing in the classroom while teaching her students than just putting her thoughts in a book. She acknowledged that as soon as it got time to chop cotton and hoe corn, her class time would be over and the children would be required to assist in that work. After that, she said she would continue to write in the book as she felt that there would be a lot to write about with the deteriorating relationships between the North and South.

CHAPTER 12

◆

The readers hurriedly looked over the few entries made in the month of March, but the one dated April 21, 1861, caught their attention.

April 21, 1861

When Papa Joe came back from Florence yesterday he said that he had some bad news to report. He said that the war has started between the North and the South. He brought in the Florence Gazette that said that on Friday the 12th that the South attacked Fort Sumter which is somewhere over close to Charleston, South Carolina. Now I don't know nothing about that place cause it aint close to here but Papa Joe says that the Confederate army needed it and wanted to keep the Yankees from having it. The paper said that the fighting started about 4 o'clock in the morning and that the Confederate batteries silenced the Sumter guns. The paper then had a story about the big demonstration that took place in Florence after the news of the Confederate victory reached the city. It says that glorious news was received, Fort Sumter surrendered and the flag of the Southern Confederacy was hoisted on its walls. The paper says that the enthusiasm was unequalled and that there were bonfires in the streets, burning of firecrackers and rockets, houses were illuminated and that there were military parading and speeches. I don't understand why starting a war and winning one little battle is any reason to celebrate. Papa Joe says that it was not glorious news to him and the South just stirred up a hornets nest and they are going to be sorry before it is all over. The paper has a long article about all the things that happened in Florence Saturday night and it was just like they had just won the war that they started and it was all over but the celebrating. There was one thing that I liked about that newspaper though. At the very top it said NEWSPAPERS and under it was written-

"A newspaper is the best history of the times that can be found, and every man that takes one should preserve the file every year, and have them sewed or fastened together. He who does this, leaves a valuable book to his children. A volume of Newspapers sixty years old, would now sell for more than the original cost; and would be read by scholars, politicians and antiquarians with great interest."

Now I am a step ahead of them cause I have been doing that since last year. I suspect that they put it in this last paper because this news of the war is history in the making. After the big article about all that dancing in the street there is another one that the people that did all that celebrating should be thinking about. It tells of Lincoln's war proclamation which means that the North is not going to take this and not do anything about it. It says, "Yesterday morning we saw an extra, of the Memphis Appeal, containing the Proclamation of Lincoln, calling for seventy-five thousand (75,000) men, to engage in subjecting the South to his rule; and to assist in retaking the Forts and Arsenals that once was called "United States Property," but have been taken by the seceded States. He has given President Davis twenty days to consider the matter in regard to giving up the forts, magnanimous. The article says "So we are going to be forced to engage in, probably, a bloody war, because we are determined not to be ruled by avowed enemies, because we are disposed to defend our rights, because we have severed our connections with a government that was oppressive in the extreme, and one in which we had not the slightest chance, or prospect of ever sharing equal rights and privileges; because we would not submit to be governed by a party, the representative of which is a disgrace to humanity, a tool–a willing tool– in the hands of a set of hell-deserving villains, who are hurrying us into a war, that they might reap the spoils. They are a disgrace to our once happy land and when they invade our sunny south, they will meet with the fate that their Prince, the Devil, is hastening them to receive. They will be received by brave men,--many more than they will be prepared to see; who have strong arms, and brave and willing hearts, who "know their rights, and knowing, dare maintain them." They may be slain, but never conquered. They will know no surrender, only with their last breath. There will be no cowering to the black-hearted minions of Black Republicanism–the invaders of the fair South, with its brave, fair and patriotic women, who say that they will not marry a man who refuses to fight for his country; its brave and loyal sons, who expect no reward, save the pleasure of assisting their enemies to "shuffle off the mortal coil," and hasten the arrival of their unworthy souls into that place "prepared for the Devil and his angels, at the foundation of the world." I wrote a lot today because I feel so bad about what is happening to our country. President Lincoln said that he is not going to let the south get away with what they are trying to do in seceding from the Union and has proclaimed that there will be war and the south has already started it by taking Fort Sumter from the Federal Government. There is one thing about what I just read and wrote. Those brave, fair, and patriotic young women sure ain't going to marry no corpse lying dead on a battlefield and I suspect that there will be a lot of those brave and loyal sons who will meet that fate.

◆

"Reverend Stone, or Papa Joe as Sarah calls him, was right when he said that the South was stirring up a hornet's nest." Raleigh was the last to finish reading the article and the first to comment on it. "He was also correct when he said that the grand celebration which brought the townspeople into the streets of Florence was a bit premature. It didn't take long before the tide started to turn toward a Union victory, and Sarah was spot on in her prediction regarding those brave young men who would never have a family of their own."

Dutch turned the page to the next entry as he was anxious to see what Sarah might say about the historic event.

April 28, 1861

I wrote a lot last Sunday because of the news of the war starting between the Southern Confederacy and the Federal Union of the United States of America. We have done a lot of talking about that this week and Papa Joe is terribly concern about what is going to happen next. He says that whatever it is that it is going to be hard on the farmers. He named a lot of things that worries him like who will buy the things that he raises on the farm like cotton and corn as a lot of it is sold to people who were friends but are now in the enemy's territory. I have never seen Papa Joe worry about something before but this war has got him to where he is afraid of what will happen next. He says that he is torn between the two sides cause he wants the slaves to be freed but he don't want to see our southern men get killed to have them freed. He says that he, and a lot of people that he knows, just want to not take sides so that they can be neutral but he says that because we live in Alabama that he is afraid that they are going to make everyone align with the Rebel army and they will make the men join up to fight whether or not they want to. He has been in touch with some people down from where mom and dad came from in the Warrior Mountains around Lawrence and Winston and Marion counties who say that they are against this war and they plan to do everything that they can to keep out of it. He says that last November on the 19th that he was invited to go to Houston, the county seat of Winston County, to meet with a group of southerners who opposed the Secessionist. He didn't go but he said that they sent word that they had nominated a young fellow named Chris Sheets to represent them in a Secession Convention in Montgomery. I don't remember all that he said about it and I want to talk to him some more and write more about it next Sunday if I have the time. I just don't have time to write any more about it today. I will try to start early and write more next week than what I did today.

◆

May 5, 1861

Last Sunday I wrote about what Papa Joe said about what all is happening in this part of Alabama what with the war started and all. It is a busy time of the year with all the farming going on but last Wednesday night we ate supper with him and Sunbeam and I asked him about what is going on in Winston County. He said that there are a lot of people that don't want no part of any war and they are getting together to organize against it. He named some of them and I remember some names like Tom Pink Curtis, Judge Oran Davis, Jiles Anderson, Howard Bates, Jerry Burns, Alf Title, Alex Underwood from Marion County, Wiley Dodd, Jack Walker, Bird Potts, Bill Weatherford, Newt Austin, George Stout, Wash Curtis, and I tried to remember all the names that he spoke of but I can't recall all of them right now. He called off a long list of names that were too many for me to remember all of them. I remember now that he said something about a fellow named Bill Looney who has a tavern in Winston County and they are talking about getting everybody that is against seceding from the Union together at his tavern on July 4th. He says that there are a sizable number of people there that are against secession from the Union but he says that there are some that think that seceding is the thing to do. He called a lot of their names cause he has stayed up on what is going on and I can't remember all of their names but I kept in mind some of them. He said that some of the biggest names on the Rebel's side are Dr. Andrew Kaiser, or it may be spelled Kaeiser, I am not sure so I will spell it Kaiser, who was chosen by the Secessionist to oppose Chris Sheets to be the candidate to represent Winston County in the convention which met in Montgomery on January 7th of this year. He said that the election was held the day before Christmas. He said that Dr. Kaiser tried hard to win but Chris Sheets won over him by a vote of almost four to one. Papa Joe said that for Chris Sheets to win by that much just goes to show how the people are against this war here in North Alabama. He said that some more names on that side are

Dick Payne and Jim Downey, who he said had slaves and
was against anyone who wanted to take them from him. He
said that one of the largest slave holders in Winston County
is Nathan Parker who they call Judge Parker because he was
the probate Judge. He said that he has a plantation in a
place called Brown Creek Bottoms and that he heard that
he is real good to his slaves but he don't want to have to give
them up. Because of that he is all for seceding and he is for
fighting a war so that he can keep them. He called some
more names of some people that he called Rebels who he
said that he was told was mean and had to be watched.
He called some names like Tobe Gibson, Ham Carpenter,
Stoke Roberts, Jim Downey, Al Gibson, Ben Humphries,
and a bunch more names and he said that they were mean
enough to kill anybody who they did not like or who would
try to keep from fighting against the Yankees. The word
from those in the hills around Winston County is that they
are afraid that there is going to be a lot of killing and it won't
be just the Yankees doing the shooting. Papa Joe says that
he is just going to mind his own business and not get mixed
up with either side or hope that he can just do his farming
and be left alone. It looks like there will be a lot to write
about and I will have more time now that it is time for the
children to get out of school to work on the farm and I will
not be teaching them. I am still asking Papa Joe to keep
bringing the newspapers from town and I am saving them
at the schoolhouse and maybe we can talk about them in
class when school gets started back up.

◆

"It has been quite some time since I read Wesley
Thompson's book, *Tories of the Hills*," Raleigh said.
"But I recall that he wrote about some of the men that
Sarah mentioned in her writings. Chris Sheet's name
will always come up while discussing the opposition to

Secession in the Northwest Alabama hill country. Bill Looney and Looney's Tavern are likewise well known in Winston County. For a period of time there was an outdoor theater that produced a play during the summer months which was called *Looney's Tavern*." Raleigh glanced toward Dutch and Abigail before he continued talking. "I suspect that I'm telling you something that you already know about and may have seen. A couple of times I went with friends and took the dinner cruise on the lake's party boat there and took in the play afterwards; they had a package deal that included the outing on Smith Lake and following that, the play in the nearby theater. It was always an enjoyable evening for me. A lot of those other people that Sarah mentioned, on both sides, played a role in the deadly conflict that divided neighbors and even families while the Civil War raged around them."

After Abigail acknowledged that she and Dutch had indeed enjoyed the play at the Looney's Tavern Theater but had never taken an excursion on the party boat, they returned to their reading.

May 26, 1861

I didn't write none the last two Sundays cause things have got so busy around here what with trying to get the crops where they will make good this year. Sunny says that it looks like the crops are going to make real good but he says that with the war a started and all that he is not sure that he will be able to sell everything because a lot of the corn and cotton was sent up north and now with them fighting the Southern army that he don't see how there will be a market in our enemies territory. I don't feel too much like writing about what is going on with the war started and all cause I just want to put it out of my mind and hope that everything gets settled soon and not too many people will get killed before this thing is over. It don't look like that will happen though because President Lincoln gave President Davis twenty days to give everything back that they took when they captured Fort Sumter and other things that belonged to the United States. That time has already passed and the word is that President Davis didn't give nothing back but is still taking everything that the Federal Government has in the south. I think that I am not going to write too much till I feel better about what is happening so as to keep my mind off it.

◆

After reading this, Raleigh looked up from the journal to say, "It's well known that the Battle of Fort Sumter marked the beginning of the Civil War. South Carolina was the first to secede, but they were soon joined by other Southern States. In the end, eleven states declared themselves to be the independent Confederate States of America. The war would go on for four years with three million Americans taking up arms against each other. Sarah didn't know just how bad it was going to get and how costly it would be to both sides. Combat and disease killed at least 620,000 soldiers, which was two percent of the population back then."

Jenny shook her head and added somberly, "There was no way that she could have known the disaster that was ahead for the entire nation, especially for the Confederacy in their defeat. She would be tired, indeed, before those four long years came to an end."

CHAPTER 13

◆

Sarah did indeed neglect her diary for a week, but apparently, after considering that she was failing to record a noteworthy period of time in North America's history, she took her pen back in hand and resumed her writings.

July 7, 1861

I didn't write none last week but I decided I would start back after the fourth of July. There has been so much happening since I wrote the last time that I won't try to write about that cept what Sunny says happened on the fourth. He said that they got invited to go to Winston County at Looney's Tavern where they had a big get together of people who don't want no part of this war that is going on. Sunny and Papa Joe didn't go because Sunny said that if they went, then that would let everybody know which side they were on and it would make it harder on the farm here when they start making every man that is able to go fight the Yankees. He said that he is not talking it but he is going to make the Rebels think that he is on their side but he is going to secretly be helping the people that the Rebels are beginning to call Tories. They are calling them that because they say that the people who do not go along with the Confederate Government are like the ones in 1776 who sided with England in the Revolutionary war. Papa Joe says that he has just the perfect place to hide out people who are wanting to get away from the people who will be searching for the ones who refuse to sign up for the army. That is not happening yet but Sunny says that it is only a matter of time before they are needing troops so bad that they will require all able bodied men to enlist. Well, I was writing about that meeting at Looney's Tavern where we got word that there were about three thousand people there. The word that we got was that people started getting there on Monday the first and there were hundreds already there before the fourth even got there. When there were hundreds more who came on the fourth of July, that made for a lot of people who were there. They said that they had a bunch of wild hogs that they barbecued and they had deer and beef and turkey that they barbecued along with the hogs. After everybody ate they said that Chris Sheets made a good speech and told how he was treated so bad in Montgomery at the Secession Convention. He was cheered by all the people that were there for him to stand up against the people who want to secede and he let them rebels know that they were foolish to think that everyone in the country goes along with seceding from the United States. He said that they were a bigger fool to expect everyone to go along with fighting against our flag and our friends. He said that they tried to force him to sign the Ordinance and to quit talking against it and he refused. After that they put him in jail and said that would shut him up and he would never be heard but he said that they were wrong there too because he was talking to thousands of people that very moment. He was cheered loudly for saying what he said and doing what he did in Montgomery to let those people there know that everybody was not going along with what they were doing. One of the things that Sunny said that he was told about was that they had made some resolutions and one of them called for Winston County to secede from the State like the State had done from the Union. They said that if Alabama had the right to secede from the Union then Winston County had the same right to secede from the State. They did not do it because after talking it over they decided that it would be better just to ask that the county be allowed to stay neutral and be left alone. There is a lot more that I could write about but I have already wrote more than I set out to do so I will just write more later on. I don't know that I will write some every week but I am not going to just quit writing.

◆

July 14, 1861

I said last week that I would not write some every week and I just don't feel like writing none today seeing as to how bad everything is getting now that fighting has started between the north and the south. There is so much happening that I thought that I ought to put some of it down while it is fresh on my mind. Papa Joe says that in Virginia and Missouri that there is already fighting going on. He said that word is slow getting here but he said that there is word that they have already had battles in May and June in Virginia at Sewell's Point, Aquia Creek, Philippi, and Big Bethel and at Boonville in Missouri. He says that they were not real big battles but that is the start of a lot worse things and a lot of people are going to get killed. He says that already this month in Virginia they have fought at Hokes Run and when he went to town yesterday there was talk of a bigger battle last Thursday at Rich Mountain in Virginia. There are some people who are keeping up with what is

happening by telegraph and he talks with them when he is
in town. He says that the Union is winning most of those
battles in Virginia and the one in Missouri at Boonville
but said that the Confederate army came out on top in
the battle at Big Bethel and one at Cartage in Missouri on
July 5th. There aint nobody around here that knows where
any of those places are where they are doing that fighting
but Papa Joe says that he is more worried about what is
happening around here. Every year Papa Joe has been
going down to Winston County the first Sunday in July to a
community church named Hope Well. He said that when
he was preaching on that circuit in the Warrior Mountains
before he moved here that he did some preaching at that
church and knows a lot of the people there. He said that
he preached mostly to the Cherokees but that in Winston
County there were a lot of people that did not like what the
government was doing to the Indians, just like they don't
like what is being done to the black slaves now, and that a
lot of them that were whites came out to hear him preach.
His circuit went on to Flat Rock so that was almost at the
end of where he went in the western part of the state and
he spent a good bit of time there. Well anyway, they had
their love feast and foot washing and the Lords Supper on
Sunday at the start of their protracted meeting that they
have every year on that date but Papa Joe said that things
are not like they always have been. There are lots of good
people there but he said that they have got crossways
with one another over whether or not the state should
break away from the Union. Last Sunday when the church
meeting started there were lots of the ones that are always
there who didn't show up because they were on different
sides. Judge Parker who is a deacon there and even Brother
Davis, the preacher didn't show up. They favor secession
and there were a lot of the ones that don't want to take

sides who did not show up because they didn't want to get caught in the middle of the dispute that's going on. Jack Walker, who is not for secession, led a prayer asking for harmony and friendship in the church but Papa Joe said that it was clear that things had changed. There is nothing that we can do about all these bad things except just stay here and mind our own business and keep on farming like we always have.

♦

"Things were beginning to get rotten in the Warrior Mountains, and they were to get worse, much worse, before there would be peace," Raleigh said after having just read about what was soon to befall the peaceful citizens of Northwest Alabama. "It is going to be much more than someone missing a revival meeting. The ruthlessness is about to begin."

July 28, 1861

I didn't write none last week cause we were busy picking garden stuff and storing it for the winter. Papa Joe got all worried about the way that some people in Alabama are getting crossways of some others because of the war that has started and he said that he is glad that everyone on the farm here gets along with one another. After he heard of what happened down in Winston County at that Hope Well Church where their protracted meeting didn't go good because some was on the Confederate side and some on the Union side but most of them just wanted to stay out of it so there weren't many who went to the meeting. Papa Joe said that he wanted everyone that would to come Sunday to the church house here on the farm. The building was full and Papa Joe, who everybody calls Reverend Stone

or Master Stone, did the preaching. He used as his text
1 Corinthians 1; 10 where the Apostle Paul says that he
beseeched the brethren at Corinth to all speak the same
thing and that they should not be divided. He preached
that he was happy that the people on the farm here was
not divided but that everybody got along good and worked
together good and because they had done that they were
having another good crop year. He said that everybody
was important to him and he would not let any of them go
hungry or lacking things that they need. He preached that
he loves them but God loves them more than any person
ever could and that God loves one person as much as he
loves another and when he looks down from heaven that he
don't see no wall separating the northern people from the
southern people and he don't see no difference between
the white people and the black people or the red people
and there is no call for what is happening with this fight that
is started between them. He preached that he has both
white and black and red people working on the farm and he
is proud of all of them and believes that God expects him
to treat everyone alike. It was a real good sermon and he
said that he wanted to make an alter call so that any of the
unsaved would have a chance to get right with God. When
he did that Sylvester and Nancy said that God had sent
Master Stone and Sunny to buy them and give them a good
place to live and they had never been baptized like the Bible
says that they should be. They said that they now know that
God loves them and they want to go to heaven when they
die so as to be with him and they wanted to be baptized.
Papa Joe said that Jesus had first bought them with his blood
and that he was glad that they were now going to belong
in his family. When they did that, Abram and Ida said that
they felt the same way about what God had done and they
didn't want to miss out on going to heaven either so they

wanted to be baptized too. They allowed that none of their kids were old enough to be baptized but there were seven more of the blacks that said that they were on their way to hell if they didn't get baptized too so there were eleven who answered the alter call. There were a lot of hallelujah's and praise the Lord's shouted by the blacks when all of this was a going on and when the last amen was said everybody crowded around them and told them how happy they were now that they were going to be saved from hell. Papa Joe said that he believed that the way to be baptized was to get all covered by water so he said that we would meet around two o'clock down at the shoals on the river at the baptizing hole and that we would have a baptizing. When we got down there, three more of the young white girls said that as long as there was going to be a baptizing that they wanted to be baptized too. About everybody on the farm went down to the baptizing and when we got down there everybody started singing. They started by singing a new song that we are learning that we like named Nearer, My God, to Thee. Then we sang Amazing Grace and Rock of Ages before the Blacks started singing some of their songs that I don't remember all the names of and words to but they can sure get going and clapping on those songs and everybody said that the baptizing was uplifting and got them in the Spirit. It was about dark before everybody got baptized and finished singing and praying and praising God. It was a good way to get everybody's mind off the war and I am glad that Papa Joe did what he did to call that meeting at the church. I guess that I will write more next Sunday.

◆

"Sarah wrote that at the baptizing they were learning a new song titled *Nearer My God to Thee*," Abigail said after finishing her reading of the July 28th entry in the journal. "I was just looking through a book that I got at the used book store, which was written by Kenneth W. Osbeck, titled *101 Hymn Stories*. I remember that I saw that song to be one of the ones he wrote about. Hold on for a minute; I want to get the book to see how old that song is."

"While you're getting that, I will serve iced tea to everyone," Jenny offered her services. "We've been reading for a good while and I'm thirsty, and I bet that you are too."

Abigail returned with her book before Jenny had time to serve the tea. She went to the contents page and found the number that she was searching for. Turning to it, she reported her find to the others.

"Author Sarah F. Adams, 1805-1848." She paused while reading to herself and then resumed reading to the others when she found what she was looking for. "*Nearer My God to Thee* is generally considered by students of hymnology to be the finest tune ever written by any woman hymn writer. Sarah Flowers Adams was born in Harlow, England, on February 22, 1805." Abigail paused again, "I have already read that at the beginning. Let me find what I was looking for."

She read a little and turned the page before speaking again. "Here it is!" She began reading again, "The hymn was introduced in America in 1844, but it did not gain real popularity for twelve years until it was wedded with the present tune." She looked up and spoke again, "Eighteen forty four plus twelve equals eighteen fifty-six. Sarah was writing this just five years after that. That was a new song to them, and I suppose that they were just learning it." Looking at the others she apologized, "I'm sorry for the interruption, but that's just the way that my mind works. Sometimes I have a question about something, and if I know that I can find the answer, I feel compelled to satisfy my mind about it."

"Amen!" Dutch exclaimed, adding, "That's my Abigail!"

Soon after, the reading continued.

August 5, 1861

I about decided that I would not do no writing today cause of that there aint nothing good to write about what with the war going like it is. Papa Joe says that it don't make no difference which side wins a battle there aint nothing to celebrate when people are getting killed like they say that they are. He says that the talk in town is about a fight that happened at a place called Bull Run which is in Virginia not too far from Washington D.C. The report from the battlefield is that last Sunday on the 21st that the Yankees attacked the Confederate army and after it looked like that they were going to whip the Rebels, the South sent in some reinforcements and ran the Yankees back to Washington. The South is claiming a big victory and Papa Joe said that the ones who are for seceding were celebrating yesterday when he went to Florence. He said that they were saying that it won't be long before the Confederate army will be in Washington D.C. and will take over running the whole country. Papa Joe says that he just listens to what everybody has to say and he don't get into talking about what he thinks. He says that he don't want to do nothing that will make them think that he is on one side or the other. He is for what the Yankees are fighting for to free the slaves but he don't want to see any of the local men fighting and getting killed so he just stays out of all the talk. Sunny and Papa Joe have their hands full here on the farm now that the corn and cotton has made good and now all of it has to be picked. They are troubled about where they are going to sell the cotton and corn like

I have already wrote a bunch of times but it is what I keep on my mind a lot. Sunny says that there is really no need to worry cause the Lord will provide. He told me that he don't want it talked but they have another secret place on the farm beside the one where people can hide out. He said that it is hid real good and it is for storing cotton and maybe corn and other things that need to stay hid. He says that he expects that the Confederate Government and their soldiers, or the Yankees and their troops, may come and take everything for themselves that they can find. We have a very large farm here and there are places where big underground storage places can be built that nobody will find. He says that we grow everything around here that we need and there aint nobody on this farm that is going to go hungry. One thing that he says that people are worried about is salt. There is no way to get salt in these parts without bringing it in which is a long way from here to where they can get it. He says that him and Papa Joe has seen this war a coming and they have been buying up all the salt that they can get and storing it in that secret place. Sunny says that he is learning a lot from his dad as to how to do things that really helps the farm. He says that Papa Joe is real good at thinking things out and keeping ahead of problems that might come up later. When he decided that he should store up a lot of salt he started working on a plan. He had a lot of pigs which he would normally sell that he held on to and let get to be big hogs. He then went to Florence to different stores that sells salt and told them his story. Now he was careful that he did not let any of them know that he was also going to the other stores doing the same thing. What he told them was that he had let his hog situation get out of hand and that he had a lot more than he wanted to keep over the winter to have to feed. He said that he was going to have to butcher a lot more than he usually does and that he needed a lot of salt to use to cure and preserve the meat. He told them that he was going to have a lot of good ham and sausage and pork chops and pork bellies and other good hog meat and that he aimed to sell some. He said that he would like to make a barter deal where he could swap some meat for salt. There is always a shortage of good pork and the store owners know that he always has the best farm goods of anybody so he made a deal with all of them to trade the hog meat for salt. He had them order as much salt as they could get at one time so he was able to get a whole lot more than he really needed. He brought in wagon loads of salt that the people that he got it from thought that he would use all of it up at the hog killings. A lot of people have not been thinking ahead and there was no shortage of it when he did what he did but now that the war has started and people have begun to wonder about where the salt is going to come from, there aint none to buy now. Sunny says that he is going to keep it quiet about all the salt he has cause he don't want to be bothered about people wanting it. He says that he hopes that it won't come down to a salt shortage but he don't see no way that it won't happen when there is fighting all over the place. Without salt there aint no way to cure and keep the pork when it is cut up and put in the smoke houses. Sunny says that the reason that they have it stored in the secret place where nobody knows where it is at is because he don't want anybody to raid this farm and carry off everything that he needs to keep. He says that there will be a lot of things that he will move to the hideout for safe keeping. I have wrote a lot today but there is going to be so much work to do now to get the garden picked and canned and the fields picked that we will be busy for a while and I won't have time to do much writing. I need to be helping can some tomatoes so I will have to stop now.

♦

Dutch chuckled at what he had just read. "Things sure are a lot different today than what they were back then. The public media has certainly changed things. Today, if one person mentioned that there might be a salt shortage because of one reason or another, you name it, the media would get hold of it and make it headline news—A SALT SHORTAGE LOOMS ON THE HORIZON! The price of salt would skyrocket and the shelves would be empty. Salt miners would be working overtime to fill every pantry in America. That is just the way things are now-a-days. There would be no waiting for an actual shortage to occur before the buying panic began."

"How right you are!" Raleigh agreed. "If a weatherman even mentions the word 'snow' in Alabama, there is an immediate run on milk, bread, flashlights, batteries, you name it."

Jenny laughed. "And ninety percent of the time it's a false alarm."

After turning their attention back to the journal, the reading continued.

August 12, 1861

Sometimes I get to studying about things and I just read back through some of what I have wrote in this book and I got to thinking that I hadn't said nothing about Flash who is Sunny's younger brother. The reason that I have not is because Flash is not here on the farm at the present time. Papa Joe was raised up in Kentucky and has family there. He decided that Flash needed a better education than what he could get here on the farm so he is now living with his grandparents and going to school in Kentucky. He has been there about a year but before he went away he grew up here on the farm. He and Woody are about the same age and they did everything together when they were growing up and Woody sure does miss him now. One summer Flash and Woody and a black boy from here on the farm took off on what they called a 'grand adventure up the river.' They were gone a month and Papa Joe required Flash to keep a record of what they did on the trip. He kept it all down and then Papa Joe read it and gave it to me so I could understand better what he needed to be taught about his composition and writings. I allowed that Flash is a very smart individual and needed to have a better education than what me and Sadie could give him and that is the reason that Papa Joe decided to send him where he could go to a good school and maybe college after he got through high school. He said that he is happy that Sunny is here on the farm so he can help him run things and take over whenever he is no longer able to manage the farm. He said that he would like for Flash to be a farmer too but he wants him to have the education to do something else if that is what he wants to do. I think that everything may turn out to be the best cause it gets him out of Alabama where he might be forced to go fight the Yankees if he was here. The word is that it won't be long before the Confederates are going to make everybody go to war who is able to fight. I just wanted to put this down since I hadn't wrote nothing about Flash.

◆

September 1, 1861

I aint wrote none in about three weeks because I have been so busy canning from the garden and drying fruit for the winter. We have done more canning this year than we usually do because Papa Joe says that he has a plan in mind that may come in handy later. There is a food cellar close to the house here that we always store our food for the winter. He says that he wants to fill it up but he also wants to hide a lot in the hiding place so if this gets took from here we will have more so we want go hungry. He has a lot of iris potatoes on lime hid there and he fixed a place to store some meat. We grew a lot more in the garden this year than we usually do so we could do that. Sunny and Papa Joe says that it is always good to look ahead cause you never can tell what will happen specially since this war is going on. Sunny has Sylvester and Abram digging sweet potatoes now and they are making places in the fields where they are digging holes and putting hay in them they are putting the sweet potatoes in that and covering that with hay and dirt so they will not freeze. They are making it look like there aint nothing there but they know where they are storing them and Sunny says that the cooks can do a lot of things with sweet potatoes like bake and make dumplings and pies and as long as we have them we won't starve. It is a little earlier than we usually do all that but Papa Joe planted some things earlier this year cause we don't know what is going to happen from one day to the next. I am glad that I am here because I still remember when I was little and hiding out to keep from getting sent out to the Oklahoma Territory that we were eating snakes and anything that we could get so as not to starve to death. I don't ever want to see times like that again. Papa Joe and Sunny are going to make sure that they take care of everybody that lives on the farm here and he says that he sure aint going to send anyone off to get killed in a war. We have a bunch of white families that live here. The talk is that they will probably make it so that all the white men here that are able go fight the Yankees.

◆

September 8, 1861

I wasn't going to do no writing today but seeing as to how it is raining and there is nothing that I can do outside I decided that I would write some about what I hear about the war that is going on. I have been keeping up with the battles that have been fought so as to be able to talk with the students about it later if we have time. When I hear something I write it down and I will write it again in this book that I am keeping for later. Sunny goes with Papa Joe to Florence sometimes on Saturdays and he talks about what he hears when he comes back. He says that the South has been beating the Yankees in most of the battles they have fought since they won that one at Bull Run. They won a battle in Missouri on August 10th at Wilson Creek after the Yankees attacked first but were beat after their General named Nathaniel Lyon was killed and another General named Thomas William Sweeny was hurt. They withdrew from the battle but the Missouri State Guard was so tired and out of shells that they did not try to follow them to fight some more. There was another battle in Virginia at Kesslers Cross Lanes on August 26 where the Confederate army surprised the army from Ohio and routed them. The fighting started in North Carolina at the Hatteras Inlet Batteries on August 28th and 29th when 7 Union ships attacked 2 small Confederate forts on North Carolina's Outer Banks. The Confederates surrendered and the Yankees took the forts. Last Monday in Missouri there was a little fight at Dry Wood Creek where the Missouri Guard troops beat the Yankees again. Sunny says that he is surprised that the Confederate army has been so successful in their battles but that the war is a long way from being over. I just looked outside and the rain is over so I need to go out and do some chores before dark. I will write more later.

CHAPTER 14

◆

Abigail suggested a bathroom break, and all agreed that one was in order. They had been diligent in their reading and a refill of iced tea was needed. After a little rest, they resumed the reading of the journal.

September 22, 1861

Here of late I aint wrote about nothing much but this war that has started cause it is what is on my mind. It is just not me but everybody is talking about what is going on and it is starting to tear up the way people feel toward one another because some people are on one side and some on the other. Sunny says that all the Rebels think that everybody should want to secede from the Union and fight the Yankees and not be no part of the United States any more. There are a lot around here that are on the other side who say that they have always been against any kind of war and they just should be left alone. I aint wrote none about one thing that is worrying all of us here on the farm. I aint wrote much about my brother, Woody, cause he has not been here on the farm since last year. It has been so heavy on my mind that I thought that today I should just put down on this paper what it is to worry about. I didn't write none last Sunday because Sunny went and picked up Woody and brought him back to the farm for a few days. I guess I will just begin where it all starts and that is when he was a baby. We were in the canyon at a secret place when Woody was born which I have already wrote about. When he was two weeks old we came out of that hiding place to another hiding place that Papa Joe had built here on the farm which was hidden so nobody could find out where it is at. That is the place where we grew up. Now maybe I am getting ahead of myself cause I need to put down something about the time that all of this happened. It was in 1838 when mom and daddy went to live in that secret cove in the forest after mother had been caught and was held in a holding pen that had been set up by the Federal Government. They were catching all the Cherokee and other Indians to make them go on a long march to the Oklahoma Territory. All this was before I was born. Daddy sneaked into the camp one night and stole mother away and they hid out for about five or six years. During that time I was born and as I wrote, Woody was born there too but it was just before we came out. Now there was no way to know any dates that things happened cause there was no way to keep up with it without calendars which we did not have, but it was around the summer of 1843 when we came out. Now the reason all of this is on my mind and I am writing about it again is that this would mean that Woody is about 18 years old. There is talk that the Confederate Government is going to pass a conscript law whenever they get everything organized and in place that will require people of his age, and of Sunny's age too, to join the Confederate army. I am not as worried about Sunny because them people who knows a lot about what is going on says that the big slave owners will have it put down that they can stay on the farms and work their slaves and not have to go fight. That won't work for Woody cause he don't have no slaves. When Woody was six years old he started going to school where Sadie was teaching and he was real smart. By the time he was sixteen years old Papa Joe said that he had learned as much as he could a going to school here and said that he wanted to send him off to college so that he could keep on learning. First he had to get some papers to show how old he was and since there were no records kept as to when he was born they put on the papers that he was older than he really is so as to get him in college. He also had the papers to say that he was Black Dutch cause they would not take him if he was Indian and supposed to be in Oklahoma. Papa Joe said that he wanted to see that he went to school where he could make a doctor cause a good doctor is needed close by in case one is needed. The only place anywhere close to here where he could get that learning is Lagrange College which is on the other side of the river down below Tuscumbia. It is a military college but the thinking was that he could do what he had to do to get to be a military doctor and then come back to Florence and open him up an office there. When he went there it was a Union military school but now the Confederate is taking it over and now there aint going to be nothing but problems. Putting down that he was older than he really is puts him at the right age that the Confederates are going to want him to go to war. Woody is like the rest of us and don't want any part of this war but now he is right in the middle of it. The reason he came here last week was so that he could talk it over with Papa Joe and Sunny to try to figure out what will be the best thing for him to do. It is really going to be a problem and I don't want to think about it anymore today.

♦

September 29, 1861

Since I wrote last week Papa Joe and Woody sat down with mom and daddy and figured out a plan to try to keep Woody from having to go to fight the Yankees which he is against anyway. What they came up with was for Woody to find a reason why he was needed here on the farm. Since Woody has been studying to be a doctor they looked for a reason why he should stay to do some doctoring here. Well, it so happened that Abram and Ida had a baby which aint right so Papa Joe had a doctor to come in from Florence to check it out to see what is wrong with it. The doctor said that the baby was born with a condition which is called mongoloid—or something like that. The doctor said that the boy will never be able to live a normal life and will probably not live to be very old. He said that the child will never be able to do any work on the farm and would require a lot of care and attention from his mother or someone else. It is not talked but he said that sometime it is best to just not care for the child and let it die because it will always be a burden otherwise and that is the reason you do not see more of them than you do. The doctor said that he has seen some who were allowed to grow up and they can be very loveable and pleasant to be around. Well what I am getting around to tell is that Papa Joe talked with Abram and Ida when the doctor was there and they all decided that there was no way that the child would be neglected so as to let it die. They named him Rufus which is not what I would have named him but it is a good name and I hope that he can keep it a long time before he dies. The doctor agreed that he would need more care to begin with than what Abram and Ida would be able to give him and Papa Joe asked him if he would put something in writing which would say that he needed constant medical attention for a period of time. Since Woody is studying to be a doctor he then would have a reason to stay here on the farm to care for Rufus and others here who are old and sickly. Since the South is ready to fight a war so that they will not have to give up their slaves, then Woody can say that since slaves are so important that a war be fought over them then it is vital for them to be in the best of health and he is needed here to doctor them and to take care of the babies and others on the farm. He is going to inform the people at the LaGrange College that there is a medical emergency at home and he will send them the statement from the Florence Doctor to verify that he is needed here on the farm. I guess we will see how that works out but they can just come here and see for themselves that baby aint right and that there is some more sickness here that people need help. Thank goodness there aint been no bloody flux on the farm yet but it is bad all around us and a doctor needs to be here just in case it gets started here.

◆

"With all the advancements in medicine today, it is easy for us to forget that a century and a half ago there were diseases that killed a large number of people," Abigail spoke up. "Diseases which the present generations have never heard of, such as the bloody flux. There are so many things that we today should be thankful for that never cross our minds. I was thinking while reading this how warfare has changed since the Civil War; not in the way of ammunitions but health wise. During the Civil War, thousands died from diseases. Today, you hear of no member of the armed forces who dies in this manner. During that war a wound would be fatal, whereas today, medics can do wonders to save a life. The suffering was great back then, but there are pain killers now which minimize the misery. Civil War troops often went hungry and without proper shoes and clothes, but today the troops eat well and are issued clothing suitable for their environment. We talk about advancement in other fields; this is an area of advancement which should never be overlooked."

Perhaps it was Abigail's motherly instinct that prompted her response to the entry regarding the "bloody flux" epidemic.

October 13, 1861

The word from Papa Joe who keeps up with the news of what is going on in the war says that there is fighting going on in Virginia and Missouri. In Virginia they have been going at one another at Carnifex Ferry and Cheat Mountain and in Missouri they have battled at Lexington and a place called Liberty. He said that they have even had a battle at Barbourville in Kentucky. He said that he thinks that they were not big battles but there will be some big ones with a lot of people getting killed before this is all over. He said that the south has been doing good in their fighting but he don't count that to be good news cause he thinks that they should not be fighting at all and there aint nothing good that can come out of all this violence and hatred. Papa Joe talked the doctor from Florence into taking that note that he wrote to Lagrange College telling them that Woody was needed to treat the sick on the farm here. The college is not that far from Florence so it was not too hard for him to do that. He has not talked to the doctor since that time to see what they had to say about him not coming back when he was supposed to but at least they know why he has not returned. Papa Joe says that he figures that those people at the college there have more to worry about than one student who didn't return because he is helping out with sick people. Everybody here on the farm is busy getting the corn pulled, the cotton picked, all the crops gathered, and hay and fodder in the barn before it gets too cold. I have been busy making sure that there are enough quilts and clothes for all the workers and Sunny has had workers who were not busy in the fields out getting plenty of stove and fire wood for the winter. So we have a lot of other things to think about beside what is going on in the war.

◆

November 3, 1861

We have been so busy getting the crops in and getting ready for winter that I just hadn't felt like doing no writing since the last time. There has been a lot of little battles in the war and I decided that I was not even going to pay no mind to what is going on in Virginia and Missouri and Kentucky when we have our hands full getting everything done here that has to be done. Papa Joe is still keeping up with the war news and I heard him talking about a battle in Kentucky at Camp Wildcat, one in Missouri at Fredericktown, and one in Virginia at Balls Bluff. He said that the south won at Balls Bluff and captured a lot of the Union troops and killed Senator Edward Baker and a bunch of other Northern solders, but they didn't do too good in the other two. The war is just a big mess and getting worse. Woody is still here on the farm and Papa Joe says that he intends to do whatever it takes to keep everyone here from having to go fight and kill somebody. I suppose that I have wrote all I feel like doing today.

◆

November 17, 1861

Papa Joe has been talking about last Wednesday's newspaper from Florence. The Gazette first wrote that

Jefferson Davis and Alex H. Stephens were elected President and Vice President of the Confederate States of America and that is not news seeing as to how they were already in office as Jefferson Davis was inaugurated on February 18 and the election was just the process that had to happen to make it official, or so I was told. But that is not what was in that paper that had Papa Joe a talking. He said that President Davis is calling upon the lord to take sides in this war. He set aside November 15 as a day of fasting, humiliation and prayer. He called upon all the preachers and people to hold divine worship at their churches and ask for kind protection over us. He issued a proclamation asking the Almighty God to protect and defend the Confederate States in the conflict with their enemies. He asked for God's almighty strength and trusting in the justness of our cause and appeal to him that he might set at naught the efforts of our enemies and put them in confusion and shame. He said to pray that he might give us victory over our enemies, preserve our homes and alters from pollution, and secure to us the restoration of peace and prosperity. Papa Joe said that the south starts a war and then when the going is starting to get rough they think that they should ask God to be on their side. He said that the slave owners are the ones who wanted this war in the first place and he thinks that God would be on the side of the north because they are the ones who want to do right by the slaves and set them free. He said that there is no way that he would do any praying to ask God to be on the side of the slave owners. The troops had better keep their guns loaded and by their side while they are kneeling down to pray, he said, cause the Lord is not going to do any shooting for them. It is tough knowing that there are southern boys getting killed in the fighting, but it is also tough realizing that anyone is being killed. Papa Joe has always been against this war and he just wants to be left along but he says that he will help the Yankees before he will help the Rebels from the south because he believes more in their cause and he thinks that we should never have seceded from the union and he still feels like he is part of the United States and not the Confederate States. He feels that the traitors are the ones who rebelled from the United States Government and not the ones who wants to remain loyal to the government that they have always lived under. There was another article in that same newspaper about what they are calling Tories. They are the people like Papa Joe who are against all that the south has done to secede from the Union and start a war. The newspaper says that there are some Tories around Chattanooga who are doing things to help the Yankees. Papa Joe says that he would never do nothing like burn bridges but he might do some of those other things if he got the chance. When all this trouble started I asked him to give me the newspapers that had something written about what was going on between the north and the south and I started saving them so as to keep the students up on what is going on in this country. I think that it is important that people here on the farm knows what is going on outside what we have here even though it has not affected us yet and I pray that it never will. After we didn't have school for a while I quit saving them papers but with all that is going on I asked Papa Joe to start bringing me papers again from town so I will be able to use them in the classes when school starts again. I am saving a copy of the paper that I just talked about and plan to keep more of them if there is something that I think the students ought to know. I have wrote a whole lot but it had been a good spell of time since I wrote last time but I have wrote enough today.

♦

CHAPTER 15

◆

"Just as I thought," Jenny voiced her previous assumption. "When we read the newspaper that had the article regarding the proclamation by President Davis, I had a hunch that it would not go over too well with Reverend Stone and Woody. To ask God to take the side of those who want to suppress and enslave their fellow men just because they were born with darker skin, is not the side that I think the Lord would choose to enable."

"We know that Sarah was responsible for keeping all those newspapers that were packed in that box," Abigail added to her daughter's comment, changing the subject. "We are not the students she had in mind to benefit from those news articles, but I am happy that Rebekah, or whoever it was, had the foresight to hang on to them and preserve them for the future. If indeed they were ever read again. We know how youngsters are and reading old newspapers is not a high priority. There was a skip of several months in the dates of the papers that were in the box and Sarah just explained why. She did not save them during that time. We have already read the papers and know that there was another skip in the dates."

Raleigh entered the discussion. "You are so right, Abigail! If I remember correctly, the next edition that she saved was the one in February 1862, when those Yankee gunboats came down to Florence and wreaked havoc on the citizens there. I think that those farmers on the plantation there were about to find out the same thing that President Davis and his army were also to become aware of. If they expected God to block the Tennessee River to keep the Federal boats from going up and down it, they needed to reassess their strategy."

"I believe that you guys may be getting a little ahead of the story in the diary," Dutch interrupted. "We are still in November and there are three months to go before the boats make their way down to Florence."

"Let's get to reading then!" Jenny proposed.

November 31, 1861

I just read back over some of the things that I have written in this book and sometimes I write things that I have already wrote about, especially about me worrying about Sunny and where he might be able to sell the things we grow here on the farm. The reason that I do it is because I just put down whatever it is that I got on my mind. It is hard to think about anything good these days cause of all the bad stuff that is happening and there aint nothing nobody can do about it except those people in Richmond and Montgomery who Sunny says aint got sense enough to get in out of the rain. He says that he figures that they must think that it is a whole lot better to be in the rain and get wet than it is to be in a battle and get killed and they rather that it be them that got wet and somebody else get killed. It just aint right that those political people who start a war can sit in their safe places while they force our fine young men out to the battlefields to be slaughtered. I think about that a lot but there aint nothing I can do about it. I wrote a whole lot the last time but we have been so busy getting all the crops in and getting ready for wintertime that I just aint had time to write no more since then. Tomorrow is the first day of December and Papa Joe has said that it is time for the young ones to get out of the fields and back into the classroom. So tomorrow being Monday the children will be back in school and both Sadie and me will be teaching again. I have decided that I won't do no more writing in this book until there is more news about what is going on in our country as the word is that there are a lot of little fights going on in Virginia and Missouri and Kentucky but there aint much going on around here so there aint much we can do but let them do their fighting and hope that it stays away from here. The bad part of it is that what I just wrote about. There are a whole bunch of young men from around here that are up there doing that fighting and lots of them are getting hurt and killed or dying from diseases or hunger. We hear a lot of names of men from around here who won't be returning cause they were killed and some are wounded and captured and they may or may not get to come back home. It will probably be a while before I do any more writing in here.

◆

February 16, 1862

The last time that I wrote I said that I wouldn't do no more writing in this book unless something exciting happened around here. Well, Saturday, not yesterday but the 8th, there was some real excitement around here.

"I stand corrected," Dutch interrupted the readers. "Looks like Sarah didn't have anything to say during those three months I talked about. But at least we know what was next to come."

On Thursday which was the 6th. Sunny told the farm workers that they could have the rest of the week off as he planned to start the next Monday getting everything ready to start farming just as soon as the weather gets warm enough. We always keep some boats on the river and Friday some of them set out some trotlines for to catch some catfish and eels. They were running their lines when there were three loaded steamers that came up the river as fast as they could go. It was not long before there were two big black gunboats that came by a chasing the steamers. In a little while they heard booms up the river which looked like it was about at Florence. After that there was a lot of smoke coming up from up that way and there were more booms like there were big guns being fired. The workers stayed on the river fishing with hooks and lines when later on the two gunboats came back down the river. On the other side of the river not too far down from where they were fishing they saw where the Confederates had set up some guns in a redoubt that they were starting to build and the gunboats stopped and shot some shells into that place. The black workers were out in their boats and the people in one of the gunboats put out one of their smaller boats and went to talk with the black workers from the farm here. They knew that the blacks wouldn't be Rebel troops and they started talking. The blacks told them that they worked on the farm here and that their masters were religious people who are against the war and that Papa Joe and Sunny has told them that they are on the Yankees side in the war. The men from the gunboat said that they had to go but said that they would like to talk with Sunny and Papa Joe if they would talk with them. The workers told Sunny about what happened and Sunny said that it was interesting. Papa Joe brought in a newspaper that I am going to keep and put it with my other ones. The paper said that the gunboats chased the steamers up to Florence and that they were set on fire so as to keep the Yankees from taking what they were carrying. There were shots fired there which is what he heard down here and the smoke that we saw was from the boats burning. There was a lot of excitement caused by all that action up there and a lot of people left Florence in a hurry. The Yankees have now brought the war to our area and we are all worried as to what might happen next. Sunny says that we are just going to keep on doing what we have always done and hope for the best. That is all that we can do. I guess I will start back writing in this book so as to keep up with what is going on.

◆

"Sunny was not the only one that found it interesting that the farm workers had a conversation with the Yankee navy men," Raleigh remarked. "That opened up a lot of possibilities for Sunny and Reverend Stone to become involved in the conflict. Now I suspect that they would not have wanted to become entangled in the war, but then Sarah has said that they are strongly against the South's decision to secede from the Union and start a war, so Sunny might have let his interest influence his action. Hopefully we can keep reading and get some answers."

February 23, 1862

All the talk around here has been about the Yankees capturing Fort Henry which allowed the gunboats to come up the river like I wrote about last week. It has been raining a whole lot lately and the river is way out of its banks and the word is that the water got up so high that it went right over the walls of Fort Henry and the Yankee's boats were able to float right into the fort. There have been some that said that they don't see how that could happen but the word is that the fort was built in a bad place and the builders were warned before they built it that something like that could happen. Now I don't know what the truth is about that but I do know that it seems like that the Federal boats didn't have too hard a time capturing Fort Henry and they were able to take their boats all the way up here to Florence. There is talk that Fort Donaldson on the Cumberland River can't hold up much longer and the north will have a water route up the Tennessee to the valley here and if they take Fort Donaldson then they can go right on to Nashville and do whatever they want to do. Whenever Fort Sumner fell last year the people in Florence were dancing in the streets and now Papa Joe says that the same streets are now all empty. People are now afraid to go out of their houses and into the streets after the gunboats fired into town. He has said all along that it was going to come to this and it will get worse before this war is all over. I worry most about the people here on the farm and especially Sunny's mother and Daddy and my parents. Papa Joe had a birthday Thursday and he turned 54 years old. He was born on February 20, 1808. Sunbeam is eight years younger than he is which makes her 46 years old. She was born the same year as my mother who is also 46 but my dad is 2 years older than she is which makes him 48 years old. My aunt Hannah is three years older than my mother and she was made to go to Oklahoma on the forced relocation of the Cherokees there but she came back and is now living here on the farm. There was a slave named Sampson who was also made to go to Oklahoma and he helped Hannah get back here. He found his wife and children and brought them to live on the farm and he is now one of the main men who helps Sunny get everything done here. Now I am writing all of this down because they are beginning to get old and a war could be bad on them and I worry about them but at least they are too old for the Confederates to try to get them to go fight the Yankees. That can't be said about Sunny and Woody and some of the young white workers that live here on the farm. There will probably be a lot of trouble before this war is over with cause Papa Joe says that there aint no way that he will let nobody make them go to war unless there are some who want to go, and there aint nobody here on this farm who want anything to do with killing nobody else no matter whether they live in the north or the south. Sunny said again that what he is concerned about now is to get the fields ready for planting when the time comes and he will cross bridges when he gets to them-if they are not already burnt down.

♦

March 2, 1862

We got the news last week that Fort Donaldson that is on the Cumberland River to keep the Yankees out of Nashville was captured by the Federal troops on February 16 and now the Yankee navy can go up the Cumberland River to Nashville just like they can to Florence on the Tennessee. The fighting is getting worse and worse and Sunny who has been keeping up with what is going on in the war just like his dad does says that the South hadn't been doing too good in the battles that have been fought since the first of this year. The Yankees have captured Fort Henry and Fort Donaldson and in Missouri they came out on top at Roans Tan yard which wasn't no big battle but they also got the best of the Confederate army in Kentucky at Middle Creek and Mill Springs and in North Carolina at Roanoke Island. He says that the South aint winning no battles and are getting people killed. I just try not to think about it cause, just like I have always been saying, there aint nothing that I can do about it anyway. Sunny says that the Federal Government has made blockades on all the Southern ports and they won't let ships bring anything in or take anything out on the Atlantic Ocean or the Gulf of Mexico. He says that it don't look good about selling any cotton or grain that has to be shipped to other countries and there won't be any markets for up north either. He says that he is going to go ahead and get everything ready to plant just like he always does and just see what happens but things sure don't look good for the south. It has been raining a lot lately and the river is way up high and the fields are too wet to plough so we will have to wait until the fields get dryer before we can plant this year. I heard Sunny and Papa Joe talking about where they might put some cotton if they grow a lot this year. He said that last year was a good cotton year and since there is a gin on the farm here they were able to gin it and hide it in the secret storage area that they have built. With all the salt and cotton and corn that they got hid there this year there might not be enough space to hide much more without having to build bigger storage areas. Sunny says again that we can't cross no bridges until we get to them and this may not be a good crop year and then we would not have to be concerned about storage.

◆

March 16, 1862

There was some excitement around here last Wednesday when there were two Federal gunboats that came up the river almost to here and fired a lot of shells into that stronghold that the Confederate army is trying to build to help protect the river. We live down the river from Florence and the boats came within sight of our farm here. There was a whole lot of noise when those big guns were firing from both the Yankee's boats and the Confederate battery that they were trying to knock out. It was real loud here and some of the blacks went down there to see what was going on. They got in their boats when they thought that it would be safe and talked to some of the Yankee navy men again. They said that there was some men on the boats who were on the ones who came down the first time to Florence. I have not been told nothing but I suspect that there are some here on the farm who are secretly telling the Yankees things about what is going on around here and they may have told them about the Rebels building the fortress that they came down here to shoot into. Now I don't know this as a fact but there has been some things done and said which caused me to wonder about it. The Confederates never got it to be more than a small redoubt and the Yankees were not going to let it get any stronger. As I say, I think that we have some spies here on the farm and they have been telling the Yankee navy men things about what is going on around here ever since that first time the blacks talked to the Yankees. I say this because I have seen some strangers come in from the river going toward the secret hideaway with some of the black men from here on the farm with them. They are dressed like fisherman and some are toting fishing poles but I don't think that they are doing any fishing. I think that they are spies, but then, I just want to stay out of all this bad stuff that is happening and keep teaching the children at school. Papa Joe went to Florence yesterday to get ready for planting season and he said that the whole town is talking about a proclamation made by

Governor Shorter the first of this month that said that there is not to be one seed of cotton planted this year to be sold. He said that he has not seen it in the newspaper yet but he was told that the governor said that he would burn every lock of cotton to keep it from falling into the hands of the enemy. He said that he went by the office of the Florence Gazette to see if that was the truth and they told him that they were writing stories about some proclamations made by the Governor on March 1st and March 6th and will publish them in this week papers but said it would probably be Thursday, the 20th before they would have it printed. They told him that the governor did say that there would be no cotton allowed to be grown this year. Papa Joe said that he has said all along that this war would mess everything up for farmers and it looks like that he had it all figured out. He don't usually go to town during the week but he said that he was going to go to Florence Thursday to get a copy of the Gazette to see what it has to say about what the Governor said about farming. If that is true like they say it is and they won't let us grow no cotton, Papa Joe and Sunny won't have to worry about building anymore storage space. Sunny has been working to get everything ready for the new crop and he said that it would be of no use for him to get the fields ready for planting if he didn't know what he needed to plant.

◆

"If there was no cotton to be grown and sold, then what were the Southerners expecting to make their clothes out of?" Dutch wondered aloud. "It looks like the South had gotten themselves into a situation where they were afraid to grow anything for fear that the Yankees would end up with it and use it for their own good. Just as they demonstrated by their foray into Florence, which prompted the burning of the Southern boats that were transporting goods."

Dutch was thinking about the farming aspect of the war, which, as Sunny and Sarah were afraid of, had been effective in keeping the oxen and mules in their pastures and away from the farming equipment. The Northern markets had dried up because of the war.

March 23, 1862

I have a copy of the last Florence Gazette that Papa Joe brought in Thursday; he got three copies and gave me one to keep. The talk about the governor not letting any cotton be planted this year is absolutely right. The paper said that the governor wanted farmers to plant crops that would be of help to the war efforts and he did not want a seed of cotton planted to be sold so the Yankees could not get their hands on it. The Gazette printed the whole proclamation because the Governor ordered that all newspapers in the state copy it twice and send an account to him. He didn't only tell the farmers not to plant more cotton than they could use for themselves but he begged that anyone who had shotguns or rifles or bowie knives plus powder and lead and balls give it to the Confederate army or if they were poor that the state would pay them for it. When Sunny read what the governor wrote he said that he was not surprised that the Confederate army has being doing so bad this year in their fighting cause they don't even have the weapons or ammunition they need to fight a war. He wonders why the South would even start a war when they don't have the guns to fight it with when they know that the Federal Government is the ones who stores the weapons needed to fight with. He says that there is no way that the south can whip the north when they don't have the weapons to fight with and the rivers and railroads are being took over by the Yankees. He is getting ready to plant a lot of corn and crops that will help feed people who have their menfolk off fighting in the war. He is not for the south getting into the war but he says that a lot of the men who are off fighting just got caught up in what the politicians got started and he will help feed the hungry as much as he can. There aint no use of planting cotton when you can't sell it and he has a lot of fields that he don't want to get growed up in weeds so he might as well do what he can to help the families who need it. He said that he don't even worry about the Yankees coming in and getting some of it cause they need food just as bad as anyone else. One thing he says that he don't want to do is to grow a big crop of food and the Confederate army people come in and get it all. He allows that they are the ones who got us in this war and they are the ones that have to be responsible for feeding their troops just as they are the ones with the responsibility of getting guns and ammunitions in their hands. He plans to grow stuff that people can eat and then give it away to anyone who needs it to keep them from going hungry. He is afraid to grow any navy beans though cause he said that the farmers have been asked to grow some to help supply the army men and he is afraid that if he does grow some and they hear about it that they will be here wanting to take it and he don't want them around here. He is growing a lot of hogs and cattle and chickens cause he says that before this war is over they will be a big need for meat and milk and eggs. Papa Joe told me that there are a whole lot of people who don't have much, if any money and he don't want people to know it but he has plenty of money in gold and silver that he keeps in the hidden room in the back of the secret hideaway where we lived while I was growing up and it won't hurt him much to give stuff away. He says that is one of the reasons why he has been careful to save because you never know what will happen next and when money might be needed. Now that there is a war going on there aint nobody interested no more in picking up Indians and moving them to Oklahoma so we don't have to be so careful as we used to be in hiding out to keep from getting sent off. As the farm got bigger and Papa Joe keep getting more workers for the farm here he kept building houses for them to live in. A few years ago he built a big one for mom and daddy because they had been living in the hideaway so as not to get caught, but there aint no more need for them to hide. Not far from their house they built a little one for Aunt Hannah so she would have a place to live. She don't ever leave the farm no more so she aint had the chance to meet any man that she wanted to marry so she lives by herself. After that long walk that she had to make to Oklahoma and then walk back she said that she has seen all of the world that she wants to see and she is happy right here living by herself. I had a lot on my mind and I have been writing a long time today but because we didn't know what to plant we have not been as busy as we usually are this time of the year so I have more time to do other things. Sadie and I are still teaching the children in school and might get to do it a little longer this year because they won't be chopping and picking cotton like they usually have to do. I need to get a good lesson to teach them tomorrow so I will start working on that.

♦

March 30, 1862

Papa Joe went to Florence yesterday and did not bring home a newspaper. He said that there weren't no paper printed last Wednesday like there usually is and he was told that they did not know just when another one would be printed. He said that they could no longer get paper and ink and they did not have the hands to help print it if they could get it. Another reason there was no newspaper printed is because paper is hard to get with the war going on and the price of paper has gone up a lot. The war has everything and everybody all scared and messed up and it is getting harder and harder to get things that are needed. It is just like Papa Joe and Sunny said when all them people were dancing in the street at the start of this war that they wouldn't be dancing long and they were right. There has been a lot of fighting this month and the north is still whipping the south in most of the fighting. According to Sunny, close to the end of last month the Confederate army was said to have come out on top way out in the New Mexico territory at Valverde but they have lost about every other fight they have been in. They lost a big one at Island number 10 or New Madrid in Missouri and now they have had a battle in Arkansas at Pea Ridge where they got beat. They lost in fights in Virginia at Hampton Roads and in North Carolina at New Bern and later in Virginia at Kernstown and in Georgia at Fort Macon. Now the reason that I know about all this is because I asked Papa Joe to get me some good maps to use at school and then Sunny tries to keep up with what is going on in the war. Every time we get some new reports of the fighting we look at the maps in class and talk about what is going on and where it is on the map. At the end of each month we talk about what went on during that month and since tomorrow is the last day of the month I want to talk to the children about what happened during the month in the war. I still keep the newspapers that Papa Joe brings in and read them in class. I think that is a good way for the students to learn how to read and it teaches them Geography too. I sometimes have them to write a short report of what they read and that is helping them to learn how to write better too. I think it is good that they know what is going on in this country cause it will have an effect on the world that they are going to have to live in. Sunny and Papa Joe are still talking about what is the best thing to do about the crops this year. They have never grown too many peanuts but Sunny says that they may plant more of them this year if they can find enough seeds. He is going to plant a lot of sorghum cane so as to make a lot of molasses cause he says that syrup can be ate when there is not much more food around' He will raise a lot of corn where one can always grind up some corn mill and make bread or cornpones and hominy and grits. Corn will also be needed for the animals to eat cause you can feed corn to the cattle and horses and goats and mules and hogs and chickens so he will grow a lot of corn and hay for the winter feedings. One of the last newspapers we got had an article asking farmers to grow navy beans so as to help feed the army. Like I have already wrote, Papa Joe had already heard about that and he said that he is not going to start planting crops on this farm like navy beans which will get the attention of the Confederate army and have them coming here to get their food, He says that he don't want them nowhere around here.

◆

"I remember reading the newspaper that had that article in it where someone had scribbled 'not on this farm' on the paper," Dutch made the observation as he read the last part of Sarah's entry. "It's plain that they didn't want to be involved in the conflict on the Confederate's side."

"We now know that at that time the war was just getting started," Raleigh said. "Those farmers may have had to do a lot of dodging before this thing was over."

April 6, 1862

We are lucky that we have not had anybody on the farm here to come down with the bloody flux but Papa Joe and the newspapers do too says that it is real bad now and especially among the soldiers in the army. Sunny says that we are lucky here when those kind of diseases start going around because we stay right here on the farm and don't get out where we can catch   contagious diseases. The trouble is that the troops are not only getting killed in the war but there are a lot of them dying from sickness. There is word that there might be a big battle in Tennessee not far from here. There are reports that there are a lot of Confederate troops who have been moved there and there is   also a big army of Federal troops who are there ready to fight them. The Federal armies have control of the State of Tennessee north of the area where they are now and have been there all winter just waiting until the right time to start their march further south. They have done took the Tennessee and Cumberland Rivers this year and are said to be ready to move on land to take all of the south. The heavy rains lately has done a lot of damage all up and down the river because of the floods. I have not been down on the riverbank but some of the workers said that they saw some cotton bales come floating by but there were some big boats out trying to pick them up. Sunny says that if they had expected to grow cotton and make a big crop this year that all the rains would set them back and have him worried but since they won't let him grow any cotton or make anything to sell that he is just going to relax and grow whatever he wants to when the time gets right. He tried to find some seed peanuts but didn't have no luck at that because it seems that they want to keep them for food. He says that there aint nobody on the farm that is going to go hungry and he will help feed as many others as he can. There is talk of an impressment act from Montgomery where the Confederacy will be able to take whatever they want for the war effort but Papa Joe says that he has a plan to keep them from getting his things if they start trying to. Those big land owners down in South Alabama has got it fixed where anyone who has 20 slaves or more, I think that is the number, don't have to go fight in the war. Papa Joe and Sunny have a lot more black workers on the farm than that. They are not printing the Gazette no longer cause of the war and hear tell is that the Yankees have come in and took over everything because they did not like what was being said in the paper. It is hard to keep up with what is going on any more. Sunny says that now people in Florence gather at a mercantile store or horse stable and talk about what they have heard. Some of that is true but there aint no truth in some of it. A lot of what we hear is told by some of the soldiers who come back from where the fighting is going on. Some of them are hurt but a lot of them are men who have had enough of the killing and leave to get away from the fighting. What the problem is that when they get back then they have to stay hid from the Home Guards who are out looking for the dodgers and deserters. I have wrote a whole lot today but I didn't have much to do after I got out of church seeing as to how we aint doing no farming yet. Sunny says that if things don't change, we can have school classes a lot longer this year than we did before cept now I don't have no newspapers that we can read and talk about.

♦

April 13, 1862

As I said when I stopped writing the last time, we don't have a newspaper no more to tell us what is going on in the war but the big talk is about the big battle that they had at Shiloh not that far from here in Tennessee. While I was writing in this book last Sunday there were people getting killed in the fighting up there. The word is that it was one of the biggest battles yet in the war and there were a lot of people killed on both sides. The latest that Sunny and Papa Joe heard was that there was probably more Yankees killed than southern troops but the Yankees still came out on top. Papa Joe has a lot to say about all this senseless killing and says that he has made up his mind that he is going to do what he can to make it as short a war as possible. He comes here to the house and talks to Sunny about what is the best thing to do and I heard Papa Joe tell Sunny that there is no way that the southern army is going to win this war and he is going to get on the Federal's side but is going to keep it a secret from the Confederate people. He says that there are a lot of people that they are calling Tories in North Alabama and especially around Winston County where Chris Sheets is the Representative in Montgomery and he was put in jail because he was against the secession of the south from the Union. When Sunny was talking to Papa Joe they decided that they would get in touch with Bill Looney and find out what they can do to help the Federal army. Sunny said that the farm here is a good location to help the Tories get across the river so that they can reach the Federal side and then we can hide them to keep from getting caught. I have decided that I am going to keep this book well hid out cause if I write about what is going on I sure don't want no Rebel a getting hold of it. I think that I will go hide it now.

I thought that I had just quit writing today when Sunny came in and said that he had just got some more news about the war. He said that the day before yesterday on April 11 that the Yankees under a General Mitchell took a big force of solders and marched right into Huntsville which is a way on up the river from here and captured the city with very little resistance. He said that means that the Federal army has control of the whole Tennessee River Valley here and they captured a lot of supplies and some locomotives and weapons. He said that is just more bad news for the Confederates and especially the people here in Alabama who support the war. Sunny says that it don't surprise him atall cause, as he keeps on saying, there aint no way that the South is going to win this war. Him and Papa Joe says that all the time and that is why I keep writing about it. More and more it looks like that they are going to be right. That is the reason that he says that any person in their right mind will be on the side of the old United States and work to get the war over with faster and get us back to where we were before the Rebels messed everything up by breaking away from the Union.

◆

"I wish that they were still printing the *Gazette* when the Battle of Shiloh was fought; it would've been interesting to read what they had to say about it," Raleigh noted. "The battle was fought at Pittsburg Landing on the Tennessee River, and now it is sometimes called the Battle of Pittsburg Landing. The battle site was downriver from the plantation and to the north of Mississippi. It was one of the major battles of the entire war and was a disastrous defeat for the Confederate Army. The battle was fought on April 6th and 7th with the Southern army winning the fight on the first day, but when Federal reinforcements came on the second day, the tide turned and the North was victorious. General Albert Sidney Johnston was killed in the battle," he said, supplementing the information that Sarah had written about the Battle of Shiloh.

"The news about Huntsville being captured by the Yankees surely didn't have the citizens out dancing in the streets like they probably were after the first battle of the war was fought at Fort Sumter," Jenny added to Raleigh's comment. "There would be more bad news for them before the war was over."

CHAPTER 16

◆

"I'm interested in knowing which battles were going on around the time of these last few journal entries," Abigail said, getting out her phone to do some online searching as Jenny had done earlier. "Particularly in Alabama. Do you all mind?"

"Go ahead," Dutch encouraged. "I'd like to know too."

After finding what she was looking for, Abigail read aloud from a web article with information on Civil War battles. "In the summer of 1862, the war picked up momentum with the Northern Army being victorious again in Georgia at Fort Pulaski only three days after their victory at Shiloh. On April 18, the Federal troops won a battle in Louisiana at Fort Jackson, and on the 25th the Union Army captured New Orleans. On April 29th and 30th, Federal troops moved south from Shiloh and laid siege to Corinth, Mississippi."

"Corinth isn't far from the Alabama state line," Dutch said quickly before his wife continued.

"Shortly thereafter, on May 2nd, the North Alabama town of Athens was entered and sacked by Federal Troops by order of Col. J. B. Turchin, resulting in his later being court-martial for the act." Abigail paused, read silently for a moment, then voiced an observation,

"Other than that, it doesn't look like any big conflict during the entire war reached inside Alabama, with the exception of the cavalry battle between Colonel Abel Streight and General Nathan Bedford Forrest in North Alabama, which was about a year later, between April 19 and May 3, 1863. It says here that General Forrest defeated Colonel Streight at Cedar Bluff, Alabama, in what became known as the longest cavalry battle in history."

Then she read on, "The Confederate Army and the Federal Army fought several battles in May and June of 1862 with some ending with no conclusive winner and the South having some success in others. At Williamsburg and Ethan's Landing, neither side could claim a victory, but the South had a string of victories at McDowell, Drewry's Bluff, Princeton Court House, Fort Royal, and Winchester. The Union gained the upper hand in the Battle of Hanover Courthouse. There was no apparent winner at Seven Pines. All these battles were fought in the month of May. The fighting continued to rage in June when there were sixteen or more battles fought in North Carolina, Tennessee, Virginia, South Carolina, and Florida."

As Abigail finished reading from the web page, Jenny gave her thoughts, "Well that does cast some light on the battles as they were being fought at that time. However, I feel that Sarah was more concerned about the battles being fought in Alabama, so this was the history she wanted to leave in her journal."

With no newspaper to read and the sharp increase in battle sites, Sarah turned her attention to the activities which were occurring in Alabama and on their farm. Her next entry reflects the change.

April 20, 1862

Papa Joe came back from Florence yesterday with some news. Last Wednesday on April 16 the Yankee army captured Tuscumbia which is across the river from Florence. The Confederate army was in Mississippi trying to keep the Yankees from coming into west Alabama from Shiloh and Corinth and they did not have the troops to come and face the Federal troops that had come into the Tennessee Valley from the north so it was not hard for them to capture Huntsville and Tuscumbia. He said that there was bad news for the men in the Confederate states. Last Wednesday the Confederate Congress passed a Conscript Law that said that all the fighting men in the Confederate army who thought that they would get to come home after one year now has to stay in the army for two more years. They also said in that law that all male men age 18 to 35 who are not already fighting in the war are subject to military service and they are going to be made to go fight the Yankees whether they want too or not. They are going to pay what they are calling Enlisting Officers to go out and find the men that are not already fighting and make them go into the war. Sunny says that what they are going to do is get a whole lot of the menfolk killed and there is going to be a lot of widows and orphans going hungry and it is all because of those rich folks down south who want to keep their slaves so they can work them to death. It just aint right that they will start a war and then force the ones who are against it to go get hurt or killed to fight it.   The word is that the south is still not doing too good in their fighting and now the Rebels just want to keep putting men in the fights so that they can get killed. Papa Joe says that the south should be able to figure out that they can't just say that they are a new nation and then expect to whip the one that beat the English to be independent and who has the weapons and supplies to fight a war. The crazy thing is that the Confederate Government secedes and then starts fighting when they don't have what they need to fight with. He tells us that he is going to get in touch with some of the men from around Winston County to see what he can do to help them keep from having to go fight the Yankees. He says that he is going to be real careful to not let the Rebels know what he is doing.

♦

April 27, 1862

Sunny keeps telling us that there is fighting everywhere now and there is a battle somewhere almost every day and there is no way that we can keep up with what is going on in the war. The Confederate army got whipped at the Pittsburg Landing and now Sunny says that opened the way for the Yankees to move down into Mississippi. He says that they have been seen around Corinth which is not too far from here but is over the state line in Mississippi. I did not write none last week because I spent the Sunday afternoon with mom and daddy and Aunt Hannah. Seeing as to how we will not be as busy here on the farm as in most years because we can't grow nothing to sell like cotton I want to spend more time with my family. During the week I spend most of the day at the schoolhouse and on Saturdays I try to do my housework and some cooking and sewing. I usually have Ida or Nancy helping me out in the house but I like to do things of my own on Saturdays. I've got to keep this book hid real good now cause I do not know when some of them Home Guards that are getting the men folks to go fight in the war might come here with their guns and go snooping around. I think that I am beginning to figure out what is going on here on the farm even though Papa Joe and Sunny are not talking about it. I have wrote before about how that I have seen some strangers come up from down on the river and meet with Sunny and Papa Joe in secret. Sometimes some of the black workers who were on the river when the Yankee gunboats came down and did all that shooting in Florence comes up with the strangers. We are so far out from anybody else with a lot of land on the river that there aint nobody else who can see what is going on. I spect that them are Yankees that are coming and Sunny and Papa Joe are secretly giving them information about what they see the Rebels are doing around here seeing as to how they are so against what the south is doing in this war. Now I don't know that what I just wrote to be the fact but this is what I suspect. I think that I am right because when I was cleaning the hideaway I found a funny looking wheel and a spy glass that had fell behind a bunk. There was also some paper with words wrote on it that made no sense. I picked them up and hid them because whoever lost them was done gone away from here already but I think it belonged to some spies. I am just going to try to not know no more than I have to so if anybody tries to make me talk I can truthfully say that I don't know nothing, which I don't. Sunny says that the ground has dried out enough that they can start planting tomorrow and they are going to plant enough corn for corn meal and grits and hominy and some to can for food and enough feed for the animals and some to give to the needy but not enough to make the Rebels interested in coming and taking it from us. He is going to plant a lot of vegetables for food but he says that he is going to let most of the land rest with no crops growing on it. Papa Joe who was a preacher said that giving the land a rest is the Bible way of doing it anyways. He says that in the Old Testament in the book of Leviticus in the 25th chapter that God when he spoke to Moses on Mount Sinai told him that they were to sow their fields for six years and the seventh year would be a Sabbath of rest for the land where they were not to plant any fields or prune their vineyards. On the seventh year they were not to even harvest anything that grew of its own accord or gather the grapes from their vines. When seven Sabbaths had passed, or 49 years, there was the year of the Jubilee for the 50th year and all the slaves were freed and all land was returned to every man's possession and every man was returned to his family. I aint got time to tell all that is in that chapter that God told Moses about the Sabbaths and Jubilees and everything and every family returned to where they were fifty years earlier but Papa Joe said that everybody should read what God told Moses when he was on Mount Sinai and this world would be a better place. He said that if they did that, then every fifty years the slaves would be free and the land returned to its rightful owners who had it fifty years ago. The Indians would then get back the land that was stole from them and all the injustice that had been done for fifty years would be righted. Sunny says that he is happy that he will not plant much of his land this year and every seventh year they should let it rest just like God told Moses that his people ought to do. I suppose that I have wrote enough today to make up for what I didn't write last week so I think that I will just go and get my Bible and read the 25th chapter of Leviticus to see what Papa Joe is talking about.

◆

"That's what she placed in the box with her journal and the newspapers," Jenny commented on the items that Sarah had found while cleaning. "The wheel thing and the coded messages inside the cigar box!"

"You're right!" Abigail responded, retrieving the items in question and laying them carefully on the table.

Jenny called a halt to their reading and reached for her smart phone. "This has been on my mind ever since we first opened the box, and I want to try to find out what it is," she said while looking at the mysterious round object. "I'm just going to search 'Confederate spy wheel,' and see what comes up," she said as she began typing on her phone.

After a short pause she reported the results of her inquiry. "It's called a 'cipher disk' and was used by Confederate spies. The CSA stands for Confederate States of America, just as we had assumed. The SS stamped in the middle most likely stands for Secret Service, although some believe it to be 'signal service.' There are only five known to be in existence, so apparently we've had a treasure in the vault this whole time that we didn't even know about!"

Abigail interrupted, "Maybe so, but this one is going nowhere but right back where it has been kept safe for the past 150 years."

Raleigh weighed in with his assessment of the items being discussed, "So those scrambled sheets of paper must have been messages which were sent but intercepted by Northern troops. Confederate runners were probably captured while attempting to deliver them. I would further venture that this was the work of Tories living a double life, pretending to be Rebels while secretly working for the Union."

"And then possibly deciphered by using the disk and the messages forwarded to the proper commander." Dutch was the next to speak. "Maybe one day we will attempt to decode and read the secret messages which apparently never made it to their intended targets."

"If we can figure out how to use the disk. Right now we are still reading what Sarah had to say, so maybe we will think about the deciphering part later," Jenny suggested.

"Let's think about that for a minute," Dutch said. "When we finish reading this, the box is going back into the vault, and I am not inclined to bring it back out to do spy work. I have a better idea. Why don't we call it quits for the day and give Abigail or Jenny time to try to decode one of those messages? Reading this old handwriting is hard on my eyes and I really need to rest them for a while."

"Good idea! Jenny is the one who has the doctorate degree. I nominate her for the job," Abigail passed the buck on to her highly educated daughter.

"Motion seconded!" was announced by all but Jenny.

"My degree is in rocket science, with no minor in espionage," she said wryly, followed by chuckles from the others.

But she agreed to work on decoding the messages, and then shortly after she and Raleigh prepared to leave for home.

"I'll see you when I see you," Jenny yelled to her parents as she walked out of the door. "This may take a while."

On Tuesday morning Jenny called her mother.

"I've lost a little sleep, but I think that I may have succeeded in figuring out this decoder. One of the codes I've been working on started to look like English. When can we get together again?"

"Let me run it by Dutch and see what he says, and I'll get back with you. He had some chores to do, but he should be back for lunch."

It was early afternoon when Abigail called Jenny with her answer. "He says that he needs to go to the bank in the morning. They close at noon on Wednesdays, and he'll be back before noon. I'll get with Angie and have her prepare a good meal for us, and then we can spend the afternoon listening to what you have dug up about the code and continue from there."

"So what did you come up with?" was the first question Dutch and Abigail asked to Jenny after lunch on Wednesday.

"It was interesting," Jenny prefaced before answering. "I lucked out in finding that General G.T. Beauregard, the one in charge of the troops fighting nearby in Mississippi, chose to use a simple code at the beginning of the war so as not to be too difficult to decipher. It had to be during this time period that the code items were left behind." Jenny paused and picked up a pad of legal papers on which she had made some notes. After studying them she said, "I think that this would be a good starting place. I will read this just as I copied it from my computer. The site was 'Overview of Civil War Codes and Ciphers.'"

She started reading, "As late as April 9, 1862-" pausing she interjected, "which is the same month Sarah was writing her entry, so this is the same code that was being used at the time the items were lost. Shortly after the battle of Shiloh, which is just up the river from here." She continued reading again, "General Beauregard used a simple code by putting the last half of the alphabet first. The 'A' would then become an 'M', 'B' an 'N', 'C' an 'O', and so on. Today it is known as 'rot13.'" Jenny looked up, finished with her reading. "So with that information, I went to work and came up with these results."

Flipping a page of the legal pad, she cautioned, "Fortunately the code is simple, but it still requires concentration. I guess this is why the cipher disk was needed, because it would be difficult to hastily write it correctly and then read it without aid. I also assume that there was only one disk available, which had to be carried back and forth with the messages."

Placing before them one of the coded messages which came from the cigar box, Jenny began an explanation of the results of her study.

It was written:

FA:SFNMFZQIOMYBSDAGZPOZFQZZDUH-
QZUZMXMIMUFUZSEGBBXUQENQRADQMFF-
MOWUZSRQMDQPEGBBXUQEUZFQDOQB-
FQPNKRAQEQZPDQUZRADOQYQZFE

"There is nothing here to show the separate words, but maybe the army had a method to separate them. I didn't, so I just decoded everything and then searched for words. Now bear with me while I explain."

Turning another page in the pad, Jenny pulled out copies she had made of her decoding work and passed them out for everyone to read.

A – M
B – N
C – O
D – P
E – Q
F – R
G – S
H – T
I – U
J – V
K – W
L – X
M – Y
N – Z

O – A
P – B
Q – C
R – D
S – E
T – F
U – G
V – H
W – I
X – J
Y – K
Z – L

"This is how the letters lined up on the disk when set for the code we're using," Jenny explained. "Next, you'll see what I translated the message to, and how I broke it up into separate segments as it began to make sense."

FA:SFN – TO:GEN

"I take 'GEN' to mean General G.T. Beauregard, the general who was stationed nearby at this point in time," Jenny clarified as they read. "Now as you read the rest, take note that the first line in each segment is part of the original message, the second line is what I decoded it to, and the third line is after I broke it up into separate words."

MFZQIOMYBSDAGZPOZFQZZDUHQZUZMXM
ATNEWCAMPGROUNDONTENNRIVERINALA
"At new campground on Tenn river in Ala."

IMUFUZSEGBBXUQENQRADQMFFMOWUZS
WAITINGSUPPLIESBEFOREATTACKING
"Waiting supplies before attacking."

RQMDQPEGBBXUQEUZFQDOQBFQPNKRAQ
FEAREDSUPPLIESINTERCEPTEDBYFOE
"Feared supplies intercepted by foes."

EQZPDQUZRADOQYQZFE
SENDREINFORCEMENTS
"Send reinforcements."

"Well, there you have it!" Jenny exclaimed after showing her presentation. "That was not easy, and I think that it would have been almost impossible for me to get the results that I did without that cipher disk. On a battlefield it would have been a time consuming task. I can also understand why they used the simple code; that is, until it was broken."

"Good work, Jenny." Her father praised her. "I'm glad that we decided to take a break and solve the mystery that was packed in the cigar box. But now I suppose it's time for us to pick up where we left off in the journal."

CHAPTER 17

◆

May 4, 1862

There is a lot happening in the war not far from here and it is the talk of the town. There are a lot of Yankee soldiers that are around Corinth Mississippi and there is a standoff between them and the Confederate troops that are there. Sunny says that the word is that there are more and more soldiers coming from the north and there are a lot more of them than there are soldiers from the south. A lot of the south's soldiers slip away from the fighting and hide out or go home because they don't want nothing to do with the fighting and risk getting sick or being killed. I asked Sunny why the Yankees wanted to fight at Corinth and take that little town and he said that it was because it is a strategic point because there are two railroad lines that cross there. He said that now that the northern army has taken Shiloh and can get their supplies off at Pittsburg Landing that they can go down to Corinth and take the railroad and that will help them to fight the war further south. He said that the south is said to be building a strong fort on the Mississippi River at Vicksburg Mississippi and the Yankees want to get down there so that they can open up that river to them all the way down to the Gulf of Mexico. The Confederates want to keep them away from there on land so there is going to be a lot of fighting to see who can keep the other side from getting control of the Mississippi River. He says that the reason the south is building their fortifications at Vicksburg is because there are some high bluffs there that lets them have a good view up and down the river and they can place their guns to shoot down on any Yankee gunboats that might be coming down the river. The war has everything in the south all turned topsy tervy and I am ready for it to end. As I have said a bunch of times before, I don't see no way that the new Confederate Government can win against the Federal Government when they do not even have enough men, guns, ammunition and supplies to even fight a war. Sunny says that is showing up now when the Yankees can get a lot more troops in the south than the Rebels can come up with in their own states. Papa Joe said again like I have already wrote that if people want to call him a Tory, so be it, but he is not one of those people who wanted to fight the Yankees in the first place. He says that he is not going to talk about him being on the side of the Union but he is going to work in any way that he can to help them win and get this war over with as soon as possible cause the north is going to be the winner whenever all the fighting is over and that is showing up more and more as this war goes on.. This farm here on the river is a good place to be cause we aint close to nobody else and there are some places on this farm where there is some dense growth of bushes and trees on the river bank where people can hide boats and go up and down the river without anybody knowing what is going on. If somebody does see them on the river they will just think that they are fisherman and give it no thought that they may be Yankee spies. Since the blacks and other workers here on the farm are not having much to do this year because we aint growing many crops they are spending a lot of time on the river fishing with trot lines and nets and baskets and set hooks and poles and lines so they are on the river more than they use to be. When I see them with somebody that I don't know it stands to reason that somebody who don't live on the farm here and don't know who lives here would not know that they don't live here. That is the reason that I suspect that there might be some Yankee spies that are coming here. I am just a going to keep minding my own business until somebody tells me to do otherwise. I had just really rather not even think about all the fighting and killing that is going on in this country but it is hard to keep my mind off it. It worries me that the fighting is so close to here but I worry more about them mean old Rebel Home Guards that are trying to get everyone that wears pants to pick up a gun and go shoot Yankees than I am about the Federal troops coming here. There aint nobody that can be meaner than those Home Guard men. I don't know why everything that I wrote about today is about the fighting but it was what was on my mind and I didn't have nothing else to write about. Since I don't want to use all my paper talking about the war and since there aint nothing much else going on except this damnable fighting I have about decided while I was writing this and trying to think about something else to write about beside the war, and couldn't, that I aint going to do no more writing in this book until I get something good to write about. I just keep writing about the same thing over and over because I can't get it out of my mind so I need to just get my mind on something else that is fit to write about. One never knows how long any of us will be living with so many people getting killed close to here in the war.

◆

"I can surely understand why Sarah was so concerned about their safety where they were living on the Tennessee River," Abigail said. "All that fighting that was going on was very near here, and this was the place where she was doing her writings. I know that if there was a war going on in those places today I would be scared to death. It is only a few river miles from here up to the old Pittsburg Landing and Shiloh. Corinth is not on the river, but it is only sixty miles from Florence on Highway 72, and we are about halfway between that, so that fighting was also very close to here. Being in the extreme northwest corner of Alabama like we are, it is not far from here to either the Tennessee or Mississippi state lines. Even though there was not a lot of fighting going on in Alabama, that certainly was not the case in our neighboring states."

"Sarah mentioned the railroads in Corinth," Dutch added to Abigail's comment. "At that time, the Mobile and Ohio Railroad ran north and south and the Memphis and Charleston Railroad ran east and west, and they crossed in Corinth. This is what made Corinth such a strategic point that both sides wanted to maintain control over it. The railroad was a vital part of the war in moving goods and troops to the battlefronts and the side that controlled the rail lines had the advantage. The same thing could be said about the rivers, so that is why there was so much fighting along the rivers and railroads.

On top of that, the Confederate troops were outnumbered almost two to one by the Federal forces," Raleigh brought up. "The Union army was said to have had one hundred and twenty thousand troops while the Confederates had only around sixty-five thousand. This was not the battle where the South could be victorious. Sarah was right when she wondered how the Southern Army could expect to get the upper hand in their battles when the Yankees could put twice as many troops on the battlefield in Mississippi. One thing about Sarah, she was a realist! She perceived that the odds were stacked against the South and there was no way that they could win that war."

May 11, 1862

Sunny came in today all upset about what he heard about what happened in Athens, Alabama on or about the second of this month. He said that it is a long story and since they have shut down the newspaper it can't be wrote up to know what it is all about but it is the talk of town how that the Yankees ransacked the town and terrorized the citizens. The talk is that they looted everything that they could get their hands on and they tore apart books and stomped on Bibles. He said that there were girls who were raped, some of them little slave girls, and they used foul language while they rifled through houses and stores. He said that he is all for the North to put an end to slavery and this war might do that if the Yankees win it but he says that this is no way that anybody should fight a war and anybody who will stomp on bibles are headed straight to hell if they don't change. He said that he heard that it all started when some men at Athens overran some Yankee guards at a railroad bridge which had been captured earlier by the northern army and they sawed through the support beams which weakened the bridge, causing a Yankee train of boxcars to crash when the bridge could not support it. The crash killed the engineer of the train and trapped two soldiers in a boxcar which caught fire and burned them alive. Sunny says that all this just shows how bad this whole business of war is and nothing good can come out of it because people get killed in a lot of ways. I just hope that this fighting gets over with soon and we can have a little peace and quiet from here on.

♦

"That is an interesting entry there," Jenny commented after reading it. "The *Gazette* had suspended their publications during this period of time, so I suppose it was difficult to really know what was happening in the battles that were being fought between the North and the South. I think that from March 19th to December 10th of 1862 there were no newspapers in Sarah's box as they were not being published during that period of time. Consequently, there was no written account of the happenings in Athens. I remember that this skirmish in Athens was discussed when I was taking an Alabama history class. It is now referred to as the Sack of Athens. A Colonel Turchin, who was already on the bad side of his superiors over the issue of confiscating the property and slaves of the Confederates, was in charge of securing the area's railroads and repairing the bridges. When the Limestone Creek Bridge collapsed due to his inability to secure it, he was angry about it and authorized the troops in the Eighteenth Ohio to sack the town as payback for the destruction of the bridge.

"As a result of his actions in Athens, he was branded as the 'Mad Cossack' and was court martialed after a lengthy trial. He, however, returned to war and stayed in the army until he had a severe heat stroke which forced him to leave the army. He returned to his hometown of Chicago where he worked as a civil engineer, never really retiring from the military. I think that he had another heat stroke after that, causing him to lose his mind, and he died in a mental hospital, a pauper. Oh, and by the way, I made an 'A' in my Alabama history class—how is that for remembering what I was taught?"

"I'm impressed," was Raleigh's only comment.

"Let's read," Dutch admonished as he turned his attention back to the journal.

May 25, 1862

We got some news this morning when a man from here on the farm got back from a secret meeting of Tories at John Taylors house down in the mountains of Winston County. Sunny sent him to report on what is going on down there. Judge John Penn gave a speech to a lot of people who were there and he said that they just wanted to be left alone and stay neutral. They are attempting to force our people to fight in the Confederate army. He said that the people of Winston County, rather than to be forced to fight for the perpetuation of slavery in the Confederate army, will abandon neutrality and join and fight for the Union army. Tom Pink Curtis, the probate Judge, then spoke and said that he wanted everyone to understand him and that he surely wanted everyone to obey the law but the law of the United States is one thing and the law of the Confederacy is another. He said that he believed that the large majority of people in Winston County never wanted to be a part of the Confederacy and they have the constitutional rights to follow the dictates of their conscience. He quoted from the Alabama Constitution that says in article 1 paragraph 4 that no human authority ought, in any case whatsoever, to control or interfere with the rights of conscience. Under 'Militia' in paragraph 2 it says that any person who scruples to bear arms will not be compelled to do so. He says that a person should follow the dictates of his conscience and if he wants to join the Confederate army he should be allowed to, if he wants to join the Union army he should be allowed to, and if he wants to remain neutral he should be left alone and the Alabama Constitution makes that plain. That is the way that I feel too. He said that if an attempt is made to carry out the threats of Stoke Roberts he thinks that a lot of citizens will go enlist in the Union army that is in the Tennessee River Valley. He said that he thinks that the attempt to secede and establish the Confederacy will come to naught because the world's sentiment is strongly opposed to the indefinite perpetuation of slavery. After he gave that talk they made resolutions and the man that Sunny sent down there wrote them down. I am going to copy them in here so as to keep them.

1. Let us be loyal to the principles adopted at the Looney's Tavern meeting, on July 4, 1861 which was one of neutrality; that is, left alone by outsiders.

2. Let us follow the dictates of conscience and obey the law.

3. Let each one keep a good loaded gun and hunt game quite a lot.

4. While we regret the circumstances, which resulted in the death of Joe Clack, we affirm that it is the duty of the men to protect the women and innocent infants in the log cabin homes and elsewhere in accordance with the law and conscience under the Constitution.

5. If the Confederate agents invade the county and attempt to force our citizens to leave their homes and county to go and fight for the Confederacy, and that against the dictates of one's conscience, this, in our opinion would justify our citizens in abandoning their position of neutrality. In that case, it would be up to the citizens of the county-individually and collectively- to take whatever action they deem necessary for their safety and security.

6. If the threat be carried out, or if, and when the

attempt is made to force us into the Confederate service, each one will have to use his best judgment to defeat the agent and escape being captured. If captured, the "Dock" Spain method to obtain release is hereby recommended, and you all know what "Dock" Spain did to procure the release of Elijah Sutherland, on last Monday. It succeeded in a great way and we think that it would again.

7. Should the confederate agents succeed in forcing some of our citizens into the Confederate service against their convictions we recommend the following, to wit.

(A) Desert and come home, if conscience dictates, join the Union army.

(B) We recommend that for each person forced into the Confederate army against the dictates of his conscience that two people volunteer and enlist in the Union army, if their conscience approves.

(C) That if the Confederate agents kill any of our citizens in attempting to carry out the threat of Roberts, the one who perpetrated the crime be punished the same way and extent.

8. In closing, we stress the following. Let us all be careful. Let us keep our ears and eyes open, and close our lips and hold our tongues. Do this at all times, and especially when the enemy and the unfriendly are near.

♦

"It so happens that I read an article written by Peter Gossett that explains the 'Dock' Spain method that Sarah copied from the report of the meeting." Raleigh tried to fill in the blanks of questions which the report might have created. "The Home Guard had captured some men from Winston County and was taking them to conscript them into the Confederate Army.

'Dock' Spain shot one of their horses in the rear which caused such excitement that the ones they had tried to conscript escaped. Joe Clack, with others, went to the home of Joe and Martha Comeens to conscript Joe into the Confederate Army. Joe was not at home, but Martha, who was pregnant at the time, was there. They confronted her in such a way as to cause her to have a miscarriage. Joe Clack later returned and stole a suit of clothes that was being prepared for the baby. When this happened, Martha's brothers, Tom and Bill Barker hunted down Joe Clack and killed him. That's the story there."

June 15, 1862

We got news from down in Winston County that a real bad thing happened last Sunday. I was not going to do no more writing for a while but I want to write this down now just to show what is going on down in the mountains where mom and daddy were born and lived before the white man ran them off. Last Sunday morning a man named Wash Curtis, Sunny says that his whole name is George Washington Curtis but they called him Wash for short, was hid out and slept under a bluff because he heard that the Home Guard was after him because he would not join the Rebel army. His brother, Tom Pink Curtis who is the Probate Judge in Winston County had heard that a bunch of them Rebels who was rounding up every man between 18 and 35 years old, and some younger and some older, to join the Confederate army, were after Wash and was going to kill him. The news Papa Joe got was that Wash was hiding out under a rock bluff in the woods and he went turkey hunting early Sunday and then went to his house to get food for himself and his horse and to see his 3 week old baby granddaughter. They told Papa Joe that the last thing that Wash got to do was to see his new granddaughter who was sleeping when he got there. He was hugging and kissing the baby girl when Wash's wife told him that she heard the Home Guard a coming. He jumped on his horse to get away but he spurred it too hard and it reared up and went in circles. The men had come from Eldridge in Walker County and lived in Walker and Fayette and Marion Counties and were not even from Winston County where Wash lived. They shot him dead right in front of his wife and daughter. When they did this, Wash's mother fainted and they had to tend to her. It is all a story that is hard to believe that there are people like this in this state. I told Sunny that I did not know who the Home Guards are and he said that they are a group of older men who are too old to fight in the Confederate army. He said that they were organized to go around and get supplies for the Confederate army but they have turned into thugs who are going around robbing and killing people. He said that the Confederate army is also paying people they call Enlistment Officers whose job it is to round up all men of eligible age and send them to fight the Yankees. Then there are the Partisan Rangers who are military men who assist the Home Guard and Enlisting Officers in doing their work of getting the new soldiers to the front lines where, Sunny says, they will be shot and killed for the rich men who want no part of the fighting. That is the kind of war that this is and it aint going to get no better. There has been a lot of rain this year and it has made the mosquitoes worse than I have ever seen because of all the standing water. The puddles are full of them little wiggle tails that make into mosquitoes, so I figure they will be bad all year. It is hard to stay outside long without getting a lot of mosquito bites and the flies are real bad too. I think about things like mosquito bites and think that they are bad but then I think that they sure aint as bad as getting hit by bullets. The soldiers not only have to dodge bullets but they have to stay out in the open all the time with the mosquitoes and flies and snakes and they don't have enough to eat or the right kind of clothes but there aint nothing that they can do about it. When it is hot like it is now they have to stand the heat and when it is cold they freeze. It puts me to mind about the place where I was born where there wasn't no way to stay out of the way of snakes and insects so you will never hear me complain about the way I get to live today. I have it good and I am thankful. I just hope that we do not lose it all in this war and it aint right that so many are not only losing everything they own but their lives too and that is what is happening in this war. I think about all this too much and I write about it too often so I think that I should not write so much.

♦

CHAPTER 18

◆

Sarah made good on her decision to halt her writings until occasions when there were news or events that she considered worthy of an entry in her journal. It took a holiday event to motivate her to open her journal again and take pen in hand.

July 6, 1862

Last Friday was Independence Day but the 4th of July don't mean what it used to. What with this country all tore apart by this war it don't seem to make no difference that we once had a country called the United States but now there is nothing but the Disunity States. Sunny says that the news is that there was fighting going on almost all the time in this country last month with people getting killed all over the place. I said that I just want to write about good things and we had a good day Friday when Papa Joe said that we were going to celebrate the Fourth of July just like we always have done. Daddy and Sunny killed a young steer and a hog and got the meat ready to cook. We had some fresh corn and vegetables and the women cooked up a feast for everyone on the farm. The children played games while most of the grown folks sat around and ate and talked. Sunny and Papa Joe don't go to Florence as often now as they did before the war because they say that there aint much to buy no longer. The price of things has gone way up because it is so hard to get goods and keep them on the shelves. Papa Joe was thinking ahead when he saw all of this coming and stockpiled in that secret storage area salt and sugar and a lot of the other things that is now hard to get. He grows most of everything else that we need. Another reason that they don't go more often is because they just dont want to be around those people who can't do nothing but talk about how the south is going to whip those Yankees and send them back up North with their tails tucked between their legs. There still aint no newspaper being printed so he can't get back no news of what is going on in the war. The holiday made me think about this country and the shape that it is in. I think all the time about our Cherokee people who they sent off to Oklahoma. I wonder how they are making out during this war and if they are trying to make them fight for this country that has been so cruel to them. We don't have many red skinned people on the farm here because they made them leave here and only the ones who suffered in order to stay here are left in Alabama. I write mostly about black people because it is them that were made to stay here to do all the hard work. The only Cherokees that are here are Sunbeam, mom and dad, me and Hannah. Sunny is half Cherokee so he counts too. I am proud to be Cherokee and will try to pass this pride on to my children if me and Sunny have any. The way that I figure it they would be two-thirds Cherokee. This was something that I was thinking about to get my mind off the war so I wanted to write it down.

♦

Sarah had been writing mostly about the plight of the Negro slaves, and she apparently was reminded of the ordeal her people had gone through only about two decades before that. The Fourth of July holiday apparently caused her to think about the things that the red people and black people had already endured in the young nation.

August 10, 1862

I have been saying that the only times I would write again would be when I had something good to write about. The war is still going strong with fighting going on last month in Virginia and Arkansas and Tennessee so that aint anything good to write about. But I am writing now because I found out last week that I am going to be a mother. Me and Sunny are all excited about that and it is a good time to be expecting to have a baby because there is not as much work to do here on the farm as in most years because we are not growing much but food for us and our animals and to give to the needy. There were some men from the Confederate army who came here in the spring and asked Papa Joe if he would plant some navy beans and potatoes and other food to help supply the Confederate army but Papa Joe told them that he had already planned to let his land rest a year like the Bible says that God told Moses to do and he thought that it would be the best thing to do for him to let his land rest since the governor had said not to plant not one seed of cotton or anything else except for one's own use. He told them that he planned to do just what the governor said for farmers to do and he allowed that it would be good to grow a little extra to help the families of the men who are away fighting as they are not at home to help provide for their wives and kids. He told them Confederate people that a lot of their soldiers are getting hurt or killed or captured and many of them are coming down with typhoid and dysentery and other sickness and their families need someone to help feed them. Papa Joe reminded them that he is a Methodist preacher and he wants to help the needed like the Bible say that a good Christian is supposed to do. They told him that the soldiers needed food and he told them that they did not need it any worse than their wives and kids do and that he would not be growing food to feed the troops. He reminded them that he did not start the war and whoever did should have plans for all that was needed before they started shooting at one another. They brought up that he and Sunny should be out on the battlefields helping fight the war and Papa Joe told them that he had more than twenty slaves just like those big plantation owners in South Alabama and if they could stay on their farms that he could too. He said that Sunny also had that many slaves and he needed to stay to help grow food for the needy families. They did not like what he said but they knew that there wasn't nothing that they could do about it. Papa Joe didn't say anything about Woody and I think that they have forgot about him right now. Woody is still here doing the doctoring and helping Abram and Ida with their mongoloid child but he is really not needed that much cause Rufus is doing fine but it is an excuse he can use if he ever needs it, and I spect that he will before the war is over. I started this writing today by telling about the baby that I am expecting. I started being sick in the mornings and so I went to Woody and told him that I thought that there might be something wrong with me. I was scared because there has been a lot of that bloody flux and typhoid and dysentery going around and especially with the men in the army and since Woody is studying to be a doctor I went to him and told him what was wrong. He asked me a few questions and then he said "I think that you might be carrying a little one in your tummy that is already causing you problems." That had not crossed my mind since I have been so busy thinking about this damnable war but when he told me that, I knew that he was probably right. I could not wait to tell Sunny and he is all excited about it. He says that he does not care whether it is a boy or a girl he just hopes that it gets here in good health. Ever since Abram and Ida had that mongoloid child it puts you to thinking that our child might be born with something wrong with it.

◆

"I don't like the use of that word, 'mongoloid', but that is what they called the deformity, if I may characterize it as such, back then. Today it is called Down syndrome, and there are some special children who were born with it," Jenny commented. "I graduated from Auburn and am a War Eagle fan, but a coach from the University of Alabama comes to mind. Gene Stallings had a son named John Mark who had Down syndrome. He was very special and everyone loved him. He died a few years ago, but he is not forgotten. Faulkner University in Montgomery even named their football field after him because he was so special. He, of course, is not the only one; it seems that most children with Down syndrome are adorable individuals and are very special people! Their life expectancy is not as long as the normal person, which is sad, but their lives are a special delight that brighten up the lives of those around them."

August 24, 1862

I am writing again because I learned a secret that Papa Joe and Sunny have been keeping for some time now, I don't know how long but that don't matter. I learned it only because they need my help along with mom and dad to keep it going. Sunny has been seeing Bill Looney from Winston County who is helping the Yankees in this war. He is the one who has been telling Sunny things like the secret meeting at John Taylor's house and the killing of Wash Curtis. Just as I suspected, whenever the gunboats first came up the river and shelled Florence, some of our blacks talked with some of the Federal navy men and told them that the owners of the farm here were not for the south's breakaway from the Union and were certainly against the Confederates going to war. Since that time Sunny and Papa Joe have secretly been meeting with Yankee spies and helping them out as much as they can. Well, the reason that I am writing this is because Sunny says, just as I suspected, that we have turned the secret hideaway that is under the bridge in the pasture into a safe place for the Union spies to stay and for the ones people are calling Tories who are hiding out from the Enlisting Officers and the Home Guards. It was first used to hide out mom and dad and Woody and me from the Federal troops who wanted to take us to Oklahoma and then we used it as a hideaway for the Underground Railroad whenever there were slaves that where running away from their abusive masters. Ever since Papa Joe built a house for mom and daddy and one for Aunt Hannah, the hideaway had been empty cept when Abram and Ida and Sylvester and Nancy and their children lived in it for a while before they got their houses built. Sunny says that it is the perfect place to hide out the ones who need it now because of the war. He said that we will have to be real careful of who uses it because they don't want no Rebel spies to bluff their way into it so they can find out what is going on. Only the ones that are certain not to be Rebel spies will be able to use it. He says that the Federal people that they help have to bring verification from their commanding officers that they are who they say that they are. Sunny wants for momma and daddy and me to keep the hideaway ready to use whenever it is needed. I know that when I write this down that I have to be real careful to keep this book hid real good cause don't no Confederate people need to read it or else all this won't be a secret any longer and we will all be in a lot of trouble. I have a good hiding place in the cellar vault where I can keep it but I will probably write in it only when I think that it is safe to do so.

◆

September 21, 1862

After church was over today I came to the Cellar Vault and got this book to write in. I aint wrote none for about three weeks now because I aint had much to write about and I got this book hid so that it is hard to get. I have been trying to think of a better hiding place that aint so hard to get to but I am afraid that it might get took If I don't hide it really good. I don't have as many sick mornings as I was having the last time I wrote and I think that the baby is doing fine and growing because I am beginning to show at my belly. Everybody is excited about the baby coming and Papa Joe and Sunbeam say that they have wanted to have a grandchild. Mom and daddy and Aunt Hannah are just as happy as anyone else and say that it will be good to have a new baby in the family. The things that worry me is that there is a war going on and it is not certain what might happen to us and our farm. As I have already wrote, when the conscript law which established the State Militia was passed they allowed for the exemption of people working in certain types of industries and occupations and for those people who had twenty or more slaves. Sunny says that this is positive proof that this is a rich man's war and a poor man's fight but he is going to use that to stay out of the fighting. He says that Papa Joe first said that he was going to claim twenty slaves and let Sunny have twenty but he got to thinking about it and changed his mind. He says that he is too old to go to war and that he don't need to claim no slaves cause they can't make him go nohow. If Flash still lived here he would have let him have half of the slaves but since he lives in Kentucky he don't need any slaves to keep him out of the Confederate army. The state of Kentucky is neutral in this war and, I am told, is under Federal control so he is in a good place with this war going on. Because of this Papa Joe is going to let Sunny claim twenty of the slaves and the Enlisting Officers and Home Guard can't do a thing about it. Since there are more than forty blacks here on the farm he says that for the purpose of the war that he is going to divide up the farm and let Woody claim twenty of them. He says that he has a lawyer friend in Florence who is against the war too and he had him draw up some papers that made it all legal. Papa Joe says that you have to take what they give you and it would be crazy not to take advantage of that part of the conscript law since those rich land owners in South Alabama are doing the same thing. Since the Yankees are in control of the river and valley here, Sunny says that it would also be crazy not to get them on our side so as not to let the Confederate people run over us and take what we have. The word is that down in Winston County the Home Guard is trying to make all the men of the age suitable for war sign up with the Confederate army and if they refuse they will kill them. Things are getting real bad down there and a lot of men are hiding out to keep the guard from getting them and make them go off to fight the Yankees. If they don't go then they get a warning that they will get shot. It is causing a lot of trouble for a lot of families and Sunny says that he is going to help those that they are called Tories to hide in a safe place. If we had done that for Wash Curtis he would be alive today so I figure that we are doing a good deed just to provide a place where those people like Wash can be safe until they get to the Federal side of the war. That is why we are keeping the hideaway ready and we have it where there are a lot of bunks to sleep in and food to feed them. Sunny says that we have made it into a dormitory for war purposes. Since it is hid real good there won't any of the rebels know about it. We didn't grow no cotton this year and the Confederate Government won't let you sell corn without getting a license from the Probate Judge and then the profit can't be more than twenty percent so Papa Joe says that he don't need the money and he is not going to sell a grain of his corn this year. He has grown a lot of vegetables and food stuff and has taken a lot of corn and had it ground into meal and has raised a lot of beef and pork and has chickens and eggs and cows to milk so he says that it won't be no problem in feeding whoever might come here. The main thing is to keep all this a secret away from the Rebels who would try to hurt or kill us if they found out what we are doing.

♦

October 12, 1862

A lot has been going on since the last time that I wrote. First there was some excitement because there was a woman spy for the Yankees that stopped by here when she was on her way to somewhere. It was all a secret and I didn't ask no questions. She stayed in the hideaway for a couple of days and then she was gone. I don't know where she came from or where she went. All I know about her is that her name is Elizabeth Van Lew. I suppose she would not be a very good spy if people knew a whole lot about her. Sunny has had Bill Looney here and they have been working to keep everything in place to help the Tories who don't want to do no killing in this war that is going on. They have been secretly meeting with the Yankee commanders and they have agreed that Bill and whoever is with him can enter their lines without getting shot. They have worked out a signal that will let the Yankees know who they are and can know that they are not the enemy. The Yankees are going to let all the Tories join up with them in the army that want to and if they don't want to fight, which most of them don't, they can go up north to work in the factories or hospitals and some of them might help in moving supplies and guns and ammunition to the soldiers who are doing the fighting, or work fixing roads and railroads. Most of them say that they don't want to be shooting and killing men in the Confederate army who are made to do the fighting that they don't want to do, so they will be busy doing other things to stay out of the battles. Sunny says that he don't consider these people to be cowards but they are people who want to stay peaceful and he says that is exactly how he feels. Bill Looney and a man named Woodruff Miles came here and said that they have got a lot of Tories and people that the Rebels call Mossbacks hid out in the woods and caves in Winston and Marion and Franklin and Lawrence and Fayette Counties and they are fighting back against the Enlisting Officers and the Home Guard men. Bill Looney had a tavern in Winton County but the Home Guard burned it down and every building that he had because he is helping the Yankees out in the war. He says that he will do everything that he can do to see that the Enlisting Officers don't have their way in making all the men go fight the Yankees that don't want to go. Sunny got with Bill and Woodruff and they got with a Yankee General named Dodge and worked out a plan to get the men to the Yankee's side that wanted to go. Since the Federal army now control all the valley here on the Tennessee River all they have to do is to get them past the Rebel pickets that are looking for them and on to the Yankee's side. There is still an old trail coming up this way from that area which is called the Freedom Trail because it was used by slaves on the Underground Railroad. The trail is pretty much growed up now but Sunny says that is better because nobody will suspect that it is being used and it was a secret trail anyway. Sunny says that General Dodge told them to bring as many as want to come and Bill Looney said that he would bring him all that he can get and he thought that would be a lot cause there are a lot of men who are against what the Confederate States has done after they let them know that they were against it to start with. Sunny showed them the hideaway that we have got ready to hide out whoever might be needed to be hid in if the Rebel troops come into this area. The Yankees have control of the river but they are away fighting somewhere else most of the time and this is still Alabama and a Confederate state and the Conscript laws apply here just like they do everywhere else in the Confederacy. The hideaway will be needed and we will use it until it aint needed no more.

♦

"I had never thought about that before." Dutch was thinking about the last comment that they had read in the journal. "There was a Conscript Law which applied to every male between the ages of eighteen and thirty-five which included all of Alabama. Yankees came into the state early in the war and captured and controlled this section of the state in the Tennessee River Valley. The Enlisting Officers, Rebels, Home Guards, Partisan Rangers, or whatever they were called, were to round up every eligible man and send him off to fight in the war. I wonder how hard they tried, or how effective they were in getting the men in Alabama who lived in Yankee occupied territory, like the farm here, to enlist.

"Were they able to carry out their terror tactics here in the valley like they did in the mountains across the river from here? Did the Yankees keep enough troops here to prevent that from happening when they were fully engaged in battles in Mississippi and so many other places? After capturing the cities here in the valley, I am sure that they kept some troops in them, but was there any who were scattered throughout the countryside to prevent the Enlisting Officers from doing their job? Who did the citizens of the towns which were controlled by the Federal Army side with, the Rebels or the Yankees? Reading this has raised questions in my mind which I never had considered before."

"Those are good questions," Raleigh replied. "I'm not sure I could answer them. Considering the reaction from the citizens in Florence when Fort Sumter was captured, there were a lot of the town's people there who were backing the Confederates, unlike the ones south of there who were in opposition to them. The *Florence Gazette* was certainly on the side of the Confederates. We saw, as we read the newspapers from the box, that the *Gazette* resumed publication before the year was over in a limited way. I understand that it did not take long after they resumed publishing the paper that the Yankee troops shut it down for good and either destroyed or moved the printing equipment, and it was years before Florence got another newspaper. Considering this, I would say that it may have been possible, but questionable, that the Enlisting Officers could have operated to some extent in the area here, with probably a lot of assistance from the citizens. Yeah, Dutch, those are interesting questions."

The journal page was turned to the next date's entry.

October 26, 1862

Sunny has talked to Bill Looney some more and he tells about some of the bad things that the Home Guards are doing to the people of Winston and Marion and Fayette and some surrounding Counties. It is hard for me to believe that there can be people like that in this world. Some of the leaders of the Home Guards got together at Mitchell's Forte which they say is in Marion County and talked about how it had got dangerous to round up the Tories and make them join the Confederate army. They came up with a plan to give the men between 18 and 35 years old a warning and if they didn't report within five days they would be considered to be traitors to the Confederate Government and they would be shot. He named Al Gibson and Ham Carpenter as the leaders in Marion County where that happened. Then he named Ben Humphries with Squire Musgrove and George Harris from Fayette County as being part of that meeting. After that they started killing the people that they called Tories who did not do what they told them to do. They killed a man named Newt Austin near Nauvoo which is in Walker County close to Winston County. They killed another man called Mr. Pugh near Double Springs in Winston County. There was a man in Marion County named Charles Cagle who had hid out in the woods but the Home Guards found him and killed him and his family found his body under a bluff and it was filled with bullet holes. It looked like that they had used him for target practice. He told about men like Stoke Roberts and Jim Beckner in Walker County who led a bunch of renegades who picked up a man for not going to fight the Yankees like they wanted him to do and they put him in jail in Jasper. When his daddy and brother went to see him in jail he was not there. They looked for him for two days before they found him dead. They had kept him in jail for five days and he still refused to go fight for the Confederate army so they put a toe-sack over his head and shot him seven times between where his galluses crossed on his overalls and then they throwed his body in a ditch. Sunny told Mr. Looney that it is that kind of things that makes him happy that he is helping to provide a safe place for those men who just want to stay out of the war that they didn't start or want to have anything to do with. Mr. Looney told of some more killings that I will write about later but I have to stop writing today.

◆

"I told you earlier that I read the book written by Wesley Thompson titled *Tories of the Hills*," Raleigh spoke as he thought about the journal entry that he had just read. "It was a good while ago when I read the book, but I remember that he mentioned some of the same things that Sarah was writing about. After reading that, it's something you won't soon forget. Such actions on the part of the Home Guards only strengthened the resolve of the Tories to resist their efforts to enlist those who did not want to fight the Yankees. They organized and began to fight back, starting their own little war which the Tories in the Warrior Mountains eventually won. Well, no one wins in a situation like that, especially the dead and their families."

"I would enjoy a glass of iced tea," Dutch looked at his wife as he suggested that she get them a beverage. "We need to stop and let me rest my eyes for a few minutes. This is old writings on old paper and sometimes it is difficult for me to read as fast as you."

The group stood and stretched their legs while Abigail served the tea.

CHAPTER 19

———◆———

After drinking their beverages and resting their eyes for a few minutes, they all were ready to read more of the journal.

November 9, 1862

For a while back in the summer I didn't write none for a while because everything was bad news what with the war going on like it is but whenever I found out that I was going to have a baby I decided that I would write about every other week. I aint said much about the baby I am carrying but I am still getting bigger so I suppose that it is growing and doing well. I aint said much about the war either but there have been a lot of battles with some big ones at Bull Run in Virginia on the last days of August which they said that the South won and another big one in Maryland on September 17 at Sharpsburg on Antietam Creek where they said that there were a lot of soldier hurt and killed and they don't really know who got the best of the fighting there. Sunny said that the word he got when he went to Florence was that when they counted up the killed and wounded that there were more than 22,000 of them with the Yankees losing more men than the Rebels. It was the first battle that has been fought on Union soil but Sunny says that it won't be the last. In August there was a battle in Virginia at Cedar Mountain plus a lot more, one in Louisiana at Baton Rouge, some more in Missouri, a bunch in Virginia, and one at Richmond Kentucky. There have been so many more in September and October that I would be wasting my time and paper trying to write about them all if I even knew anything about them. As I have said before, we have enough going on around here without worrying about stuff that is happening in other states. We was hoping that there would not be any of them Enlisting Officers that are still around here but there is word that they have been up here on this side of the river going after men of age to go to war. Papa Joe says that he expects that we might see some of them before long and he is getting everything ready to hide out men so the Enlisting Officers won't know just who all is here. He has been in touch with General Dodge on the Yankees side and General Dodge said that he would send some troops to stay around here if we are afraid. Papa Joe said that might cause suspicion and give away what he is doing to help the Federal troops so he turned that down. General Dodge says that he needs as many people as he can get to help him on the railroads and he said that he will take any of the men that don't want to get in no fights and they can work on the railroads in Mississippi that they captured but was torn up when the Confederate soldiers moved out.

♦

"Sarah talked about General Dodge, but I don't know who he was or what connection he would have in sheltering the men escaping the Home Guard," Abigail wondered.

"I don't know much, but I can say a little about the man," Raleigh ventured to inform his mother-in-law. "His name was Grenville Dodge, but I know very little about his early life other than that he called Council

Bluff, Iowa his hometown. The reason that I know this is because he served as a United States Representative from that area. Another reason that I am familiar with the name is because he was the person shaking hands with Samuel Montague in the center of the famous picture of the Golden Spike Ceremony at the completion of the Transcontinental Railroad. The story goes that when he was escaping a war party in the Black Hills of Wyoming while working for the Union Pacific Railroad, he realized that his escape route was suitable for a pass to build the railroad through the hills. He was promoted to the position of Chief Engineer for Union Pacific and was responsible for the completion of the railroad to the West Coast.

"As for his involvement in the Civil War, this was before his work for Union Pacific, although he was involved in the railroad business before the war. At the beginning of the war, he joined the Union Army and was sent to fight in Arkansas at the battle of Pea Ridge in March of 1862. He was wounded in that battle and as a result, he was appointed to Brigadier General of Volunteers and placed in command of the District of Mississippi involved in protecting and building the railroad in the Mississippi District. This is why he was the person whom Bill Looney and his helpers contacted to assist the Tories who were escaping the Enlisting Officers and Home Guard.

"I think that I read somewhere that later in the war he joined Sherman's army in Atlanta and fought with him there. In the Siege of Atlanta, he reportedly played a critical role in the Battle of Ezra Church in July 1864, in Fulton County, Georgia. He was later shot in the head by a Confederate sharpshooter during the siege while he was looking through an eyehole in the Union breastworks, but he survived this wound also. After the war, he resigned his military position and went to work for the Union Pacific Railroad. That is the extent of what I know about the man."

"She also talked about the Battle of Sharpsburg, which is normally called the Battle of Antietam today," Jenny entered the conversation. "One of the few things that I remember about the Civil War is that the battle there was the bloodiest in the history of our country. The total number of casualties on both sides was said to be around 22,717. The Northern Army's casualties were 12,401 and the Southern Army's count was 10,316. On the Northern side, there were 2,108 killed, 9,540 wounded, and 753 captured or missing. The Southern side had 1,546 killed, 7,752 wounded, and 1,018 captured or missing. Those numbers stick in my mind because I studied them in a history class at Auburn, and the teacher thought that it was important enough for us to learn them that we were told it might be on a test. I spent the time to learn them and then they were not on the test, which sort of hacked me off, although I must admit that it did make me think about how bad the fighting and loss of life really was in the Civil War."

"You two have really filled me in on what I was wondering," Abigail spoke once again. "I'm surprised that you know that much, and that explains the role of General Dodge in the activities which Sarah is writing about. She had more to say so we should read some more."

November 23, 1862

Sunny says that the report from down in Winston County is that the Confederate army is so hard up for solders that they are making every man that they can find sign up and go off to war. It don't matter how old a man is, if he can walk they say that he has to go fight. Bill says that Chris Sheets was elected once again as the Representative to the State Legislature in Montgomery and when he went back this month they expelled him from the Legislature and throwed him back in jail and called it treason. He had not been out of prison long because they had put him in jail the first time he went down there to represent the people of Winston County. He was elected by the people of Winston County by a big majority over Judge Parker and still the State throws him in jail. Bill says that Jonathan Barton who went with Chris Sheets and Willis Farris to Montgomery wrote Tom Pink Curtis and Tom Gartman, who was the father of Chris's girlfriend at that time, and the folks of Winston County, a letter last Wednesday, which he just got Friday, telling what had happened. Bill said that he took the time to sit down and copy the letter so the people in Winston County could see what is going on with our people that we elect. He is here now and asked me if I would write out another copy so that we could have one. I will stop writing now and copy that letter for Bill. I just might copy it twice so that he can have an extra one. School is still in session and I will be teaching tomorrow so I think that I will help Bill now and finish this later. I will try to write this letter out in this book tomorrow so as to keep it.

♦

November 25, 1862

I didn't have time to do no writing yesterday because we had to get the students to help tote up some wood for the heater in the schoolhouse as it has done got cold but I let them out a little early today because I wanted to get this letter wrote in my book. I will write it just like he brought it to me. This is the third time that I have copied it and it makes me very unhappy every time because of what they are doing to a man that the people elected to be their voice in Montgomery.

Montgomery, Alabama
November 19th, 1862

Mr. Tom Gartman
Houston, Alabama

Dear John and Folks of Winston County,

It is with regret that I assign myself the task of writing you because I know that you are going to be greatly disturbed when you hear of the criticalness of events here in the State Legislature.

When Chris Sheets appeared in the Chamber of the joint session, he was greeted with boos and jeers from those present until it seemed an eternity of bedlam had broken out.

Chris was very calm and possessed all the time. He continued waving and smiling to the whole audience as long as it lasted. Finally when the speaker had restored order, the Chairman of the Committee of Credentials, asked him if he had been duly elected. Chris told him that according to the due process of law that had been in operation throughout the duration of the war he had received a majority of votes in the county and was looked upon by the people as being the duly elected official to represent them in their State body. They then asked Chris what his attitude was toward secession and the Confederate States and Chris told them that it was the same as it had been from the first.

At this, the members of the Legislature pounced upon

him with the viciousness of a pack of hyenas and actually, I thought they had beaten and torn him to pieces. At last, I saw a bunch of them dragging him from the chamber. He had lost his hat and shoes and his coat was gone. His suspenders were dragging on the floor and his shirt was ripped open to the tail. Willis Farris and I followed them till we could see what they were doing with him and saw them throw him like a dog, into jail. They called it arresting him but it was nothing short of brutal violence.

Then the Legislature went through a sham pretense of expelling Chris from the body, on what they claimed was treason and punishable by death.

I haven't got to talk with him since they threw him in jail to see how he is getting along. But a Negro attendant at the jail told me that he thought the man was pretty sick.

We are hoping that they will remain quiet and that there will not be any lynching. They have been threatening him though, and I shouldn't be surprised for it to happen.

If you people there could get the people of the adjoining counties to appeal to the State Legislature in his behalf, it might spare him.

We will try to stay here and see how things go and write you about them when we can.

I hope that there have not been any killings in Winston by the home-guards since we left. Good Luck and pray for us.

Very truly yours,
Jonathan Barton.

When you read this you can see why Tom Gartman and Bill Looney wants everybody to see a copy so that they can know what is going on in Montgomery with the

Confederates in control. This is no way that a civilized nation should act and I am proud that Papa Joe and Sunny does not support this kind of violence. I think that those people in Montgomery are fools to start with if they think that they can whip the Yankees who are already showing that they will pretty well do what they want to with the Southern army before it is all over. They have already took everything they wanted in this part of the state. Bill said that he is here because Tom Gartman wanted him to leave that day to take a copy of the letter to Colonel Streight or General Sherman or General Thomas and see if the Yankees can do something to get him out of jail. I suspect that the Confederate people in Montgomery are going to meet their match if one of them Yankee Generals gets involved in this.

◆

November 30, 1862

This is the last day of the month and I just wrote some Tuesday   but there is so much going on now that I will try to write every week if I can. Before Bill Looney left Sunday to take that letter to General Thomas who is in Huntsville he told about some more of the killings that the Home Guard is doing in the mountains where mom and daddy came from. I have already told about Newt Austin getting killed, Bill said that they hung him before they shot and killed him. Another man named Mitch Kanidy was killed by the Home Guard after he ran to try to get away from them. They said that he was shot so many times that his guts was running out of his stomach. Sunny says that the Home Guard is killing every man that won't enlist in the Confederate army. He says that they will catch a lot of them and first give them five days to join up with the Rebels. They are arresting them and putting them in the Stamford Prison which is an old log house that they have built to use for a prison. It is in Marion County close to Mitchell Forte and the word is that it is dirty and crowded and they are just about starving men to death that they have in there. Bill Looney says that the Rebels are after him but he stays away from where they done burned his tavern down cause they would catch and kill him. He talks about men like Stoke Roberts and Ham Carpenter and says that they had just as soon kill a man as tell him howdy. They are causing terror wherever they go throughout the hills and counties around Winston County and people are afraid of them. Woodruff Miles and Lum Thunderburk have already led over 200 men to Decatur to join up with the Union army. Bill says that they are working up an Alabama Union Cavalry and a Colonel Spencer will be over them. Papa Joe said that he got word that he needed to be more careful because they pulled most of the Yankees troops from the valley here to go up and fight with General Bragg when he invaded Kentucky. He says that this really opens up the way for the Rebels to do whatever they want to do around here.

♦

"Sarah hadn't told the half of it yet!" Raleigh weighed in on the actions that were Sarah's concern regarding the senseless bloodbath that the Home Guards were inflicting on the Tories. "The Home Guards in Winston, Marion, Fayette, and even Franklin and Lawrence counties, intended to exterminate every man in those counties who did not, after giving him five days, sign up to join the Confederate Army. They waged a war of their own, and there were numbers of men that they killed, many of them in a form of torture.

"At the ending of the year of 1862, there was a brief pause in their slaughters because they wanted to get their candidate, Nathan Parker, a former Probate Judge of Winston County, elected to represent Winston

County as State Representative. They thought that if the Home Guard was less active, they would have a better chance of winning the election. When Chris Sheets won by a landslide, they resumed their butchery. In the spring of 1863, the Home Guard, assisted by the Partisan Rangers, was very active again. From what I have heard and Wesley Thompson and others have written about, there were some slaughters involving torture so horrendous that I don't understand how any human could carry out such hideous acts. I could describe some of those slaughters that happened after Sarah wrote these entries we have just read, but she may do it for me, so let's keep reading."

December 7, 1862

We are busy hiding out people who want to stay out of the war and away from the Home Guard that are looking for them. Sometimes they need a place to hide while they are on their way to join up with the Yankees. The Federal troops have pretty much taken over this valley so we have not had much trouble here on the farm from the Confederates but there has been a lot of trouble in the Warrior Mountains. They took most of the Federal troops out from here to go with General Bragg to invade Kentucky so they asked that we help hide out the ones who come up with Bill Looney from the area of Winston County. We have an old black man named Sampson who is helping Papa Joe in hiding out the ones that Bill brings in. Sampson was made to go to Oklahoma as a slave when the Cherokees were run out of the state. Now they made a lot of slaves go on that march to Oklahoma so as to do a lot of the work and my Aunt Hannah was made to go too because she was Cherokee. While they were walking all the way to Oklahoma, Sampson helped Aunt Hannah out a lot and she says that she thinks that she would have died if Sampson had not helped her. After they got there they ran away and came back here by using the Underground Railroad so Sampson knows how to hide people out because he did that. They use the river to keep what they are doing a secret. The blacks here on the farm are doing a lot of fishing and trapping and staying on the river a lot. Whenever there is somebody to be hid out they meet them on the south side of the river and dress them like they are fisherman. They put them in a boat and make like they are running gill nets or trot lines but they go bring them across the river and lead them up to the secret hideaway. They stay there until they can move them to where the Yankee's are. It is working out real good and we hadn't had no problems and I hope that it stays that way. The soldiers that left here went up to fight in Kentucky and they had a big battle at Perryville and Sunny says that it depends on who you talk to as to who was the winner and he says that the troops will probably be up there a while longer since they were not able to do everything they wanted to do. That fight was on or about the 8th of October so maybe we will know soon when they might get back which will make it easier on us. The war is still going strong with fighting in a lot of states but they hadn't been much fighting going on in Alabama. The Yankees who are in charge of the river valley here have really helped us and General Dodge and General Sherman told Colonel Spencer to use the Alabama Union Calvary to help protect this place if they are needed. Papa Joe still says that he don't want them on the farm here now so as to not cause suspicion as there are a lot of people around who are on the Confederate's side.

◆

December 14, 1862

There is still so much going on around here that I don't have a chance to write about it all. We are excited about the baby coming but there is still a lot of things to think about now beside taking care of a baby. Sunny says that with most of the Yankees gone from here that he has got word that they have started printing the Florence Gazette again but he don't have a copy yet. He says that when he goes back to town that he will get me a copy so I can read what they have to say. Sadie and I are still teaching the children that are here on the farm and they are learning real good. I tell Sadie that I think that it won't be long before all the slaves are freed and then the education that the children that we are teaching will help them to be able to go and do things that no blacks have ever been able to do before but they will need an education to get ahead. Papa Joe has done good by building the school and teaching the ones that have grown up on the farm and he has been doing it since I was a little girl. Some of the ones here about my age that have grown up and went to school here are very smart and I think that if they are freed that they have a chance of getting a good job. Papa Joe says that when the North wins this war that he is going to have a talk with some of these Yankee Generals that he has been helping out and see if there might be some work for them up north and maybe with the government in Washington. He will tell them that they have as good an education as any blacks that they can find in the south and he thinks that some of them from the south ought to be given a chance to do what has always been done by white people. It would make me proud to see some of the ones that I have grown up with, and later some of the ones that I am teaching, to get away from farming and go out and get good jobs just like white people do. Whenever I think about this I also think about the Cherokee people over in Oklahoma and wonder what kind of education the young ones are getting there. I hope that it is enough that they can do good too but I don't think that they will even let them go off the reservations there to work somewhere else which just aint right. We have not seen Bill Looney in a while but Woodruff Miles did come by and give us some news. I wrote about what they did to Chris Sheets in Montgomery and how that Bill Looney took a copy of the letter to General Thomas in Huntsville. Bill said that the General said that he would tend to that and he went and gave General Crook orders to arrest an old man named William McDowell from Huntsville who they say is rich and is a Confederate Major. They found him and arrested him and told the ones that are holding Chris Sheets that if he is killed that they would kill Major McDowell. They said that he would be held as hostage as long as Chris Sheets is in jail. Major McDowell is being held in jail in Huntsville and if somebody kills Chris then he will die too. That is a hard way to do it but things like that happens in war. I am glad that they did that cause if they didn't then they would have killed Chris Sheets. If it is good for one side, it is good for the other one. Sunny says that he is going to go to Florence Saturday and see if he can get a copy of the Gazette and if he does I will write about it next week This is all that I want to write today.

♦

December 21, 1862

Sunny went to Florence yesterday and brought in a copy of last week's Gazette but there weren't much to it. It was only about half the size of what the paper use to be and they just mainly said that they are going to try to put out a paper every week but it will be hard because about everybody that knows anything about putting out a paper is off fighting in the war. They said that because they did not have the help that they needed to put out a full size paper that they would do the best they could with what they have. It says that the price of the paper cost up to four times what it did before the war but everything has gone up about that much. The one thing that they promised that caught my eye was that they will try to get a price current list of goods and chattels, they spelled it chattles but Papa Joe says it is misspelled like a lot of other words are in the paper and should be spelled chattels. Papa Joe says that some of them newspaper folks need to come here and get some schooling cause there are lots of words misspelled and writing errors in the paper and they could take a lesson from some of our blacks who went to school here on the farm. He taught me how to write and he went over everything that I wrote and corrected it. He don't want me to make any mistakes. It is getting close to Christmas time but there is not much to celebrate about seeing as to how the war is so bad. The Confederate supporters have been all excited lately because they said that they won a big victory in Virginia at Fredericksburg but Sunny points out that they have been losing more battles than they are winning. He said that the Yankees won a big battle in Arkansas at Prairie Grove after the Confederates won a smaller one at Cane Hill. A couple of weeks ago there was a little fight in Tennessee at Hartsville where the Confederates did good so that fight and the one at Fredericksburg has got the people all excited and they say that the tide is turning and it won't be long before the South wins this war and sends the Yankees back up north a licking their wounds. It has been going back and forth like this ever since the war started and the Rebels will be excited one day and gloomy the next one when they get war news of another defeat on the battlefield. I try not to keep up with what is going on in the war any more but just enough to know when it might be over cause I am tired of the North and South a fighting one another. We have kept it a secret but we have been hiding out some Federal Spies in the hideaway while General Bragg has most of the troops in Kentucky. Sammy says that we have a Spy Sanctuary here but he hopes that it is not needed long and some more of the Federal troops will be sent back to the valley here to help protect the people who are on their side in the war cause it can be dangerous if there are not many of their solders around. I still keep what I am writing hid real good just in case some of those mean Home Guard men come here. Sunny says that there are other things going on around here but he said it would be best if he not talk it to anybody including me. That is alright by me cause the less I know the better off I am cause there aint nobody that can make me tell anything that I don't know nothing about in case them Home Guard men come around.

"I thought that we would complete our reading today, but I have read just about as much as I can enjoy today." Dutch rubbed his eyes as he spoke. "This is exciting and I am just as anxious as the rest of you to finish this, but I have reached my limit in reading today. I propose we finish this tomorrow. There is not too much left for us to read. The crops are all in, and the ground is wet, so if you will come here for breakfast in the morning we will finish our readings."

All were in agreement.

CHAPTER 20

◆───────────◆

Raleigh and Jenny were at the big plantation house of her parents early the following morning. Angie, the cook for the Riddles, already had a pan of large buttermilk biscuits in the oven when they arrived. It was a simple breakfast of ham, fried eggs, gravy, grits, sorghum syrup with butter, and biscuits, but it was typical of the breakfasts that were served each morning at the Riddles' household. Sometimes there were pork chops, bacon, or sausage served as meat, but the biscuits, gravy, grits, and eggs were pretty well standard fare. After enjoying the meal, the journal was opened and they continued reading.

December 28, 1862

This is the last time that I will write this year as Thursday will be New Year's Day. It has been an awful year with the war going on the whole year and it is sad to think that there are a lot of fine young men who died or were wounded during the year. I know that I have wrote this before but it is what is heavy on my mind that this is all a senseless slaughter caused by a bunch of rich slave owners who are exempted from going to war and getting shot at. I have said it before but It is what they say it is, a rich man's war and a poor man's fight. I thought about this last Thursday when it was Christmas but it didn't seem like Christmas because of everything that is going on. The war has made it to where there aint no Christmas things that are being sold in the stores. Sunny went to Florence to look for some Christmas gifts but said that he could not find anything decent in the stores that would be good to give at Christmas time. The prices of everything that the stores have for sale now are doubled or tripled or more to what they were before the war started. He brought in 2 more Gazette newspapers which were published on the 17th and the 24th and they are still little to what they were before the war. The first one did give a price list of what things are costing now and Sunny says that people can't afford much unless they have a lot of money. He says that the store owners want to be paid in gold or Yankee dollars or else the price is higher if you pay in Confederate money. Papa Joe says that makes a lot of sense since the Yankee Greenback is always going to be good no matter who wins the war cause the northern states are not going anywhere and their money will be good no matter what, the only difference will be that the south will have their own money too. If the Confederates lose the war, which he says they will, then their money will be worthless. He says that just shows how much the merchants really believe that the Confederates will be able to win this war and they think that it won't be long before the Confederate money will be worth no more than the paper it is printed on. Sunny says that we have plenty of gold but there aint no way that he is going to let anyone know about it. He also said that he is not going to take any of that Confederate money for payment cause it is worthless. There was a small article in the paper that said that they wanted to buy several hundred pounds of pork and Papa Joe says that we have several hundred pounds of pork that we can sell but he aint going to take no Confederate money for it. We have a lot of hogs here on the farm that we can kill and the weather is cold enough that we can do that. The newspaper also told about the shortage of salt and Sunny says that if you could find some at the stores that the prices are so high that you could not afford much. Sunny say that Papa Joe was real smart when he bought up all that salt when you could get it and we have plenty of salt to do whatever it is needed for. There is a shortage of pork because the other farmers don't have any salt to put on the meat to keep it from ruining. This is the reason they have to advertise to get several hundred pounds of it. Papa Joe got everybody on the farm here together before Christmas and told them that because of the war that there would be no Christmas gifts but we would have a feast and enjoy the day. It has been in the past that every year he and Sunny would go to town and buy Christmas gifts for everybody, but it was different this year. He says that at least we are all alive and well and that is more than can be said for a lot of men who were alive last Christmas. I just pray that next year will be a better year than this one was.

♦

January 4, 1863

It is a new year and the way that I figure it we should have a baby coming about the middle of March if we stay alive that long. Sunny went back to Florence yesterday and brought back a copy of the Gazette which was published on the day before New Year's. There were two articles in there that we talked about. The first one was about the year 1862 and it says that it shall go to its grave shattered and heart broken. It says that 1862 has left to history a mournful duty and that the south cannot be charged with wanton and cruel misdeeds. What would you call the despicable slaughters that the Home Guards have been carrying out in Winston and Marion and Fayette Counties? I cannot think of anything that would be more wanton and cruel than what they are doing to the ones there who just want peace and asked that they be allowed to remain neutral. Then there is all the fighting and killing that the south started at Fort Sumter. What could the South expect after that but a year that would go to its grave shattered and heartbroken? Did they expect the Union to roll over and give up? There was another article that tells of the large number of Confederate soldiers who are absent from their duties in the war. Me and Sunny read it and talked about it too. The question is asked in the piece "what has become of the patriotism, pride and principle of a young man, who can, and will abandon his command, his country and himself?" Sunny said that the question should be; who abandoned whom and what happened to the patriotism to the United States like it was before the war? He says that it is the Confederate Rebels who are being unpatriotic. They think that just because the rich people in the south wanted to be unpatriotic to their country that everyone else should be unpatriotic too and secede from the Union. Everybody that grew up in this country of the United States and wants to remain loyal to it should be allowed to do so without getting killed for not joining any army. The war is still going strong and I suspect that this New Year is not going to be any better than the last one. Papa Joe had raised some turkeys and geese for us to eat on New Year's Day and we had another feast. There were plenty of black eyed peas that we had raised and hog jowl and everything that you are supposed to eat on New Year's Day to make it a good year but I don't think that will help this year but I sure hope it does. We had a lot of Tories and spies hid out over the holidays and they ate with us and everybody had all that they could eat. The hideaway has been a busy place with people coming and going and Sampson has kept everything going good but it has took a lot of work to do it. Mama and daddy and a lot of the other workers here on the farm has helped him and there aint been no trouble yet which is good. We still go to church every Sunday morning and there have been more going now than there were before the war started. I guess that if they get killed because of the war they want to be sure that they make it up to heaven where there won't be any wars, but nothing but love. Papa Joe says that he don't see how those people who just want to fight over money will ever make it to heaven cause there sure aint going to be no fighting, or money, up there. Sunny says that heaven and hell are both getting filled up fast seeing as to how many people are getting killed in this war. He says that there are good ones who don't want to fight that get killed and go to heaven and there are others who don't want to do nothing but fight and kill that are going to go straight to hell. This is all that I want to write this Sunday.

◆

January 18, 1863

I didn't write none last week because I was not feeling well and didn't even go to church. The baby is getting bigger and I get tired easier than what I use to. Sunny told me that I have just got to start slowing down but it is hard to do because there is so much that has to be done around here. He has got Ida and Nancy to come help me do the work that I have been doing. The children are very helpful too and I really like to have little Rufus around because he is such a lovable child, I don't know what our child might be like but if it is born mongoloid or with some other problems we will just love it like Abram and Ida does Rufus. Woody is still here on the farm with us but General Dodge has talked to him about going up north to be a doctor up there. He could help doctor the wounded Federal troops but Woody says that his interest is in helping young kids who are disabled as he has worked with Rufus. He is interested in this because of what a hard time we had when we were little. He says that there should be someone who will dedicate themselves to help young children who start life at a disadvantage. He had that little saying that helped him out when times were so hard and I can still remember it because he said it a lot. I will admit that it is sort of amateurish but he was little when he wrote it and I think that it is a pretty good thought. I think maybe I wrote it down before but I want to write it again.

"Helpless we begin our life
Dependent on a man and wife
Nurtured then by love and care
We must each our burdens bear
Helpful then we must become
Troubles will surely fall on some
With the golden rule to guide
Help is always by your side
Always do unto others as you
Would have them do to you."

Woody is talking about going on up north to get away from here if the Home Guard does come around trying to make our men go to war. He says that if he does he intends to come back just as soon as it is safe and he wants to start doctoring like he has in mind. Sunny did not go to Florence last Saturday and get a paper but he went yesterday and got one that he said had just been printed. He said that the people at the Gazette says that it is so hard for them to get a paper out that they have to run late sometime to get it on the streets. The paper had another sad article in it about James Southerlin who died on January 2 in the battle at Murfreesboro. James was one of the few persons that Papa Joe liked to have come here to the farm because he said that he was a good Christian young man and everybody liked him. This is just another case where good men die in a senseless war. I have wrote a good deal this week but I am thinking that I will not be writing so much anymore because I am about to run out of paper in this book.

◆

"I had noticed that she was getting toward the end of the sheets left in her journal. It is certain that she will not be able to continue her Sunday writings in this book for much longer. I was hoping that she would be able to lead us through her experiences during the entire war, but she will run out of paper first. This is the only journal that was in the box, so we will just keep reading and see what's left." Abigail flipped through the remaining pages as she spoke. "It is filled all the way through the last sheet so she still had a little more to say. I also noticed that her writing was getting smaller so as to be able to crowd as much in it as possible."

"At this point we now know that the war is about half over," Raleigh commented in response to his mother-in-law's observation. "The first battle at Fort Sumter was fought on April 12, 1861, and the final battle before the surrender of the Confederates was at Appomattox, Virginia, on April 9th with the formal surrender on April 12, 1865, exactly four years later. If Sarah can lead us through a couple more months, the war will be half over. Of course she had no way of knowing that when she was doing the writing. She was obviously hoping that the war would soon end and everything would be back to normal before the year's end, but there would be a lot of bloodshed on the battlefields for the next two years. I also keep in mind that there would be a lot more killings in the Warrior Mountains of Alabama before everything was settled. I just hope that the slaughters did not spread to the farm here. There was probably enough drama left to fill another journal."

"Don't forget, there's another box in the cellar vault! I wonder..." Dutch said reflectively, "Let's finish reading this one and see what she had left to say."

February 8, 1863

Because I aint got much paper left I have decided that I won't write every week so I can save some if there is something that happens that I want to put down on paper. I wrote about reading the advertisement in the paper where somebody wanted to buy several hundred pounds of pork. Sunny went into town to find out about that and when he found the man who wanted to buy it Sunny said that he told him that he wanted him to pay in gold or Federal dollars. Sunny told him that the last Florence Gazette that we got had a long article about shinplaster and he considers Confederate dollars now nothing but shinplaster. He told him that it don't have nothing to do with how people feels about the war but the Confederate money is new and if the South don't win the war, and they are not doing too good in fighting it, that the money will be worthless. He told him that he could provide the pork but he would have to be paid in gold or Yankee greenback dollars. He said that the man said that all he had was Confederate money and that was the official currency of the new Confederate country and that it should be accepted. Sunny told him that he was a businessman and he had to make sure that he carried out his business on a sound basis and that he would not sell the pork to him. He told me that the man was not happy because he would not take Confederate dollars but he said that he was not going to give his stuff away and he thinks that this would be what would happen if he took the Confederate money which he says is nothing but shinplaster. Sunny did not bring in another paper because he said that he could not find one and he said that there is not enough in the little paper now to fool with getting one. He said that he is not even sure if they are going to keep publishing it seeing as to how hard it is to get the work done now that the war is going on. He did say that there was a good piece in the last paper he got about the sale and exploration of corn. It is something that he already knows about but it had a little more information in it than what he had heard about. Nobody can sell corn without first getting a license from the Probate Judge and it can be sold only in that county and is good for only one year. The profit from the corn can be no more than 20%. The miller also must get a license and he cannot sell any corn that he does not get as a toll for his grinding. Sunny says that he and Papa Joe have a secret which they have kept for a year or more now. I did not know nothing about this but it makes sense to me. He says that he has got with General Dodge and that General Dodge has a business friend up north who needs cotton and can't get it because there aint none coming up from the south since the embargo that has been placed on the transport of goods from here to the north. He told me that the man's name is Thomas Clark Durant and that General Dodge is furnishing him information as to where to get cotton. He said that they have captured most of the railroad lines down here in Mississippi and Alabama in the Tennessee River Valley, and they are in control of the waterways and that he has a way to get the cotton back up north if he can get it. At first they were able to confiscate some that they could find on boats or in warehouses but that is all gone. Sunny calls it stealing but it seems that anything can be done during wartime. General Dodge is the head man over the railroads so he can do what he wants to do about what they are hauling. The railroads are bringing troops, military supplies, guns and ammunition down here and he don't want them to go back empty. Papa Joe says that he don't see no reason why the people up north where it is cold cannot have the cotton to make them some clothes out of. I hadn't heard nothing about all this cause I don't keep up with the farming business but Papa Joe and Sunny has a lot of cotton hid out in that secret storage place and wants to do something with it. The way that it is working out Sunny says is that they will even get a lot more money for the cotton than they normally would because it is so scares now that farmers can't grow it anymore. They do not tell me a lot of things because of what I have wrote about before that the less I know the better off I am. Sunny says that they know of other farmers who have cotton and he has given their names to General Dodge. He tells me that they have a way of loading boats on the river here at nighttime and fix it so that the boats look like they are hauling logs and nobody knows what is going on with them shipping cotton. That is all that I know about that part of it and that is all that I want to know. I suppose I should not write all of this down but it is what is on my mind so I will write about it and keep this book hid really good like I always do. I could write more today but I don't want to use up too much paper.

◆

February 22, 1863

Last week was a terrible week here on the farm and everybody has been crying and asking why something like this has to happen. Sunny says that he thinks that everything that happened was because the man that he would not sell the pork to and take that Confederate money from got mad and went to the Home Guards to have them get even. He says that it was a big mistake to answer that ad in the paper and if he had it to go over again that he never would but what has been done has been done and there aint nothing that he can do about it now. It just shows how ruthless this nation has become since the south seceded from the Union. Before that there was the United States government that took all the land away from the Indians who were the rightful owners and ran them off to Oklahoma and now it is the south now that is doing just as bad. I been thinking about why we support the Federal Government in this war when we did hate them because it was under them that the red men lost their lands, but then mom and dad says that it was really the southern people from Georgia and Alabama that made it so hard on the Indians, so the southern people have to be blamed just as much as the northern ones. I think that the south is to be blamed for this war and that is the reason I am on the other side. I guess I have been writing this part because it will be so hard to tell what happened here last Thursday. It all started when some guards that we had here on the farm came running and said that there was a bunch of Home Guards and Partisan Rangers with Enlisting Officers that were headed this way. Papa Joe and Sunny ran and told everybody who could be sent off to fight in the Confederate army to run to the secret hideaway and hide. They all got hid before those men got here and some of our guards went out to find some Federal troops who could come and help us out. The Home Guard and those other men got here first and Papa Joe and Sampson met them in the road and asked them why they were here. They said that they had come to get all the men who were here on the farm that was of the age required by the Confederacy. They lied and said that they had given them a five day notice and that they were going to take them back with them. Papa Joe told them that there wasn't nobody here that had been given any kind of notice and that it was obvious that he was too old for the army and so was Sampson. He said that the farm now belonged to Sunny and since they had more than 20 slaves that the law exempted him from going. He said that there were black slaves on the farm but they did not have to go nowhere and that they would stay right here where they were needed on the farm. After that they ordered Papa Joe to bring every man on the farm to them so they could look them over, and this included Sunny. There are some young white workers on the farm here and Woody is here too but they did not know that. Papa Joe told them that he wasn't going to bring anybody out for them to see and that they should be on their way out of his farm. What he said made them mad and so they told him that they would kill him if he did not do what they told him to do. Papa Joe said that they would just have to go ahead and kill him because he wasn't going to go get any man away from their farm work. This made them madder and one of the Home Guard men raised his gun and told him to do it now or he would shoot. When Papa Joe told them no again, the man with the gun started to pull the trigger. When Sampson saw that he was really going to shoot he jumped between the gun and Papa Joe and the bullet hit him right in the heart and Sampson fell over dead. Right about the time that this was happening there were some Yankee Cavalry soldiers that could be heard galloping toward the farm and the

Home Guards scattered and got away. Sampson was such a good man and he died to save Papa Joe's life. Papa Joe and Sunny picked out a nice place in the cemetery where our family is buried and had some of the farm workers dig a deep grave to bury him in. I don't know what all it was, and I didn't ask, but Papa Joe collected a lot of valuable things and put them in a big metal box and put it in the grave with him. He ordered that the grave never be reopened and that Sampson's family will always have a place here on the farm. Sampson's wife, Lucy, and his three children are living here on the farm and Papa Joe says that they can live here as long as the farm is here if they want to stay. If it was not for Sampson then Aunt Hannah would probably have died on the march to Oklahoma and he helped to get her back here, and now if it was not for what he did, Papa Joe would be dead. Sampson has saved two lives and had to die for it. This is not good for me as I will have the baby in a month or two and I don't feel well anyway. I was hoping that this year would be better but it is getting off to a worse start than last year what with Sampson getting killed. It will probably be a while before I feel like writing anything else.

◆

March 29, 1863

It's a girl and she is healthy and beautiful. You can tell that she has mostly Cherokee blood cause her eyes are brown, her hair is black and she has red skin. Sunny said he did not care if it was a boy or girl but I know that he is real happy with his little girl. He told me that if it was a girl that I could name her and if it was a boy that he would give him a name. I named her Rebekah because it is a good Bible name like my mother's name, Eve, her sister's name, Hannah, and my name, Sarah. After I got to thinking about a name I came up with Rebekah because she was the daughter-in-law of Sarah in the Bible. I aint wrote none since Sampson got killed cause I just aint felt like it. The last time I wrote I said that I probably would not write none in a while and I decided to wait and save my paper until after the baby got here so I could put some in here about it. There has been a lot that has happened since then that I could have written about but I just never got to where I wanted to do it. The big thing still is the war that is going on and there is no end in sight to it. Sunny don't go to Florence much more since he went to see about selling the pork and it ended up with Sampson getting killed because they got mad at him because he wouldn't take that worthless Confederate money. He says that he is afraid now that if he goes to town that the Home Guards will get him and either make him go fight against the Yankees or kill him for not doing it. He says that he thinks that they are on to him helping out the Yankees and it is dangerous for him to leave here. Papa Joe says that it was a mistake for him not to have General Dodge keep some troops here for our protection and now there are Federal solders here all the time staying in the hideaway. General Dodge is moving on away from here but before he leaves he wanted to speak to Woody. He told him that he knows that Woody wants to be a doctor and he will help him get more education to be one but he has another job for him while the war is going on and there is still an embargo of cotton from the south. He said that Thomas Clark Durant, his friend who is smuggling cotton up north, needs somebody from the south who knows about farmers here to help him in his smuggling business. At first Woody said that he didn't want no part of that but after he thought about it he reasoned that the people there needed to have clothes and since that don't have nothing to do about the war he agreed to help him out. According to General Dodge, there is a lot of money to be made and Woody will be well paid for what he does. Since the Rebels did what they did to Sampson, I don't care what people do for the Yankees because I want them to whip the Rebels bad. I told Woody to go ahead and help those people out and that would be a better thing to do than doctoring now. I told him that he also should get away from here where they can't make him join the Confederate army. We are getting word that the Home Guard has been getting even meaner now that Judge Parker did so bad in the election and Chris Sheets was reelected. I could write more but I want to save as much paper as I can.

♦

April 12, 1863

I decided to write today because it has been two years since the Confederate army took Fort Sumter and people were dancing in the streets at Florence. Now we don't even go to Florence no more because it is not safe to do so and the people there are all scared of what will happen next since the Yankees have moved in and control everything that goes on there. Papa Joe says that there is no reason why we should go to Florence because all the stores have run out of most everything that people need and we have all we need right here on the farm. Papa Joe saw all this coming and he stocked up on whatever we might need before everything started getting scarce. Rebekah is doing real good and I am staying with her most of the time to make sure that she gets what she needs. Ida and Nancy are still helping me and they help take care of Rebekah too. Little Rufus has really taken a like to the baby and he is so gentle with her. Rufus is such a delight to be around and Ida says that it is alright for Woody to leave and go work for Mr. Durant getting cotton so that the people up north can stay warm and have something to wear as he has helped Rufus out just about as much as he can. It is farming time again and Papa Joe says that he don't care what the Confederate Government says, that he is going to plant his crops again this year just like he has always done. He says that they probably won't even know about it what with the Federal troops keeping everybody run away from here but if somebody does say something about it he will say that he is growing it legal because a farmer can grow enough cotton and corn for their own use and he said that is just what he will be doing. He says that he will not be lying because his own use will be in letting Woody have a job and that is a good purpose even though Woody will be helping out Thomas Clark Durant. Sunny says that if they don't respect this farm enough that they would come here and kill an old black man when they were aiming at the old man who owns it, then he has the right to disrespect anything the Rebel Government might tell them to do. This means that all the farmhands are busy getting the seed planted so as to have a good crop year. I will write more later on.

◆

"She won't write much more. She doesn't have a lot of paper left." Abigail was once again assessing Sarah's paper supply.

"She saved enough to make sure that she could write a little about her baby," Jenny said. "I'm thinking that baby may be somewhere up our family tree."

"It is certainly a possibility," Abigail replied. "She was obviously anxious to finish the book, so we should go ahead and finish our reading, and then we might have a little discussion about what she had to say in her writings."

May 3, 1863

Rebekah is doing good and still keeping me busy. The crops are all planted and Sunny says that he thinks that by giving the land a rest last year that it will make the crops even better than they were before. He says that God made the land and he knows what is best for it and back in the olden days of the Bible he told them that it needed that rest every seven years. Sunny told Woody that he could have the cotton and extra corn that is stored in the secret hiding place and all that we grow on the farm this year to do with what he wants to. Papa Joe says that he is glad that he has a cotton gin on this place so he can grow and gin his cotton without having to take it off the farm. He said that he wishes that he had a grist mill but there is not the kind of creek on the farm that could turn a water wheel to grind the corn. Woody is not around here much as he is now working for Thomas Clark Durant and he spends a lot of time up north. What he is doing is much better than having to go to war and kill people which he is opposed to. He is making a whole lot of money but that is not as important now as getting this war over with so that things can get back to normal, or as close to normal as they can be. Sunny says that the Home Guards have been real bad this spring and most of the people are fed up with them. He told about one fellow that they killed which has made a lot of people mad. There was a good old man that everybody liked named Jack Walker who would help out everybody that needed help that they killed. They found Jack and his boy named Bill hid out in the woods in Winston County and they shot and hurt Jack but Bill got away. They did not give Jack the five days' notice that they were supposed to but they chopped him all to pieces with hatchets. He said that the preacher named Brother Haley who lives there said that they chopped off his arms and his legs and left him butchered up. I don't even want to think about it. Another man they killed was even worse than that. That mans' name was Henry Tucker and he had been in the Yankee army for over a year and went home to see his wife. When he was home ole Stoke Roberts and his gang rode up and he hid in a big meat box and his wife throwed a quilt over it. The Home Guard forced their way into the house and searched until they found him. Henry tried to run but had no chance to get away. They tied him up with a big rope around him and took him to a place called Bald Rock in Winston County. They had him tied up real good with a rope around his neck with the ends loose on both sides and throwed him on a horse and took him a good far piece away from his house. It got dark while they were doing all of this and Sunny said that he was told that ole Stoke Roberts went to an old dead pine tree and split up some pine and built a fire. While four men pulled Henry by the ends of the rope around his neck off the horse and drugged him on the ground, they built up the fire really big. They cut off a limb of the old pine tree up as far as they could reach while Henry was begging them just to kill him with a gun or ax and not to torture him but that didn't do no good. They tore his clothes off him and left him buck naked. Then they tied his hands behind him and cut a gamboling stick and then cut him behind his heels for the gamboling stick. A gamboling stick is a long stick about four feet long which is sharpened at both ends that farmers use when they are butchering animal. They hung Henry up by his heels on the limb like they would when they butchered a hog. Henry again begged them to shoot him or knock him in the head but Stoke told them to skin him alive. Their knives were too dull to do that so Stoke told them to castrate him and they cut off his pecker and everything down there and Stoke stuffed them in

Henry's mouth. Stoke then took a knife and bored into his eyes and flipped both eyeballs onto the ground. They then took an ax and broke both of his jaws and pulled his tongue as far out from his mouth as they could and cut it off with Henry screaming as loud as he could, he was heard from a great distance away. After that Stoke cut the hide around his head and pulled it over his face and tied it. If that was not enough, they then split up a big bunch of long pine splinters and drove them in his stomach and bowels and heart and as he was dying Stoke bashed his head in with a chopping ax. There are more bloody stories like this but I have wrote enough about that one that anyone can see what is going on right close to here. Sometimes I just wish that the Yankees would just come on down and wipe out all those Rebels in that part of the country but then I think that a lot of good folks would get killed too so this carnage keeps going on. Sunny says that people like Stoke Roberts, Ham Carpenter, Jim Downey, Jim Mooney, Al Gibson, Mell Thomas, Harm Davis, and he named a lot of others that I don't remember, have killed a lot of people. Sunny says that it was part of that bunch that came up here and killed Sampson. There is a Confederate Colonel named John T. Morgan who gave permission for some Partisan Rangers to go into Winston, Marion and Fayette Counties to hunt Tories. He put Stoke Roberts in charge and there has been a lot of bloodshed since.

◆

"I see that there is only one more page left, so I know that she did not finish the story of the Tories in Winston and surrounding counties." Raleigh felt compelled to fill in a few blanks, prematurely starting the discussion that Abigail had suggested. "I remember reading about the encounters between the Home Guards and the Tories in some papers recounting the accounts of the conflict

in Winston and surrounding counties.   One of them
is the book that I've already mentioned several times
before, *The Tories of the Hills*. After the time that Sarah
was writing this, the people in the mountains soon had
enough of the tortures and bloodshed which had been
imposed on the good citizens there who just wanted to
remain in peace. They banded together and declared
war on the Home Guards, and a big bear of a man named
George Stout assumed leadership of the opposition
to the atrocities inflicted by the band of outlaws. The
Tories went on a mission to get every Home Guard
man that had anything to do with killing those who
had resisted their efforts to make them go fight for
the Confederate Army. They pretty well succeeded in
killing and sometimes inflicting torture of their own to
those who had earlier been so ruthless. Sarah named
some names, and I think that most, if not all of them,
met death at the hands of the Tories.

"When the Tories caught Ham Carpenter, someone
suggested that they do to him like Stoke Roberts had
done to Henry Tucker, but they said that even though
he deserved it, they had to remember that they were
still human beings. It took an inhumane, merciless,
coldhearted individual to do that, and they would kill
him in a way more humane. They tied him on a horse
with a rope under its belly, and when they got to where
they were taking him, they cut the rope and jerked
him off the horse onto his face. They then tied a rope
to his ankles and threw the end over a tree limb and
drew him off the ground. John Mitchell was the one
this time who was giving the orders. Ham Carpenter
had earlier run John's pregnant wife out of her house
and caused her to freeze to death in the snow after he
had looked for John but failed to find him. A little boy
there had begged Ham to go get John's wife and bring

her back to the house, but he refused, saying, 'let the bitch die.'

"This is the kind of people they were. Mitchell was determined to get even. He said that he would make it as hot for Ham as he had made it cold on his wife. They built a fire under where Ham was hanging and put some green pine tops on the fire. The smoke began to smother him, and he began coughing and sneezing. After sneezing violently for a period of time, the men let the fire die down under him. They lowered his head nearer to the coals and left him hanging. He had killed his last Tory.

"There are many more stories to go with this one, all happening later than her last writing date, but I will only mention a couple more. One had to do with Jim Downey who had earlier killed Tom Pink Curtis, the Probate Judge of Winston County, for his money. Judge Curtis was killed when a mob of Home Guards went to his house and demanded money which he refused to give them. He said that it was not his money, but it belonged to the people of the county. There was a fire burning in the fireplace, and they got a poker and heated it red hot and stuck it deep into his flesh. When Judge Curtis still refused to give them the money, Jim had the poker reheated to where it was red hot again, and another man grabbed it and stuck it into his chest. This set his clothes on fire; he began to fight but the judge was no match for the group of men that were there. The poker was reheated again, and one of the men stabbed him between his shoulders which paralyzed him. His wife came running and gave them the money, and they started to leave but returned. They got him and dragged him outside, then they tied him up and threw him on a horse and rode away. The judge was found the next morning lying on the bank of a creek with his feet frozen

in ice, which they had to break with an ax to free him
of. To get even, the Tories went to Jim Downey's house
at night time and shot him as he ran out of the house.
They then set it on fire and threw his body inside and it
burned with the house.

"Al Gibson, another one of the thugs, got it at the
hands of the Tories too. Fifteen or twenty of the Tories
raided the Mitchell Fort in Marion County and tore the
doors down. Al Gibson was hiding in there and they
caught him. George Stout was the Tory leader; they shot
Al where he couldn't run and rode off with him. Ham
Carpenter and his men found Al's body lying beside a
branch of water. He had an iron railroad spike driven
into his mouth, through his head, and into a tree root.

"A man that was passing when the bunch of Tories
came along said they told him that they were going to
kill every Home Guard and every Rebel in the country.
They carried out that threat. They also burned some of
the Rebel's businesses, a thread and cloth factory in Bear
Creek that belonged to Lang Allen, and Harm Davis's
Gin on Sponge Creek. Harm was a very active member
of the Home Guard. They later caught him and burned
his feet off before they killed him while trying to get
him to tell where he had hid his money. The leaders of
the Home Guards, Jim Mooney, Al Gibson, Jim Downey,
and Stoke Roberts were all killed by George Stout's gang
of Tories before Ham Carpenter met his end at the
hands of John Mitchell. Well, I have said enough. Let's
finish reading the rest of what Sarah had to say. It won't
take much longer."

Raleigh had no sooner stopped talking before he
spoke again. "Oh yeah, I almost forgot. I was going to say
something about that George Stout that was the leader
of the Tory gang. Before it was all over, he got it too. He
had been responsible for the brutal death of an invalid

boy in the Kelley family, which caused them to go after him. He had a large farm in Marion County with a fine yoke of oxen. After bargaining to buy the yoke of oxen from him, they were to return with the money the next morning. The Kelley's waylaid him at his barn when he went out to feed the oxen. They fired thirty bullets into his head and body at close range.

"When this was reported to the community, there were several men who formed a posse to kill the Kelleys. After they had traveled several miles toward the Kelleys' homes in Kelley's Cove, a man named Andrew Mitchell, the man Mitchell's Fort was named after, thought over what they were doing and stopped the men. He told them that they might be able to kill some of the Kelleys, but some of them would probably get killed too. By this time the war was over; Mitchell said that they should forget about it. That the killings had to end somewhere and it might as well be now. He told them that George Stout had done some good things, but that he also did some bad things like killing the Kelley boy, and he probably got what he had coming. All of the posse turned around and went home. That was the last of the war slaughters that happened in the Warrior Mountains. The long war had ended, and it was time for some peace in the embattled land."

May 31, 1863

I decided to write today for the last time in this book. It is just as well that I am out of paper because I would not be able to write any longer about the news which was appearing in the Gazette. The Federal troops have returned to Florence and they let Sunny know that it would be safe for him to go shopping in town because they had run all the

Home Guard men back to the mountains. He came back here and said that the Yankees have destroyed the presses at the Gazette and they won't be doing any more printing of newspapers any time soon. I suppose that they didn't like what the Gazette was printing about the war and I can understand why; the editors were big time Secessionist who continuously published anti-unionist views. I have got just enough paper left to put down again for the last time how I feel about what is going on with our Country. I keep hearing about the fighting that is going on between the north and the south and about all the bloodshed in the Warrior Mountains in and around Winston and Marion County and I think about Sampson getting killed. It seems that the lives of people are not worth as much anymore as land and cotton and the money it can bring to make the rich even richer. It goes back to when I was born when land was worth more than the people who had lived on it for thousands of years. Thousands of our native people died when they were made to leave and go out west. Now there are a lot of people dying because of the greed of men who values money more than the lives of those men who have to die for them to get and keep it. I have wrote a lot about all that killing and when I found out that I was going to have a baby I got to thinking about what this country will be like when it gets to be my age. Now that Rebekah is here it scares me to think about it. When she gets as old as I am, if she don't die or get killed first, or as old as Papa Joe is, what kind of country are we going to have? We are in the middle of a big war that has torn apart the country that I grew up in. No one knows just when or how this war will end and it is certain that there will be a lot more people to die before it is over. I just pray that it will end soon and Rebekah, with all the other students that I am teaching in school and all the young people everywhere in this country, can grow up in a country where life is the most important thing and everyone will be respected for who they are. I pray for a homeland where, as the founders of our country intended, all men are created equal and It don't matter their skin color, or rich or poor, or young or old, or north or south, or east or west, or whatever their religion or political views might be, they can live in a nation in which they will be proud. Our country now, with its people fighting everywhere, is not one that anyone would be pleased to claim as their homeland and maybe when this war is over people will come to their senses and strive to make it a United States that Rebekah will gladly claim as a citizen. We are now seeing the results of greed and hatred which has no place in a strong and great nation. It is my prayer that peace be restored throughout this great land that God has given us.

◆

"That is the end of the journal, but it's not the end of the story," Jenny commented at the end of the last journal entry. "Sarah would endure two more years of war before the conflict was settled. Her assessment of the outcome was never in doubt. Her wishes that all might be free were fulfilled. I am sure that many of her students stayed on the farm and made their contribution in helping make this farm the prosperous operation that we have today. I am also confident that others left as free individuals, and with the education they received in the little schoolhouse on the Stone Plantation, that they made a contribution to the healing of a divided nation. One that Rebekah would 'gladly claim as a citizen.'"

The secrets of what the boxes might contain had been revealed. The journals, letters, and old newspapers had been read once again. Jenny closed the journal from which they had been reading and a moment of quiet ensued as the readers collected their thoughts.

Abigail was the first to break the silence. "It is shameful that people today are not more aware of the struggles that our ancestors endured to create this great nation that we call home. Perhaps, with future generations in mind, many gave their lives for the cause that they felt to be worthy of that ultimate sacrifice, while others were given no choice but to place themselves in harm's way."

Jenny replied, "It all started when the early settlers of this land wanted to be independent and freed from the yoke which England had placed upon them. Many offered their life for this freedom. Following that were battles fought to secure lands that would unify the United States. Then there were the world wars that claimed the lives of many of our young men."

Abigail nodded. "I suppose that we might say that there was a period of time when our nation had what I would classify as 'growing pains.' This journal was written during that time. It was a time when greed reigned supreme and it certainly was not our finest years. Greed toppled human rights, causing the removal of our people from their homelands and the suppression of slaves who were brought here to help in the development of newly acquired lands. A devastating war was fought because of this greed. I'll put it in woman's words. When we examine our nation's history, it has not always been a bed of roses. There were periods when there were more thorns than flowers."

"Well, Abigail," Dutch was the next to comment. "Looking at it in a man's perspective, we are fortunate that here on the farm we have not allowed greed or the suppression of others to be a factor in our success. We owe a debt of gratitude to our ancestors who made the efforts to avoid the fray and went about the business of working hard while making an honest living. This is probably the greatest factor that brought this farm through the early years, and later the depression, to the successful farming operation that we have today.

"What a thoughtful thing those girls did by making the effort to put on paper those things which were foremost on their minds as they struggled through difficult times. There are very few families who have been fortunate enough to open journals that give a glimpse into the lives of ancestors who lived over one hundred and fifty years ago."

"Even with all that has been revealed so far, there is still another box in the cellar vault," Raleigh reminded them. "I wonder what may be in it!"

About the Author

Wheeler Pounds grew up in rural Alabama, and he has always possessed a deep connection to the outdoors and his Native American heritage. He is a member of the Echota Cherokee Tribe of Alabama, of which he is the chief of the Blue Clan. For thirty years he was employed by the State Board of Pardons and Paroles and was an adjunct instructor of Criminal Justice at Faulkner University.

Since retiring, he has been able to devote time to his favorite hobby of being an avid hiker. He has backpacked the majority of the National Parks in the United States but maintains that his favorite is Bankhead National Forest, which is near his home. He is also a committed husband, father, and grandfather and has dedicated a significant portion of his life to volunteer work.

Wheeler resides in Walker County, Alabama with his wife, Judi, where he spends time with family and friends and continues to foster his passion for nature.

Read more from the *Secrets of the Cherokee Hideaway*
by Wheeler Pounds

ISBN: 978-1934610640

ISBN: 978-1934610794

If you enjoyed this book, try these other titles from
Bluewater Publications

Die Like Men
Tim Kent
ISBN: 978-1934610626

The Secret of Wattensaw Bayou
M.E. Hubbs
ISBN: 978-1934610763

Betrayed
Tim Kent
ISBN: 978-1934610817

Never Smile Again
Tim Kent
ISBN: 978-1934610688

www.ingramcontent.com/pod-product-compliance
Lightning Source LLC
Chambersburg PA
CBHW020537020726
47494CB00006B/1797